AMONG THE DEAD

AMONG THE DEAD

A Rachel Carver Novel

J. R. Backlund

CROOKED LANE

NEW YORK

Published in the United States by Crooked Lane Books, an imprint of The Quick Brown Fox & Company LLC.

Crooked Lane Books and its logo are trademarks of The Quick Brown Fox & Company LLC.

Library of Congress Catalog-in-Publication data available upon request.

ISBN (hardcover): 978-1-68331-273-4
ISBN (ePub): 978-1-68331-274-1
ISBN (ePDF): 978-1-68331-276-5

Cover design by Craig Polizzotto
Book design by Jennifer Canzone

Printed in the United States.

www.crookedlanebooks.com

Crooked Lane Books
34 West 27th St., 10th Floor
New York, NY 10001

First Edition: August 2017

10 9 8 7 6 5 4 3 2 1

For Wanda and Thu

1

Wednesday

Yellow light from a greasy bulb above the stove. Tomato sauce bub-bling over pasta in the droning microwave. The smell of melting cellophane.

Dylan Gifford was trying to focus on anything but the man dying in front of him. There were short gasps and wet coughs and twitching hands, all signs that it was coming to an end. It would be over in a matter of seconds. Gifford couldn't change that now, even if he'd wanted to, and that realization made him shudder.

Irrevocable.

It was strange to have a word like that pop into his head. It just wasn't part of his vocabulary. But it stayed there even after he looked away and tried to force it out of his mind. Made him think of his cousin Clayton, who he'd punched in the ear when they were teenagers.

Clayton had called Gifford's momma a whore, which was jus-tification for a severe beating. But a single hit had sent that boy to the ground, crying and cupping the side of his head. Ruptured eardrum is what the doctor had said. Damaged his hearing for life. Half of Gifford's family disowned him after that, and he never saw Clayton again. It hadn't bothered him before, but it did now.

The microwave beeped three times, and there was silence.

Gifford steadied himself, pulled the dishrag off the man's face, and leaned in to inspect. The black knife handle protruding from the man's chest was perfectly still. There was no sound of breathing. No air moving across Gifford's cheek.

His instinct was to run, to get out of the house and escape into the woods. But instinct was careless. There were rules to follow. He stood up, scanned the kitchen, and went through his mental checklist.

Cover his mouth and nose. Check.

Use one of the kitchen knives to finish him. Check.

Make sure he's dead before you leave. Check.

And don't forget the bat . . . shit.

It would have been a major screw-up to run off without the Louisville Slugger. He searched the floor and found it tucked into the toe-kick space beneath a cabinet. It must have rolled under there after he had dropped it, too preoccupied to notice. He picked it up and decided to wipe it down, just in case any of the man's hairs had stuck to it. *Check.*

He looked around for a few more seconds and figured it was time to leave. He dropped the dishrag and walked slowly to the back door. The groaning floorboards complained too loudly, making him cringe with each step. He knew there was no reason to worry—no one else in the house—but it seemed wrong to disturb the quiet.

He reached the door and cracked it, felt a stream of cold spring air pushing in. He turned his ear to the opening and heard a breeze jostling the trees, insects calling in the distance. But there were no voices, no sirens, no barking dogs . . . He worried a lot about dogs.

He peered into the sliver of night and saw thin clouds covering the moon. They gave off a gray glow, which was just enough light to see across the property to the tree line. He could be halfway down the trail before needing the flashlight in his pocket. He drew the door open, took a last look at his handiwork, and then ran for the safety of the woods.

2

Rachel Carver's head snapped up, and she realized she had nodded off again. The third . . . maybe fourth time since she'd arrived at the Blackstone Estates mobile home park for her weekly visit. She was sitting in her Camry, in the guest lot between the sales and leasing office and the community mailboxes, waiting.

She'd gotten there earlier than usual, too anxious to sit around in her apartment after another sleepless night. She checked the time on her phone and rubbed a kink in her neck. A moment later, the old woman appeared on the sidewalk, pushing the stroller against a frigid wind. The toddler in the seat endured the ride quietly, pink faced and bundled in layers.

They were returning from their morning trip to the playground at the other end of the community. As soon as Rachel saw the little boy, she had to look away. It was almost a reflex. A familiar sting of guilt, still too strong to face head on.

As they crossed in front of the Camry, Rachel could hear the old woman yelling muffled words of encouragement beneath her scarf. She might have been telling her grandson that they were almost home. Or she might have been telling herself. When they finally reached the single-wide, she unbuckled the child and carried him up the steps and inside.

The stroller stayed on the concrete patio, as it always did— she was too weak to carry it in by herself. In the afternoon, she would come outside and cover it with one of those fifty-gallon, lawn-and-garden-type trash bags to protect it from the pollen and the spiders. At least, that's what she had done last week.

A silver sedan turned into the parking lot.

Right on schedule, Rachel thought as she grabbed the envelope lying on the center console.

The sedan pulled into one of the guest spots, and a large woman with a round face and a black, shiny bob stepped out a moment later. She was a social worker from the Wake County Division of Social Services. Her name was Eva Santi. Rachel approached her as she struggled to dislodge an oversized handbag from the floor behind the driver's seat.

"Good morning, Agent Carver," Santi said with a grunt as the handbag broke free. "Wish I could say I'm surprised to see you here." She shut the car door and brushed past Rachel, heading for the old woman's trailer. "I don't suppose it would do any good to tell you, again, that you shouldn't be here."

"I know I've been a pain," Rachel said, keeping pace. "And I'm not here to try to see the boy. I was just hoping you could give this to Mrs. Bailey for me."

She sped up to get in front of Santi, blocked her path, and held out the envelope.

"Oh, for heaven's sake . . . This is completely inappropriate, Agent Carver. If you want to—"

"I'm not an agent anymore."

"What . . . ?"

"I quit. More than a month ago."

The look of irritation on Santi's face softened. She stared at the envelope for a few seconds and asked, "How much is in there?"

"Two hundred."

"And how do you know I won't just keep it?"

"I guess I'll have to trust you."

"Don't go trusting me too much." Santi took the envelope and slid it into her handbag. "Anything else?"

Rachel glanced at the trailer. "Have you had any luck finding him a home?"

"Are you kidding? A two-year-old with no disabilities? No developmental disorders? At least none that we know about. I won't need luck. People will be lining up to adopt this kid."

A chime from Rachel's phone announced an incoming text message. She flicked the mute switch with her thumb and stuffed it into her back pocket. "Then why is he still here?"

"These things take time," Santi said with a shrug.

Rachel held her gaze, demanding a better answer.

"I shouldn't be talking to you about this," she sighed. "The problem is we can't find the father. We know he doesn't want the boy, and we've started the procedure to terminate his rights, but . . . like I said, it takes time."

"Would it help if I found him for you?"

Santi chuckled, shook her head, and said, "I know this is personal for you, Agent Carver. Especially with . . . what happened. But you really need to let us handle it. Go home. We'll make sure the boy is taken care of."

"I'm not an agent anymore," Rachel repeated, but Santi was already walking away, climbing the steps to knock on the old woman's door.

Rachel went back to her car and checked the message on her phone.

"Hey, Rachel. Need your help with something. Call me when you get a chance."

It was Danny Braddock, an old partner from her time as a detective with the Raleigh Police Department. They had worked together in the homicide unit until Rachel had decided to move on, taking a job as a special agent with the State Bureau of Investigation. But they had remained close friends, at least until Braddock had moved away in an attempt to save his marriage. His wife had wanted to be closer to her family, had wanted Braddock to be around more. "Maybe we'll finally be able to start a family of our own," she had said. They divorced a year later.

Rachel called him, and he answered on the second ring.

"How've you been?" he asked.

"Not bad," she lied. "You?"

"Could be better . . ." His voice was tense and distracted.

"Everything okay?"

"Yeah, sorry . . . I got something here. Thought maybe you might be able to help." He seemed to be dancing around a question. "Are you busy? I mean, have you started a new job yet?"

"No. Haven't really been looking."

"Really?" He sounded surprised.

Her eyes drifted back to the trailer. "Been a little preoccupied."

"Well . . . if you're interested, I might have some work for you."

"What kind of work?"

"Consulting on a murder case."

She thought for a moment about how enticing that sounded. "I don't think that's a good idea, Danny."

"Why not?"

"It's just not what I do anymore," she said without conviction.

"I'm pretty desperate, Rachel. Anything I can say to change your mind?"

Braddock worked for a small sheriff's office somewhere west of Asheville near the Tennessee border. Lowry County, if she remembered correctly. A quiet mountain community. The kind of place where people didn't kill each other very often, save for the occasional hunting accident.

"Are you not getting any help from the state?" Rachel asked.

"They're sending us a tech to help with the crime scene, but all their investigators are tied up right now. Might be a week before we get one. I can't wait that long. I need someone now."

"Sounds like you're in a tough spot."

"You have no idea."

Rachel could feel herself being drawn in, almost compelled to say yes. She missed being a homicide investigator, in spite of the job's considerable downside. There had been long hours and periodic bouts of insomnia, an ever-increasing dependence on caffeine and alcohol—sometimes together—all accompanied by the complete absence of anything resembling a social life. And Rachel had made all of it worse by burying herself in her cases, allowing them to consume every aspect of her existence.

Her apartment was a perfect example. Crime scene photos on her coffee table, medical examiners' reports on her couches, autopsy photos on the kitchen counter by the coffeemaker . . . She had been living among the victims, making them part of her daily routines so that she never lost sight of her obligation to them. Her commitment. A promise that had driven her to the point of obsession. She never would have given up on it, never would have abandoned them, had it not been for . . .

"Tell me about the case," she said, looking away from the trailer.

"We discovered the body this morning," Braddock said eagerly. "Doesn't happen very often around here. Especially not like this."

"Not like what?"

"The victim was killed inside his home. He lived alone. No signs of forced entry. No witnesses, no suspects . . . your specialty."

"I have a specialty?"

"You've got a talent, that's for sure. All I've got is a pair of detectives who spend most of their time working larceny. There's no one around here with your expertise."

"Aw, Danny, you're making me blush," she said, her mood lightening a bit.

"I mentioned we'd pay, didn't I?"

"Flattery *and* money? You're making it hard to say no."

"I'll have to work it out with the sheriff. Daily fee plus expenses?"

"Sounds about right." She thought about the prospect of turning him down, of spending the next few days trying to track down a deadbeat dad, torturing herself for things she couldn't change. Or she could say yes and get away for a while, bury herself in a new mystery. The money was a nice incentive too. It had been nearly six weeks since she'd resigned. Six weeks without a paycheck, and she had all but drained her pitiful savings account. "How long will it take me to get there?"

"About five hours or so, depending on traffic."

"I'd better get moving."

"Wait. Don't go taking off just yet. I still need to make sure Ted's gonna be good with all this."

"Well damn, Danny. You got me all excited and everything."

"I know. Just give me twenty minutes, and I'll call you right back."

3

Braddock could hear the conversation between the two sheriffs as he approached the open door. His boss, Sheriff Ted Pritchard, was rocking in his chair, staring blankly at his glass-topped wooden desk with puffy eyes. Pritchard's cousin, Sheriff Lee Harrelson of Buncombe County, sat across from him and seemed to be doing most of the talking.

"You never know what that bunch of damn fools is gonna say or do," Harrelson said. "But I wouldn't go trusting a single one of 'em."

Pritchard noticed Braddock standing in the doorway and waved him in. "Have a seat, Danny." Then to Harrelson, "Lee, you remember my chief deputy, Danny Braddock?"

The heavyset Harrelson reached over as far as his broad midsection would allow and shook Braddock's hand. "Good to see you, Danny. Wish it was for a better occasion."

"Ain't that the truth," Braddock said and sat down. "Good to see you, Sheriff."

Pritchard said, "Lee was just telling me what he thinks of our friends on the county commission."

And Harrelson continued, "They can all go to hell, as far as I'm concerned." He looked at Braddock. "And I wouldn't have a bit of trouble telling each one of 'em just as much." Back to Pritchard. "They didn't have any right to try and scapegoat you the way they did last year. But to a man, they'll try and do it again if this case doesn't get solved real quick. Mark my words."

Pritchard rubbed his eyes with his thumb and forefinger and asked Braddock, "Have you heard anything back from Sanford yet?"

Braddock had called the State Bureau of Investigation within an hour of learning about the body. The special agent in charge of the Western District office had taken his time responding. "Just a few minutes ago. He said we can expect a crime scene specialist within the hour. Also said he might be able to free up an agent toward the end of the week, but he didn't sound too sure about it."

Harrelson said, "Hopefully that'll be enough to get the job done. Y'all got your work cut out for you, that's for sure. But I've known Sanford for a few years. He's a good guy. He'll do what he can to help." He gripped the arms of his chair and lifted himself to his feet. "Well, boys, it's a long drive back to Asheville. I'd best be on the road."

"I appreciate you coming all the way out here to see us, Lee," Pritchard said. "You sure I can't convince you to stay for lunch?"

"Nah, Tee Pee. I appreciate it, but I reckon my fat ass could use a break from the barbecue sandwiches for a while. Y'all be good."

Braddock waited until he was sure that Harrelson was out of earshot before he said, "Tee Pee?"

"Always hated that damn nickname." Pritchard drummed his fingers on his desk. "Danny, how many murders did you work when you were in Raleigh?"

"Eight," he said.

"How'd they turn out?"

"Five arrests. Four convictions. One got off. The others went cold before I moved. One of them was closed two years ago."

"Did they get a conviction?" Pritchard asked.

"No. The suspect was shot and killed. Tried to rob the wrong guy."

"Any of those cases like this one?"

Braddock shook his head.

Like many of the sheriffs in Western North Carolina, Pritchard had never been a homicide detective. His previous law enforcement experience was limited to seven years as a state trooper in the

Highway Patrol, which his wife had complained was too dangerous. So he had taken a job as the Lowry County Manager. When
he'd run for sheriff, Braddock had supported him. Now, confronted
with what was shaping up to be the most difficult case of his career,
Braddock hoped that his boss recognized how ill equipped they
were to handle it.

Pritchard rubbed his eyes again and sighed. "So this ex-SBI
agent you want me to hire as a consultant . . . what's her name
again?"

"Rachel Carver."

"Right. And how do you two know each other?"

"We worked together in homicide, before the SBI recruited
her."

"Recruited her? I didn't know they did that."

"Apparently, the special agent in charge of the Capital District
took a liking to her."

That caused Pritchard to raise an eyebrow. "Is that so?"

"It's not like that, boss. She's good. Hands down the best investigator I've ever met."

"Fair enough." He stared at his desk for a moment and asked,
"You really think we need her?"

Braddock shrugged. "The state's not exactly jumping through
hoops to send us any help. With everything else that's been going
on around here . . ." Braddock didn't have to use the word *scandal*.
He knew it would be the first to enter Pritchard's mind. "I think
it'd be a smart move to bring her in."

Pritchard thought about it for a few more seconds, raised his
hands in a gesture of surrender, and said, "All right, Danny. I don't
know how I'll pay for it, but what the hell."

4

The three-hundred-mile trip required five Monster Energy drinks, a possible UTI—from holding it in too long between stops—and a power nap in a McDonald's parking lot just west of Greensboro. Shortly after 2:00 PM, Rachel steered her Camry off the Great Smoky Mountain Expressway and headed into the center of Dillard City. She turned onto Main Street and found a one-story brick motel two blocks down called the Fontana Lodge. She parked, sent Braddock a text to let him know that she had arrived, and went to the office to get a room.

"How many nights will you be with us?" the clerk asked. He was short and spindly. Bald, save for a few wispy strands. Had tawny skin dotted with liver spots.

"Not sure," she said. "Can I just pay by the night?"

"Sorry?"

"I'm not sure how long I'll need to be in town."

He stared at her for a moment, open mouthed and confused. "You mean, you don't have no idea at all?"

She glanced out the window. Aside from her Camry and a small pickup parked in front of the office, which she suspected was his, the parking lot was empty. "Does it really matter?"

"Well . . . I gotta put somethin' in this computer."

"Let's just say three nights."

"All right then. Three nights."

"Yeah, for now."

His mouth fell open. He stared at her for another moment and said, "Well . . . what d'ya mean, 'for now'?"

★ ★ ★

The room smelled like leather and fried chicken. Rachel guessed the furniture had been there since the early 1980s, along with the matching floral-patterned drapes and bedspread. She spun the knob on the through-wall air conditioner and welcomed the musty air. She laid her briefcase on a lopsided table, hefted her rolling suitcase onto the bed, and unzipped the main compartment.

A shower would have made her feel like a new woman, but a text from Braddock said he was on his way over. She settled for washing her face in the sink and applied a fresh coat of Secret. Then she added a black single-button blazer to her jeans and white T-shirt. Standing in front of the mirror, she liked the way the jacket hugged her waist, happy that her Brazilian jiu-jitsu classes were holding an otherwise unhealthy lifestyle at bay. But her hair was another matter. It looked flat and oily, almost black in the dim lamplight. She pulled it back and cinched it into a ponytail. Decided it was best to stop looking.

She grabbed her briefcase and her last can of Monster Energy and went outside. Braddock was waiting in the parking lot, leaning against the side of a black Chevy Tahoe. He was taller than she remembered, and he'd lost weight. She guessed at least twenty pounds, which gave his oval face some much-needed definition, his brown eyes more prominence. He was dressed in a black snug-fitting sweat shirt and a pair of those utility cargo khakis that men in law enforcement were so fond of wearing. His service automatic was clipped to his belt. There was a gold badge embroidered on the left side of his chest. The writing beneath it read, "LCSO."

"Welcome to Lowry County," he said. "Hope the drive wasn't too rough on you."

"I'll survive." She hugged him and suddenly felt too short and out of shape.

He glanced at the oversized can in her left hand and smiled. "I forgot how much you like that stuff."

★ ★ ★

Main Street ran alongside the Tuckasegee River on the way out of town. After a couple of miles, the tree line fell away from the road, and Rachel took in the expanse of the Appalachian Mountains. The rolling hills looked like an ocean of green waves, each one cresting higher than the one before it. A forest-covered tsunami rose in the distance. Pine, birch, chestnut, hickory, white oak . . . every type of tree that Rachel could think of fought for exposure on the crowded mountainsides.

"Do you ever miss living in the city?" she asked.

"Not even a little bit."

The thin lines at the corners of Braddock's eyes deepened. There was the hint of a smile, perhaps even contentment.

A handheld radio sitting in a cup holder in the center console chirped. A garbled voice followed. Braddock turned the volume down and said, "So I guess I should let you know what you've stepped into by coming here."

Rachel didn't like the way that sounded. "Uh-oh."

"Yeah." He glanced at her and smiled. "It's nothing too bad. Just politics as usual around these parts."

"Okay."

"You see, Ted . . . Sheriff Pritchard . . . he's in his first term, and it's been a rough ride so far. A few years back, the county commission voted to build this big, expensive new jail. Cost around nine million bucks. Was way more than we needed, but the last sheriff pushed hard for it. He said we would get money coming in from the surrounding counties if we built the facilities to house their inmates."

"I'm guessing it didn't work out that way."

"Took you all of ten seconds to realize what the commission couldn't figure out in two years' worth of planning. The damned thing's been less than half full since it opened."

"That's gotta sting a bit."

"Yep. And when Ted was running against the previous sheriff, he wasn't afraid to use that to his advantage. The problem is, since the commission approved it, his campaign made *them* look bad too. But not bad enough, as it turned out. Four of the five were reelected. And that's made things tough on us. They've kept the budget tight and looked for any excuse to criticize us."

Braddock turned onto a stretch of rough asphalt that was barely wide enough to make two lanes. The nose of the Tahoe dove as they dropped into a valley. A quarter mile in, the road burrowed into a dense forest.

"And last year," he said, "we gave them exactly what they were looking for."

"What happened?"

"A kid from the local high school went and beat the absolute hell out of this other boy. Put him in the hospital. It was bad. The DA wanted to charge him with attempted murder. His parents sold their business, mortgaged their house, brought in this big-name attorney from Charlotte. The DA got nervous. She said we needed physical evidence to make it stick. So we did another search. The house, the property, and most importantly, the crime scene, which was a trail through the woods behind the high school. The victim used to walk it every day to get from his house to the school and back.

"The suspect claimed he hadn't been on the trail at all that day. Said he had gone home a different way. We had two witnesses who said they saw him follow the victim, but there was also a girl who swore up and down that she saw him going home the other way. So during our second search of the scene, one of our detectives happened to find the suspect's school ID card buried under some leaves. It was a little outside of where we had looked the first time, but close enough that it could have been kicked away in a scuffle. We felt really good about it until the kid's lawyer showed up with some videos of us searching the house."

"You're kidding." She knew what was coming.

"Nope. The suspect's parents had planted nanny cams around the house, including in the kid's bedroom. And on that video, the same detective who found the ID at the crime scene can be seen pocketing something he picked up from the kid's dresser."

"Wow. What happened?"

"Ted fired the detective, of course. The chief deputy resigned, and I took his place. But we couldn't save the case."

"That sucks."

"Yeah. Since then, the commissioners have done everything they can think of to get Ted to resign, but he's been hanging in there. Now we've got a killer on the loose."

She thought about how stressed out he had sounded on the phone. "You said it doesn't happen very often. How many murder cases have you worked since you moved here?"

"None."

She almost asked if he was joking. "In five years?"

"Hell, Rachel, we've only had three since then. The last one was drug related, so the state came in and took it over. The two before that were investigated by the detectives who are no longer working for us on account of the aforementioned shit storm."

"Damn, Danny."

"Exactly. I have two detectives left, and neither one of them has any experience in homicide. Which is why I need you. We've got to be as thorough as possible, and we can't afford to have any missteps. So, as much as I'd love for you to help us catch the bad guy, you're really here to make sure we don't fuck this thing up."

Rachel slumped in her seat. Her last case as an SBI special agent had ended in a political mess. The last thing she wanted was to find herself in the same situation all over again.

Braddock chuckled. "What's the matter? Starting to feel a little pressure?"

"Actually, yeah. I kinda wish you hadn't told me any of that."

5

Braddock turned onto a dirt driveway, eased past a parked patrol car, and emerged into a clearing. A small ranch house sat in the center atop a gentle rise. It was brick with yellow trim, and it had a metal carport that looked like it had been added as an afterthought.

Three more law enforcement vehicles were parked on the grass. The first was a black Tahoe, like Braddock's, but with yellow stripes and the words "Lowry County Sheriff" painted across the doors. Next was a white Explorer with an SBI logo on the doors and the words "Crime Scene Search" painted near the back. Last in line was an unmarked Crown Victoria. Braddock parked beside it and reached into his back seat to retrieve a notepad.

"Victim's name is Dean McGrath," he said, looking over his notes. "Thirty-one. Divorced. Lived alone. No children. Found early this morning by a guy claiming to be the victim's friend. Guy named Adam Butler. Call came in at six thirty-two." He flipped to the second page, looked it over for a few seconds, and then flipped back. "A deputy was first on the scene. Arrived at six forty-three. He found Butler in the front yard, still on the phone with the operator. He went in through the side door over there by the carport, found McGrath lying on the kitchen floor, face up, with a knife in his chest."

"Sounds painful," Rachel said. She looked toward the carport and imagined herself approaching the house as the first responder.

"I thought so too. EMTs showed up a few minutes later and pronounced him dead. Looks like he'd been that way for a couple of hours. ME estimates time of death to be between two and four in the morning based on rigor, lividity, liver temp, and all that other witchcraft. But McGrath was a bartender in town. He worked last night, and the owner says he usually left the bar around three after cleaning up. There were no signs of a struggle. No signs of forced entry."

"Interesting." Scenarios began to play out in her mind.

Victim throws a drunk out of the bar. Drunk follows him home. Victim lets him inside? Probably not.

Victim doesn't lock his door, and the drunk barges in? Would have been a struggle. Try again.

Victim meets a friend at the bar, invites him home for a few after-work beers. They get into an argument. Then a fight. Things go too far. The friend kills him, cleans up the evidence, and calls 9-1-1? Maybe.

Braddock tossed the pad in the back seat. "Shall we have a look?"

"Are the crime scene techs done?"

"Let's find out."

They got out of the Tahoe and started toward the house. A deputy jogged up to them holding a clipboard in one hand and a pen in the other. "Can I get you to sign in, Chief?"

"Ladies first," Braddock said.

Rachel took the clipboard and filled in her name and the date, checked her phone for the time and wrote it down, left the space for "Agency/Department" blank, then handed it over to Braddock. While he was signing in, she tried to bring up a bird's-eye view of the crime scene, but as soon as she opened Google Maps, a message appeared—there was no network connection. She held her phone up, stepped away from the vehicles, and spun in a circle.

"I wouldn't waste your time," Braddock said. "We use the only carrier that works down in this valley. If you had it, you'd know by now."

"Hmph." She slid the phone into her back pocket.

"What are you trying to do?"

"Just wanted to look at the area from overhead."

"I'm sure you'll get a good signal back in town. If not, we'll let you use a computer at the office. I don't imagine the Fontana Lodge has free Wi-Fi."

Braddock led Rachel into the carport, which housed the victim's red Ford Ranger pickup. A baby-faced man with a buzz cut and a thin mustache leaned against the front end. He wore black slacks and a white polo shirt that was too tight for his muscular frame. Braddock introduced him as Detective Shane Fisher.

"They almost done in there?" Braddock asked.

"I believe so," Fisher said. "Wasn't much to collect but a few prints and the dishrag."

"Dishrag?" Rachel asked.

"Yes, ma'am. We found it on the floor next to the victim. Appeared to have some blood on it."

"When was the body picked up?"

"About a quarter after nine."

"That reminds me," Braddock said. "The pathologist is off for the next few days. As a courtesy, she agreed to stay late to do the autopsy today." He checked his watch. "She's going to start at three thirty. You need to be there in case she has any questions."

"Roger that, Chief," Fisher said. "I'll head that way as soon as we finish up here."

Though he didn't look too happy about it.

A few minutes later, the crime scene technicians emerged from the side door. The first one out, a stocky, red-haired man, gave a quick nod as he walked past them carrying a collection kit. A tall, muscular woman stepped out next. She had closely cropped black hair and appeared to be American Indian. She was holding a clipboard and had a bulky digital SLR camera hanging from her neck.

"Hey, boss," she said, sounding tired.

"This is Carly Brewer," Braddock said to Rachel. "She works for us." He leaned in close and lowered his voice. "She does CrossFit."

Carly rolled her eyes.

Rachel introduced herself, and Braddock asked, "Are we good to go in?"

"Yeah," she said. "Didn't get anything new while you were gone." She nodded in the direction of the Explorer, where the other tech was stowing his equipment in the back. "Our SBI friend says it's one of the cleanest homicide scenes he's ever seen."

"Meaning the killer cleaned up after himself?" Rachel asked.

"Meaning he didn't make much of a mess to begin with."

"Really? No castoff, no bloody prints, no tracks?"

She shook her head. "Nothing that we could find. And we just about sprayed the entire kitchen with Hemascein."

Rachel was surprised. She had worked dozens of stabbing cases in her career, and they had all been quite messy. The victims who had left the least amount of blood evidence were the ones who had done most of their bleeding internally. They were usually able to move after the attack, or at least call for help. And they usually died on the way to the hospital. But McGrath had died lying on his back, with no sign that he had tried to get help or struggled with his attacker.

Carly patted the camera on her chest and said to Braddock, "Boss, I gotta run. I need to make sure these photos get to the pathologist before the autopsy."

Fisher said, "I'm outta here too, Chief."

"All right," Braddock said. "Call me right away if she finds anything worth talking about." When Fisher and Carly were halfway to their vehicles, he leaned over to Rachel and said, "Shane's a good guy, but I think he's a little squeamish."

"Is this Carly's first homicide too?" she asked.

"Yeah. She's a good tech. Really good with prints and a hell of a photographer. But this is too much for her to handle on her own." A perplexed look fell on Braddock's face as he watched the SUVs and the unmarked Crown Victoria drive away. "You know, I just realized that she's the only one who doesn't call me Chief. I wonder if it has anything to do with her being a Cherokee."

★ ★ ★

Rachel stepped into the kitchen and smelled something rotten.

"Is that from the trash?" she asked.

"Food in the microwave."

"So he was making dinner when he was attacked."

"Looks that way."

She scanned the room, starting high and working downward. The ceiling, the lights, the walls, the cabinets, the counters, another door that led to the backyard . . . When she got to the floor, she saw the only sign that there had been violence: a mottled pool of blood where the victim had died.

She circled the stain, noticed diagonal lines that resembled the impressions of folded or bunched-up fabric. "He was wearing a shirt?"

"Sweat shirt."

"How many wounds could you see?"

"Just the one."

Rachel thought there were likely more, but they could be hard to see when examining a blood-soaked body at a crime scene. Once the body was washed, the pathologist would count and measure each wound.

"What kind of knife was it?"

"One of those," he said, nodding toward the counter behind her. She turned and saw a knife block sitting in the corner by the fridge, an empty slit where one of the largest of the set should have been.

"Okay," she said, "we have this one bloodstain, the body, the knife, a few prints, and a rag."

"Yep."

"Anything else?"

"We bagged his phone, his keys, and his wallet. They were laying on the counter."

She paced the room, noticed the creaking floorboards, and said, "Would have been hard to sneak up on someone in here. Who talked to the friend?"

"Shane did. This morning while we had him here."

She thought for a second and asked, "If McGrath got home after three in the morning, why would his friend come over at six thirty?"

"Shane asked about that. Butler does handyman work around town. Apparently, he was on his way to a job and came by to borrow a saw of some kind. I think McGrath used to work in construction too. There's a bunch of tools locked up in the shed out back."

"Does Butler have an alibi?"

"Yep. He was home with his live-in girlfriend at the time. Shane talked to her, and she confirmed it."

Rachel processed that as she took another look around the kitchen. Her eyes found a window, and she asked, "How about the canvass? Did the neighbors see anything?"

Braddock smiled. "We talked to everyone that lives on this road, but the nearest house is three football fields away."

"Must be nice." She looked back at the blood, tried to imagine what it might have been like for Butler to find his friend dead on the floor. Then a thought struck her. "Danny, did you know the victim?"

"A little," he said. "Met him a few years back. Would see him around town every now and then."

"Sorry."

He shrugged. "There're only about two thousand people in the whole town. You stay around here long enough, you'll get to know all of 'em eventually."

"Which means we might be talking to two thousand people."

"If you say so."

"You said you wanted to be thorough."

"I'm going to regret asking for your help, aren't I?"

"Without a doubt. In the meantime, you need to get everyone who's working on this case in the same room so we can go over everything we have so far. Maybe after the autopsy."

"I can arrange that."

"When are you planning to release the house?"

"I'm not in any hurry."

"Good." She thought for a moment about all the work that was ahead of them. "I sure hope this doesn't turn out to be some kind of random thrill kill or serial case."

"Me too," he said, and there was the hint of genuine fear in his voice. "Where do you want to go from here?"

"Wherever we can find people who knew Dean McGrath."

6

Braddock had his other detective pulling records and searching for next of kin, so Rachel wanted to focus on the victim's coworkers and friends. For a bartender, those two groups were often made of the same people, which meant that the best place to start was the bar where McGrath had worked.

"I need to check in at the office first," Braddock said. "I'll probably be close to an hour. Anything you want to do in the meantime?"

"Would you mind dropping me off at the motel? I could use a shower."

"Sure thing. I'll be back to pick you up as soon as I can."

He left her at the door, and she went in feeling a little shaky from caffeine withdrawal, if there was such a thing. She showered for as long as there was hot water, trying to make sense of what she knew about the murder. When she got out, there was still time to spare, so she decided to lie down and close her eyes for a bit.

When the knocking woke her, she was naked beneath a wet towel and had sucked some of her hair into her mouth. She spit it out and yelled, "Hang on!" Had to remember where she was.

She dressed as quickly as she could and let Braddock in while she brushed her hair.

"Man," he said. "I thought this place looked bad from the outside."

On the way out to the Tahoe, he offered to put her up in a bed-and-breakfast across the river.

"I'm good," she said. "Any news?"

"Nothing yet."

Which was to be expected.

★ ★ ★

The Riverside Pub was on the eastern edge of Dillard City next to an auto parts dealer. There were four motorcycles parked in front, all of them large Harley-Davidsons. Braddock turned onto the side road and said, "Let's see who else is here."

"Is this a biker bar?" Rachel asked.

"When the weather's right. We get a lot of bikers coming through this area, especially now that it's starting to warm up. They like to ride the backroads through the mountains. If you're still here this weekend, you'll see them at your motel."

In the parking lot behind the building, a red, beat-up Dodge Durango sat by the back door. Braddock parked next to it. "We can go in through there."

"Let's walk around to the front," she said.

They followed the side road back to Main. Rachel stopped at the corner and surveyed their surroundings, hoping to spot a public building or a bank or a gas station, but there were none in sight. There was a hardware store and a flower shop directly across the street. She asked, "Do you think either one of those has a camera pointed this way?"

"I doubt it, but we can check."

"You should canvass this area, in case there was anyone around who saw him leaving."

When she turned to face him, Braddock was already on the phone with the patrol captain arranging for a deputy to go door to door for a three-block radius. He finished the call and put his phone away, looking a little sheepish.

"Don't worry, Danny," she said, fighting the urge to smile. "It'll come back to you."

"Thanks, *former* Special Agent Carver, I'll keep that in mind."
He walked over to the door and held it open. "Can we go inside
now?"

"No need to get testy."

He gave her a half smile. "At least you're starting to earn your
keep."

They stepped inside, and their eyes needed a moment to adjust
to the dark interior. It was wood paneled and decorated with old
license plates and pictures of women wearing bikini tops and cutoff
jean shorts. The four bikers were sitting at the bar. Southern rock
played on the jukebox.

"Afternoon, Deputy Danny," came a voice from behind the bar.
It was hoarse and stuffy, as if spoken by a man with severe nasal
congestion.

Braddock cocked his head to one side and said, "Smiley? Is that
you?"

"Hell yeah."

"I thought you were working over in Whittier."

They walked past the bikers and met Smiley by the beer taps.
He looked miserable with a red nose and watery eyes.

"Nah, I quit that gig last month."

"You don't look so good," Braddock said.

"Goddamn pollen." Smiley touched his nose with a bar napkin.

"Can't you take some allergy medicine or something?"

"Momma's got me drinkin' this tea she makes"—he sucked a
breath through dry lips—"with honey she ordered online. Says it'll
cure me, 'cause it comes from California or somewhere."

Rachel said, "I don't think it works that way."

"Well, now you just ruined my whole damn day." He looked at
Braddock. "Y'all figure out who killed Dean?"

"We're working on it," he said. "Thought we'd come by here
and talk to whoever might have seen him last night."

"I saw him when he came in. You know, to start his shift."

"How did he seem to you?" Rachel asked.

"What d'ya mean?"

"Was there anything unusual about his behavior? Did he seem nervous or afraid of anything? Anyone?"

Smiley shrugged. "Not that I could see. But I really didn't talk to him much."

"Did you see him interact with anyone? Outside of what he would normally do as a bartender?"

He shook his head, dabbed the napkin under his nose.

"How well did you know him?"

"Not too well. Just met him when I started workin' here."

Rachel pulled a Steno pad and pen from her inside jacket pocket and made a couple of notes.

Braddock asked, "What time did you leave outta here last night?"

"Just after seven."

"And where did you go?"

"Home."

"Did you go anywhere else after that?"

"No, sir." He didn't appear bothered by the question. "Mom will tell you. I was there all night. Laid up in bed with this damn hay fever."

"Well, we sure appreciate the help, Smiley. Who's working tonight?"

"You're lookin' at him."

"You gonna make it?" Rachel asked.

He shrugged again and dabbed his eyes.

"I feel for you, bud," Braddock said. "But look here, you keep your ears open for me, all right? Let me know if you hear anything that could be useful to us."

Smiley had a sneezing fit but managed to get a nod in. Rachel and Braddock started to leave, but he held up a finger asking them to wait. He sneezed again, then sounding even more pitiful than he had before, said, "You know, there wasn't too many people around here that liked that asshole."

"Why not?" Rachel asked.

"'Cause he owed most of us money."

Braddock: "How much did he owe you?"

"Fifty bucks. But that ain't shit compared to some."

Rachel: "You think someone might have killed him over it?"

"Wouldn't surprise me. He was always pissin' someone off about it. And how in the hell could he manage to hang on to his house and all that property workin' here?" He wiped his eyes with the backs of his hands. "I know I couldn't do it."

7

Braddock treated Rachel to an early dinner at Lexington Barbecue, which he said was the only Carolina barbecue worth having.
They ate outside on a patio that overlooked the river. The gentle
sound of water flowing over rocks was putting Rachel to sleep, so
she asked for the most potent soft drink she could get. When the
server returned with a Mountain Dew, she drank a third of it at
once.

"You look like you're starting to fade," Braddock said. "Rough
night last night?"

"I'll be fine," she said.

He nodded, stayed quiet for a minute, then asked, "So what do
you think of our little town so far?"

"It's nice." She was too tired to come up with anything better
to say. "How about you? Do you still like living here after all these
years?"

He smiled. "You know, when I first moved here, I thought
I would hate it. I mean, the scenery's amazing and all, but I thought I
would get bored out of my mind in a place like this. But then . . .
I don't know. I just sorta fell in love with the place. I think it actually bugs Mandy that I like it here even more than she does."

Rachel had been wondering if he would bring up his ex-wife.
"Does she still live around here?"

"No. She moved to Asheville when we separated. I think there
was a part of her that—"

The server, a teenaged girl in a tight red T-shirt and black jeans, appeared at the end of the table and said, "Can I get anything else for you all?"

"I think we're good," Braddock said.

She turned to leave, then stopped short and stood a step away with an uneasy look on her face.

"Everything okay, Amber?" he asked.

"I'm sorry, Mister Braddock, but . . ."

"It's okay," he said with a polite smile. "What's the matter?"

"Well . . . it's just that my mom's been readin' online about the murder and all . . ."

"Yeah?"

"And she knows that you eat here every now and then."

"Okay?"

She looked over her shoulder and bounced on the balls of her feet like a small child needing a potty break. "She made me promise that, if I saw you here, I'd tell you . . . I mean, it ain't me sayin' it . . . but she said for me to tell you that you all should be out tryin' to find that murderer instead of sittin' here eatin' barbecue."

Braddock laughed. "Is that exactly how she said it?"

Amber looked around nervously. "Not exactly. She said you should be out tryin' to find that murderer instead of sittin' here stuffin' your faces."

"Yeah, that sounds a little more like her."

Rachel gave him a stern look, reminding him that it was never a good idea to ignore criticism from a concerned citizen.

He straightened up and said, "Well, Amber, tell your mom that we're doing everything we can."

Rachel's expression said, *Is that the best you can do?* He shrugged, so she decided to step in. "Amber."

"Yes, ma'am?"

A pang of sadness from being called "ma'am" again. She pushed it aside and said, "Tell your mom that the Lowry County Sheriff's Office has devoted all of its resources to ensuring the fastest possible resolution to this case."

"Yes, ma'am."

"Also tell her that the sheriff has requested and received additional assistance from outside law enforcement agencies including the State Bureau of Investigation and the State Crime Lab."

"Yes, ma'am."

"But, Amber."

"Ma'am?"

"Everyone needs to eat."

"Yes, ma'am."

Rachel smiled, and Amber shied away. But Braddock suddenly looked morose. He said, "Sounds like you've said that a few times before."

"Once or twice."

He looked toward the water, seemed to be lost in thought for a moment, and said, "I really do love this place. But if we can't solve this case, my days here might be numbered."

8

The Sugarlands Distilling Company in downtown Gatlinburg, Tennessee, was packed with tourists waiting for the next round of free samples. Gifford slipped into the crowd unnoticed. Carrying a small plastic bag containing twelve dollars' worth of fudge wrapped in white paper, he drifted along the edge of the room and pretended to examine the rows of mason jars filled with various flavors of moonshine. His right hand, buried in his pocket, clenched the burner cell, waiting for it to vibrate.

After his second trip around the perimeter, he stopped at one of the bars to watch a salesman deliver a speech about the latest variety of apple-pie-flavored spirits. It sounded good, but the phone buzzed in his hand just as the tiny plastic cups were being filled. He strolled outside, stopped at the edge of the street, and spotted the tank-green Jeep Wrangler a few seconds later. It rolled up to him, and he felt his heart speed up as he climbed into the passenger seat. They were already moving when he closed the door.

"I did good, didn't I?" Gifford asked. He kept his eyes on the storefronts and restaurants passing outside his window. Confectioners and T-shirt vendors and souvenir shops. A place to buy cheap samurai swords and ninja throwing stars.

"You did good," the driver said.

"Done it just like you said, man. Went real smooth too. Slicker than baby shit. Just like you said it would."

The driver veered into the left lane and sped up, and Gifford realized he was talking too much. He kept his mouth shut for the rest of the trip, which took them through town and into the Great Smoky Mountains.

★ ★ ★

Despite his forbidding demeanor, Derek Bishop was in a good mood. Gifford had performed better than expected. In fact, he had done such a good job, the Lowry County Sheriff's Office had hired an outsider to assist with the investigation. The consultant, according to his source, was a woman who excelled at solving difficult cases. Especially those that lacked physical evidence or a witness who could identify a suspect. And that was exactly the kind of case that Gifford had given them.

Everything had gone according to plan, but the woman made Bishop nervous. There was still work to be done, and once the body count started to go up, she would be looking for patterns. If she looked hard enough, she would find one. Bishop couldn't let that happen, so he had begun to think of ways to modify his plan. But changes would create complications. He needed time to work out the details. For now, he would keep things moving forward, which meant giving Gifford his next assignment.

Bishop steered the Wrangler into Newfound Gap, a scenic over-look straddling the border between Tennessee and North Carolina. He pulled into a spot near the end of the second row and took a few seconds to look around. The edge of the parking lot lined the top of a bluff that offered a commanding view of the mountains to the south. Dozens of people milled about the walkway, pointing at objects in the distance and trying to capture the scenery with smartphone cameras before the sun went down, all of them too preoccupied to notice two men planning a murder.

"You did good for your first time," Bishop said. His eyes continued to scan. "But it was an easy mark. The next one's going to be more complicated."

"No problem, man. I can handle it."

Bishop responded with a look that said he was unimpressed, and Gifford's Adam's apple jumped.

"I swear, man. I got it. You can count on me."

"We'll see." Bishop reached into his pocket and withdrew a small slip of paper. He unfolded it and held it low. "This is your next target."

Gifford studied the sheet. His mouth moved silently as he worked to memorize the name and address. After more than a minute, he said, "Got it."

"You sure?"

"Positive."

He slid the paper back into his pocket. "We don't have much time. It needs to be tonight." A few seconds passed in silence as his eyes moved from mirror to mirror, making sure no one was getting close enough to overhear them. He said, "And this one won't be home alone."

9

After they finished eating, Braddock took Rachel to meet Sheriff Pritchard. They sat across from him in his office and listened as he recapped a phone conversation he'd had with the district attorney an hour earlier. The call had not gone well.

"I'm pretty sure that's the first time I've ever been called an injudicious moron," he said.

Braddock laughed.

Pritchard ignored him and said, "But I guess I have myself to blame for that. This morning, I gave an interview to some kid from the Waynesville Ledger, and I just couldn't resist telling him about the high-dollar, out-of-town expert we hired to help us catch this killer."

Rachel felt the urge to object to the term "high dollar" but decided it was best to let it go.

Braddock said, "I wish you hadn't done that, boss."

"So do I," he said. "Knew it was a mistake as the words were coming outta my mouth. But, you know, I actually thought I wouldn't have to worry about it till tomorrow morning. Part of being in the digital age, I guess. Little bastard probably wrote that damned article on his cell phone while he was still sitting in the parking lot. And, of course, the DA is checking the local news sites every hour."

"You might consider doing the same," Rachel said.

"Are you serious?"

"Yes, sir."

Pritchard laughed. "Miss Carver, once you get to know me, you'll learn that I don't have the patience to sit in front of a computer all day."

"I can't blame you for that, Sheriff. But what I really mean is that you should assign someone to track how the case is being reported in the media and have them save any articles they find."

"Well, that's a thought," he said, leaning back and rocking in his chair. "Any other advice?"

"I think you need to change your overall approach toward the media."

"How so?"

"There's a lot of pressure on you right now, and you're going to be tempted to try to give them something new every time you talk to them. But doing that sets the expectation that something significant will develop every day and that the case will be solved quickly. You need to start thinking long term."

"How long term are we talking?"

"There's no way to know for sure."

"But if you had to guess," he said, "based on your experience, what kind of time frame are we looking at?"

She thought for a second, trying to decide how to phrase a realistic answer that wouldn't send him into a state of panic or depression. "We could catch a break at any time. A witness might walk in here tomorrow and solve the whole thing for us, but you can't run an investigation based on that kind of wishful thinking. You need to be prepared for the possibility that it could drag on for months or even longer."

"Okay." Pritchard smiled, but there was tension in his jaw. "So, aside from refining my media relations strategy, what else do I need to do?"

"Have you assigned a case officer?"

Pritchard looked at Braddock, who nodded and said, "Shane."

"He's going to be overwhelmed," she said. "Especially in this early phase. You have another detective, the patrol units, plus Danny and me, and each one of us is working a different angle.

We're all going to have information to contribute. Then there's the crime scene techs, the crime lab, the medical examiner . . . Detective Fisher is going to have a tough time keeping up with all of it. You should assign someone to help him manage the paperwork and create an indexing system."

"What do you mean by indexing system?" Pritchard asked.

"It's a way to track every item of interest that turns up as part of the investigation. Every name, address, vehicle, whatever . . . anything that appears in a report or in someone's notes, you log it. You create an entry for it and update the log any time that item comes up again. That way, you'll have an easy way to track it and cross-reference your documentation. You won't have to rely on an investigator's memory of what's in the case file. The old-fashioned way was to use index cards, but I'd recommend a spreadsheet. It's easier to search."

"All right," Pritchard said. "Anything else?"

"Meetings."

"Like the one we're going to have tonight," Braddock added.

Rachel said, "We should have one at the end of each day for now. Everyone who's involved will be there and get updated on any developments. That's also a good time—"

Braddock's phone rang. "Sorry," he said as he withdrew it from his pocket. He checked the screen before he answered. "Hey, Shane. Everything all right?" The skin around his eyes tensed as he listened. "Okay . . . okay . . . yeah . . . all right, we're on our way." He ended the call and said to Pritchard, "We gotta run, boss." Then to Rachel, "Looks like you get to meet Mister McGrath in person after all."

★ ★ ★

Harris Regional Hospital was a thirty-minute drive from the sheriff's office. Fisher was waiting in the corridor outside the autopsy room. He led them inside and introduced them to the pathologist, a tall, lean woman in her fifties named Cynthia Breyer.

"Glad you could join us, detectives," she said, holding the front section of Dean McGrath's ribcage in her left hand. The rest of the body lay on a stainless steel table in front of her. A second table to her left held her instruments, tools, a scale, a section of McGrath's skull, and a bowl containing his brain. "Give me just a second, and I'll show you what I've found so far."

Carly Brewer approached, thumbing through images on her camera screen. "Hey, boss," she said without looking up.

"How's it going?" Braddock asked.

"Better now. I'm a little embarrassed, though. Had to run out when she started working on the head."

"I don't blame you," he said. "I did the same thing the first time I saw an autopsy."

Rachel knew he was lying. She had been with him at the time. Even though he had stayed quiet for more than an hour afterward, he had made it through the procedure with no problem.

"You hangin' in there, Shane?" he asked.

"Yep," Fisher said. A trace of pride in his voice. "I'm good."

"Okay," Breyer said, "let me get all of you over here on the opposite side of this table, if I could."

Rachel stepped up first. The others moved in behind her. The body lay face up, its internal organs exposed by the Y incision and removal of the breastplate. Breyer's gloved hands gripped the edge of the table as she tilted her head forward to look over the top of her glasses. She said, "Obviously, the ME will have the final say about what ends up on the certificate, but I don't think there's any doubt that the victim died from massive hemorrhaging that resulted from a single stab wound to his chest."

"Just one?" Rachel asked.

"One's not enough?" Fisher said.

Breyer smiled. "It's unusual, I agree. Especially given the fact that he didn't seem to put up much of a fight. But take a look at this." She grabbed the flap of skin, muscle, and fat that rested on the victim's chin and pulled it down to cover the top of his chest. Rachel saw the wound immediately. It was held closed by a piece of clear tape. Breyer pointed to it and said, "The wound is significantly longer than the width of the blade. By nearly an inch. Also, if you look closely, you can see a couple of smaller lacerations branching off where the edge of the blade was."

Rachel leaned in. She could see the extra lines. They left tiny slivers of skin at slight angles from the main cut.

Breyer lifted the flap and set it back on the chin. She reached over to the side table and returned with the breastplate. The sternum and ribs—the web of bone, muscle, and cartilage—looked too much like something that might be packaged in the meat department of a grocery store. Rachel forced the thought out of her mind as Breyer set it in place.

"You can see the same thing here as well," Breyer said, pointing to the slit where the knife had penetrated. After everyone got a look, she put the breastplate back on the side table, then used her index fingers to probe the organs. "And in here, we can start to make sense of that. Look at the damage the killer caused in here." She lifted a lung with one hand and shifted the heart around with the other. "There's a puncture to the ventricle wall, the aortic valve is shredded, the pulmonary artery is almost completely severed. And this lung . . . just look at it."

"What a mess," Braddock said.

Rachel asked, "Do you think that means the killer was moving the knife around while it was still in his chest, trying to cause more damage?"

"That's exactly what I think," Breyer said.

"The wound is pretty high," Rachel said. She raised her hand as if she were holding an imaginary knife. "But the angle of the blade doesn't look right for an icepick grip." She turned to face Braddock. Pretended to stab him, then moved her hand around to simulate what the killer might have done.

Braddock cringed. "I can almost feel you doing that."

"I don't think it happened that way," Breyer said. "When I removed his sweater, I noticed that all the blood that seeped from the wound seemed to run toward the shoulder and neck. There was none running down the abdomen."

"But that would mean that he was already on his back when he was stabbed," Rachel said.

"Exactly. There's something else I need to show you." Breyer stepped around the corner of the table and stood next to the head.

"When I did the external exam of the scalp, I didn't see anything unusual. There's a lot of purple discoloration on the back of his head that's consistent with livor mortis—just the blood settling at the lowest point. So I didn't bother to look too close. When I examined the skull, I found a small fracture right here . . ." She bent forward and pointed at a shaved spot on the scalp just beneath the incision she had made to expose the skull. "At first, I thought it might be from his head hitting the floor during the attack, but I figured it was better to be safe than sorry. So I shaved this area, and lo and behold . . ."

Rachel crouched and turned her head to get a good look. Braddock peered over her shoulder and asked, "What are we looking at?"

"See those two blotches?"

They were small, each the size of a fingertip. They would have been longer had they not merged with the purple mass of pooled blood. Rachel said, "Tramline bruising."

"I'll be damned," Braddock said.

Breyer looked over her glasses at Rachel. "Something tells me you've seen your share of the dead."

Rachel smiled, and Fisher said, "Well, I haven't. Would someone mind telling me what the heck you all are talking about?"

"It's a bruising pattern that forms as a result of blunt-force trauma from a cylindrical object like a pipe or a baseball bat," Breyer said.

Rachel turned to Braddock. "How much time do we have before the meeting?"

He looked at his watch. "Two hours."

"Good. I want to go back to the house."

★ ★ ★

They pulled into the dirt driveway forty-five minutes later. The deputy met them as they were getting out of the Tahoe. They signed in and went inside through the carport. The rotten-food smell hit them as they entered the kitchen. Rachel wrinkled her nose and said, "The killer was already in the house, waiting for McGrath to come home."

"Had to be," Braddock agreed.

She looked around the kitchen. "But he wasn't just hanging around in here waiting for him to walk through the door. McGrath had time to get leftovers out of the fridge and heat them up in the microwave before he was attacked." She moved from the kitchen into the living room, then down a narrow hall. There were five doorways to choose from: three bedrooms, a bathroom, and a linen closet. She looked inside each one, found McGrath's bedroom at the end of the hall. Then she backed up and went into the bedroom nearest the living room. There was a queen-size bed in the center, stacks of cardboard boxes lining the far wall. A guest room doubling as a storage space. "Was this door open when you guys got here?"

"I don't know," Braddock said. "I'd have to ask Shane."

"This is where I would have hidden." She held her hands together by her right shoulder, as if she were holding a bat. She stared through the doorway and tried to put herself in the killer's mind. "I'd stand here in the dark and wait for him to come down the hall. He'd have to walk by this door to get to his bedroom. I'd come out behind him and . . ." She stepped into the hallway and took an imaginary swing. "It would have been easy."

"Except it didn't happen that way."

"No," she said and moved back into the bedroom. "Because I hear my victim come home, but he doesn't go to his room. He's moving around in the kitchen. I hear the fridge open and close. I hear a drawer and cabinet doors. It's taking longer than I thought it would. He might be in there for a while, cooking and eating. I'm nervous. Impatient. I want this to be over with so I can get out of here. I start to have doubts about my plan of attack."

She slid through the doorway and eased down the hall into the living room with Braddock in tow. They turned the corner to the kitchen. She could see McGrath standing in front of the microwave, his back to her. She raised the imaginary bat, stepped forward, but a noisy floorboard stopped her.

"Doesn't make sense," Braddock said. "He was hit on the back of the head. Like he didn't know it was coming."

She took another step into the kitchen, caught the odor of putrid meatballs in tomato sauce. Saw the bloodstain on the floor and fought the urge to gag. Then she looked at the microwave. It was small and white and old. A cheap model even when it was new. She walked back into the hall toward the bedroom and said, "Go turn on the microwave. Stand in front of it, and let's see if you can hear me coming."

He nodded and disappeared into the kitchen. She heard him touch a couple of buttons, and it started humming. As she tiptoed around the corner, she was amazed at how noisy the little appliance was. Almost as loud as a hair dryer. She was able to approach Braddock and stand just behind him, yet he didn't react. She reached out and grabbed his shoulder.

He flinched and said, "Jesus, Rachel," then turned and fixed his eyes on the bloodstain.

"You okay?" she asked.

"Yeah, but this little exercise of yours is starting to freak me out."

The time on the microwave ended. *Beep, beep, beep*, and there was silence.

★ ★ ★

On the drive back to the office, Braddock got a call from Fisher. After listening for a couple of minutes, he said, "All right. We'll see you in a few." He dropped his phone in the cup holder. "That was Shane giving me an update."

"Anything good?" Rachel asked.

"Not really. Tina—our other detective—just got back from notifying the family. McGrath's mother and sister over in Franklin, about thirty-five miles from here. Said it was tough, but they didn't have much to say. She also did a record search this morning. Found out our victim was arrested once for public indecency about four years ago. Drunk, pissing in a bush on the side of the street."

"Sounds like we might have a short meeting."

Braddock smiled. "Somehow I doubt that."

10

Rachel was seated between Braddock and Pritchard on one side of an oval conference table as the others began to file in. Braddock introduced her to Tina Pratt—the other detective—when she entered the room. Fisher arrived a minute later and took a seat next to Pratt, directly across from Rachel. A tall man in uniform, who looked to be in his sixties, sat down at one end of the table.

"Rachel," Braddock said, "this is Melvin Curtis. He's our patrol captain."

Curtis smiled broadly, tilting an uneven mustache. His thin, deep-set eyes nearly disappeared.

Another uniformed deputy, a petite woman with blonde hair who looked a little overburdened by her utility belt and sidearm, sneaked in and found a chair at the other end next to Carly Brewer, apparently trying not to be noticed. Braddock leaned toward Rachel and said, "Her name's Melissa Howard. She'll be helping Shane out with the paperwork."

Once everyone was situated, Pritchard cleared his throat and said, "All right. I think everyone here has met by now, but just in case"—he pointed a thumb at Rachel—"this is Rachel Carver. She has a lot of experience in tough homicide cases, so we're lucky to have her. You may or may not have heard that the SBI is taking their time sending us an investigator, so Danny went and found us one."

A few chuckles around the table.

"Right now, we're focused on catching whoever killed poor Dean McGrath. But you all know even better than I do that there's a lot more to it than that. We need to catch the bastard, but we need to do it right. The last thing we want is for some lawyer to stroll into the courthouse and destroy our case because we didn't cover our butts. We all know what that's like. Miss Carver is here to make sure that doesn't happen." He turned to Rachel. "Anything you want to add to that before we get started?"

She looked at the detectives. "It's my job to pick you two apart. To scrutinize every move you've made every step of the way. And I'm going to suggest that you do some things from this point forward. Things that will make a lot of extra work for you. Before this meeting is over, you'll probably want to tie me up and force feed me the case file. But when you're sitting on the witness stand, you'll be grateful for every note you wrote, every picture you took, every sketch you made . . . because every aspect of this case, from the way you document what you find at a crime scene, to the canvass, to the handling of physical evidence, to the interrogation of a suspect . . . all of it will be under the microscope. I know you're experienced detectives, but in a case like this, even a veteran can make a mistake that might cost a conviction. I've seen it happen."

Fisher fidgeted in his seat, looking agitated. Rachel's eyes met his as she said, "So we need to be sure we don't make any more."

"Any *more*?" Fisher asked. "What mistakes have we made?"

In her peripheral vision, she saw Braddock straighten in his chair. She smiled and said, "Were you there this morning when Carly and the SBI tech started processing the crime scene?"

"Yes."

"Did you leave at any point before they finished?"

"For about an hour or so," he said. "I met with the deputies who did the canvass, then stopped to get coffee for everyone. But Tina was there."

Pratt nodded and said, "That's right. And I stayed until he got back."

"I see," she said. "And during all that time at the house, did either of you two need to use the restroom?"

"Yeah," Fisher said. "I did."

"Okay. I didn't see a portable sanitation unit there. Did you go in the woods?"

"Uh . . . no, ma'am," he said, turning a little red. "It wasn't really something I could do out there."

More chuckling.

"So does that mean you left the house to drive somewhere else?"

"Of course not."

"Then I'm confused. Where did you go to use the restroom?"

"I used the one in the house."

"Before the crime scene process was complete?" she asked.

He opened his mouth to speak but stopped himself as he realized his mistake. His face turned a shade darker, and he shrank in his seat.

Rachel said, "We have a lot to talk about."

★ ★ ★

Rachel had been lecturing about the proper way to handle a crime scene for nearly twenty minutes when Pratt said, "Okay, obviously there are some things we could've done better, but what does this have to do with where we are now?"

"Two things," Rachel said. "First, we may still find another crime scene related to this murder. Second, our killer may not be finished yet. If either one of those happens, we need to be ready."

The room went quiet, and it struck Rachel that Fisher and Pratt had not been prepared to hear that.

Melvin Curtis, the patrol captain, spoke for the first time. "Are you saying this could be a serial killer or something?"

"We don't know," Braddock said. "But we can't rule it out. All we really know is that the killer planned this ahead of time and knew what he was doing."

"But I thought McGrath was stabbed with one of his own kitchen knives?"

"He was."

"Doesn't that contradict what you're saying? I mean, it seems to me like he came a little unprepared."

"I don't agree," Rachel said. "Every house has kitchen knives in it. He could have counted on it being there."

Curtis had a look of skepticism.

"Think about what the evidence tells us," she said. "There was no sign of forced entry, which means he may have been skilled enough to pick the locks on one of the doors. So maybe he goes inside and searches the kitchen. He's studied the victim's routine and knows how much time he has. He finds the knife, but he leaves it alone, knowing it'll be there when he needs it. Then he hides and waits.

"There was no sign of a struggle. The victim was taken by surprise, hit from behind with something like a pipe or a baseball bat, probably hard enough to knock him out because it caused a small fracture on his skull. Does the killer keep hitting him? No. He knows better than to rupture the scalp and send blood flying everywhere. So he goes for the knife, which can never be traced back to him. With the victim lying unconscious, flat on his back, he stabs him in the chest. But he doesn't pull it out and try to stab him again. He doesn't want to risk getting blood on himself. Instead, he moves the knife around inside the wound, causing as much damage as he can.

"When he's done, he doesn't even bother to take it out. He just walks out the door without leaving so much as a bloody footprint. And I'm willing to bet none of the fingerprints found at the scene are his either. If I'm right about all that, then we're dealing with someone who's smart and disciplined, and that's a bad combination for us."

"Damn," Curtis said. "Sounds like you know quite a bit after all."

"It's just a theory," Braddock said, "but it fits."

Pratt asked, "What part of that tells us that this could be a serial killer?"

"It's more about what it doesn't tell us," Rachel said. "The fact that the killer appears to have been so calculating makes it seem like there wasn't any emotion directed specifically at the victim. If he had been stabbed a dozen times, or if his face had been beaten to a pulp before he was stabbed, that might suggest that the attack was personal. That there was some hatred or pent-up anger. But this doesn't look like it was fueled by rage. It was almost . . . surgical. That doesn't mean it was a serial killer. It just means that we can't ignore the possibility."

Pritchard sighed. "Wouldn't that just be my luck. A damn mass murderer getting his start on my watch."

"We're assuming he's getting his start," Rachel said. "He might have done this before somewhere else."

"That's a good point," Braddock said. "I'll put in a call to the SBI when we finish here and tell them what we're thinking. See if they have anything with a similar MO. They might even decide to run it past the FBI in case our guy is from out of state."

"In the meantime," Rachel said, "we need to focus on the victimology and hope that the motive *was* something personal. That'll be our best chance of finding a suspect at this point."

Braddock said to the detectives, "Which means you two are gonna get to know Mister McGrath real well. Starting first thing tomorrow morning, go back to the house and go through it from top to bottom. Then talk to his friends, family, coworkers, acquaintances . . . We want to know who he was hanging around with, where he spent his time, what he did when he wasn't at work . . . We need to get warrants for his financial records, his cell phone records . . . any and everything you can think of."

Rachel said, "Your goal is to collect as much information as you can about McGrath and what was happening in his life. And get it from every source you can. When you have no suspects, no witnesses, and no forensic evidence, all you can do is get to know the victim." She looked at Fisher. "This is your case, and it's your town. You know the people you'll be talking to. Don't be afraid to follow your instincts. Everyone at this table is here to back you up."

Fisher nodded, looking a little more enthusiastic. "I'm on it."

Curtis said, "I hate to throw a wrench in these works, especially with something so trivial, but we had a couple of calls come in today. I was planning to pass them along to you, Danny. One was about a stolen ATV, and the other was Sue Bethany saying that someone broke into her shed again. Although she can't say for sure whether anything's missing."

Pritchard closed his eyes and pinched the bridge of his nose.

Curtis asked, "You want me to just have a couple of deputies look into it for now?"

Braddock was about to answer when Fisher said, "I was here when the call came in about the four-wheeler this morning. I can run by during lunch tomorrow and talk to the owner. Shouldn't take long."

"And I live down the road from Sue," Pratt said. "I'll call her up when we leave here. Maybe swing by and talk to her on my way home."

"All right," Pritchard said. "But you two don't go wasting too much of your time. *This* is everyone's priority right now. Besides, we all know it was probably just Sue's boy up there borrowing a damned Weedwacker or something."

★ ★ ★

After the meeting, Rachel approached Carly and asked for copies of all the photographs she had taken.

"There's a bunch of them," Carly said. "You have a thumb drive?"

"Yep."

"Awesome. It would take forever to e-mail them all."

She followed Carly to her office, which was only slightly larger than a janitor's closet. A wire-framed shelving unit stood against the far wall. It held heavy-duty plastic cases for camera equipment and unused evidence collection kits. A desk was pushed against the wall to the right, leaving only enough room for a single chair. Carly dropped into it and moved a mouse around until her workstation came to life, then she logged in.

Rachel dug through the pockets of her briefcase. She found the drive and handed it over. Carly plugged it in, and a new window opened on her desktop. She copied and pasted the file folder, sat back while the progress bar worked its way to the right, and said, "Old server. Might take a minute or two."

"No problem." A few seconds passed in silence. Rachel leaned against the desk and asked, "How long have you been doing CrossFit?"

Carly looked at a spot on the wall, thinking. "I guess it's been about three years or so."

"You like it?" Rachel almost cringed as the question slipped out. She was terrible at small talk. "I mean, of course you like it or you wouldn't still be doing it."

Carly smiled. "Yeah. It's fun. Challenging. More interesting than running on a treadmill."

"I could see that."

"Danny mentioned that you train jiu-jitsu. How long have you been doing that?"

"About nine years."

"What got you into it?"

"Raleigh PD brought an instructor in once to give a seminar. I loved it. I went to his school and signed up that same week."

"Good way to work off the stress?"

"There's no better therapy in the world than trying to choke someone out. And it's more interesting than running on a treadmill."

Carly laughed. "That's awesome. What belt are you?"

"Brown."

"You must be pretty good by now."

Rachel shrugged. "I can hold my own, if I'm having a good day."

"Well, Danny said you were *really* good."

She laughed. "He did, huh?"

"Yep." Carly smiled. She looked on the verge of winking as she said, "He's had a lot of nice things to say about you."

Rachel felt flushed, unsure of how to respond. Luckily the task bar disappeared from the screen, and Carly said, "All done." She took out the drive and handed it back.

"Thanks." Rachel dropped it into her briefcase and started backing toward the door. "I'd better go find Danny."

Another smile. "Yeah. You should do that."

★ ★ ★

Rachel found Braddock in the hall just outside the conference room talking to Pritchard and a tall, heavyset man in a sport coat and khakis. The man had thick white hair and a red face with spider veins on his cheeks. Braddock waved her over and said, "Rachel, I'd like you to meet Commissioner Lawton Jones."

Jones reached out with a puffy hand and shook Rachel's. "It's nice to meet you, Miss Carver. I've heard a lot about you."

"My pleasure, sir. I hope I'm not interrupting."

"Not at all," he said.

Pritchard said, "Lawton's here on behalf of the county commission. They want to know how badly we're screwing things up."

Jones laughed. "That sounds a little paranoid, Sheriff."

"What is it they say? It's not paranoia if they're really out to smear your name and run you out of—"

"So, Commissioner," Braddock said quickly, "I wish we had more to tell you, but we're really just getting started here."

"That's all right, Danny," Jones said. "I understand. I just wanted to stop in and see if there was any news." He turned to Rachel. "Tell me, Miss Carver, when you were working for the SBI, did you ever come to a little town like ours and help the locals solve a murder?"

"More than once," she said.

"Well, in that case, I'm glad you're here. People in this area are pretty scared, as I'm sure you can imagine."

"Yes, sir, I can."

"This kind of thing is unusual for us, but some folks are saying that we should expect to see more of it. Especially with all the outsiders we get riding through here."

"Outsiders?"

Braddock was fighting back a smile, as if he knew what was coming.

"The bikers," Jones said. "Coming in and out of town every weekend. I'm not saying they're all bad, mind you, but there's definitely a criminal element there."

"I see," she said.

"I've heard all sorts of stories from people. Drugs, prostitution . . . things I hate to even repeat. And everyone knows they're the reason we have such a problem with the crystal meth now."

"Okay."

"That's something I'd be checking into, if I were you."

"Right." She looked to Braddock for help, but he seemed to be enjoying the exchange. She said, "I'll make sure Danny and I look into it personally."

11

Rachel and Braddock decided it was best not to be seen enjoying another meal in public, so they picked up chicken sandwiches from McDonald's and took them back to the Fontana Lodge. They ate at the lopsided Formica table and talked about the case. When they were finished, Rachel took her laptop computer from her briefcase and powered it up so she could load Carly's crime scene photos. She inserted the thumb drive, opened the folder to a gallery of tiny thumbnail images, and selected a few at random.

"You were right," she said. "Carly did a good job with these."

Braddock sipped an iced tea and stared at the floor, looking weary. Rachel opened a photo that showed the body lying on the kitchen floor and zoomed in to get a closer look. After examining it for a couple minutes, she closed the screen and fell back in her seat. "I need a break. I'll take a look at them in a little while."

"In a little while?" Braddock asked. "You go right ahead. I'm so tired, I can hardly see straight."

She smiled, thought about the meeting and the encounter afterward. "What's the deal with that commissioner?"

"Lawton? He's a real estate developer. Owns a bunch of land all over the western part of the state. He's pretty wealthy, though you wouldn't know it to look at him."

"Doesn't seem to care much for bikers."

"Been going on about that for years. Says they're bringing in meth labs and driving down property values."

"Any truth to it?"

"Some. We see a little gang activity every now and then, but nothing like what Lawton would have you believe. They do make and sell meth, but they're not the only ones. Either way, the majority of the bikers that come through here are just regular people. Weekend riders. The truth is we'd really miss them if they weren't around. They bring in a lot of money for the local economy."

"You ever see any gang activity at the bar where McGrath worked?"

Braddock shook his head.

Rachel thought for a moment and said, "Hmm."

"Uh-oh. Don't tell me you're starting to take Lawton's biker thing seriously."

"Maybe. Maybe not. Like you said, they're not the only ones around here dealing meth. And McGrath wouldn't be the first bartender to sell drugs on the side. We know he was having money problems."

"That's true," he said. "I guess we can't rule it out."

"That's the problem," she said, rubbing her eyes. "We can't rule anything out yet."

"You should get some sleep. We can talk to Shane about the drug angle in the morning."

"Had enough for one day?"

He nodded toward the bed. "If I don't get outta here soon, you're going to have to share that bed with me."

She thought about her conversation with Carly and laughed. It came out louder than she'd intended.

"I didn't mean it like . . ." His face turned red.

Her face turned red.

He said, "Okay, I'm gonna leave now."

They said good night, and she showed him out. Then she leaned against the door and thought about how good he'd looked walking away.

★ ★ ★

A few minutes later, Rachel stood in front of the mirror and leaned in to examine her bloodshot green eyes. Fine lines were starting to form beneath them, but the rest of her skin was holding up well for a sleep-deprived thirty-eight-year-old with a poor diet. She even had a little color, despite the fact that she rarely spent time in the sun.

She turned off the vanity light and climbed into bed. Pulled the computer onto her lap, thinking she might browse the photos. The little clock at the corner of the screen said it was 9:17. Her eyelids felt heavy. She changed her mind, set the computer aside, and switched off the lamp on the nightstand. She was nearly asleep when the phone rang.

The caller ID said, "Bryce Parker," who was a reporter for the *Raleigh Herald*. It had been nearly four months since she had last spoken to him. She let it ring two more times before deciding to answer.

"Hi, Rachel," he said with the kind of overly courteous tone that suggested he was desperate for a quote. "How are you?"

"Good. What can I do for you?"

"Well, I was wondering if you'd had a chance to look at the report that SBI released today."

"What? No I . . . I'm out of town right now, Bryce. I don't know what you're talking about."

"Oh . . . I assumed . . ." He was quiet for a moment, then said, "Sorry, Rachel. I thought they were keeping you in the loop—"

"What report?" she asked, getting impatient.

"Lauren Bailey," he said.

Rachel sat up in the bed, felt a black hole swallow her heart.

"The report on the internal investigation came out today," he said. "I was hoping you might have a comment."

She tried to answer, but the words stuck. She swallowed with a dry throat and said, "I don't . . . I think I need to read it before . . ."

"Of course," he said. "No worries. Hey, if you want, I can e-mail it to you."

"Yeah . . . thanks."

"I'll send it now. And if you get a chance to read it tonight, I'd love to hear back from you."

"Sure."

"Great. You have a good night, Rachel." Then he was gone.

She sat in the dark and tried to fend off the memory, but relentless images poured into view. A child, hardly a toddler, sitting on a floor in a soiled diaper. The deputy, sidearm gripped in his outstretched hands, trying to yell over the little boy's piercing screams. Lauren Bailey waving a handgun too large for her stubby fingers.

Rachel held her weapon low and tried to calm things down. Tried to talk to Bailey, to reason with her for the sake of her son. Bailey was distraught and desperate. Sounded intoxicated. Almost incoherent. Her only clear words proclaimed her innocence. She didn't want to go to jail. Didn't think it was right. Didn't think it was fair.

She turned to walk away, perhaps toward her kitchen. Maybe the hallway to her bedroom. But the deputy stepped forward and yelled his commands. Told her to stop, to drop her weapon, to get on the floor. Bailey turned and raised her hand, looking like she might have wanted to give him the finger, but there was a gun in that hand. The deputy hesitated, so Rachel opened up on her, putting eight rounds in her center mass, just like she'd been taught. And Bailey fell. The deputy ran up to secure the gun, then checked for vitals, then called for help. Rachel scooped up the child and headed for the door. She was outside talking in soothing tones as Bailey died on the floor.

Back in the Fontana Lodge, an e-mail alert sounded on Rachel's phone. Parker had sent the report. She wasn't ready to read it, so she set it on the nightstand and turned on the light and the TV. She propped two of the pillows against the headboard and sat up to flip through the channels, knowing that she would be lucky to get any sleep at all before morning came.

12

Gifford had the route memorized. He turned his Sierra pickup onto Everly Street and crossed the river. He cruised past the dark store-fronts and climbed the hill leading away from the center of town. A half mile later, he saw the feed store on his right and took the next left. He drove slow, almost idling once the road turned to gravel. Then he found it. He flicked off the lights and veered to the right, following the tire-worn tracks by feeling as much as by moon-light. Once he was deep enough beyond the tree line, he killed the engine and stepped out.

He stood next to his truck and listened for a moment. Satisfied that he was alone, he clicked on his flashlight and started walking. After nearly five minutes headed mostly downhill, the path ended at the bottom of a valley. Directly ahead was a steep rise. He scaled it quickly, zigzagging between half-buried boulders. He used the trees to pull himself along, thankful that he was still agile enough to climb like he did as a teenager when his favorite pastime was exploring these wooded hills.

When he reached the ridge, he turned off the flashlight and kept still until his eyes adjusted to the light. Ahead to his right, he could see a gentle slope that led to a stream. Beyond that, a short incline to a wall of trees, vines, and shrubs. He descended carefully, testing the ground with his feet before committing his weight. A bad step on a rock or in a hole could take him out of the hunt, and he had too much to lose to let that happen.

He jumped over the water and jogged up the sandy embankment, feeling his confidence grow until he tripped on a root, cursed at himself, then continued more cautiously. At the top, he found a gap between a pair of trees that let him see the road. He ducked behind a sweetshrub and listened for approaching cars. A short sprint and he would be safely in the woods on the other side. He checked his watch, felt good about the time. Once he made it across, the house would only be a hundred yards away.

★ ★ ★

It was slow going through the dense forest. The tree canopy hid most of the moonlight. Gifford had to use the flashlight more than he had wanted, but it was starting to get late. When he finally reached the edge of the backyard, he only had a few minutes to get in position.

He watches one of those adult cartoon shows on Comedy Central every weeknight, Bishop had said. *His wife will be in the bedroom watching HGTV. You won't have to worry about her, if you do it right. As soon as the show is over, he'll walk the dog in the backyard. It's a Chihuahua. Nothing to be afraid of, but it'll bark. Might bring the neighbors outside or the wife downstairs, so make sure to shut it up as soon as you get a chance.*

Gifford slipped on his leather gloves and stepped into the open. He kept his eyes on the windows as he approached the back of the white two-story house. He moved to the corner and crouched down, putting his back against the wood siding.

You won't need the bat this time. He keeps an old ax handle by the side door to the garage. He used to use it to chase away the neighbor's bulldog. But don't worry, that thing's dead now.

The neighbor's house had a single light on in the back, but he couldn't see any movement. His heart raced, and he had to take a few deep breaths to slow it down. He found the ax handle leaning against the doorjamb, exactly where it was supposed to be. The old piece of gray wood felt good. His confidence swelled again with a weapon in his hand. He moved back to the corner and waited.

A few minutes later, he heard the back door open. Then there was a man's voice urging a little dog outside to do its business. He called it "Beau."

"Come on, Beau. Hurry up now, li'l man."

Beau's nails made light *tick, tick, ticking* sounds on the wooden steps. Then the back door closed and heavier footfalls descended. Gifford tightened his grip, peeked around the corner, and saw the man standing just a few paces away. He stepped out to make his move, and Beau saw him instantly.

"What's the matter, li'l—"

The man caught sight of Gifford just before the ax handle hit its mark. The blow sent its victim reeling, but he was still conscious. Beau jumped forward like he might bite Gifford on the ankle, barking and growling and snarling. The man fell against the wall. He used one hand to steady himself and tried to raise the other for defense, but Gifford's second swing was too fast, knocking him onto his back.

Beau caught the leg of Gifford's jeans, trying to pull him away. Gifford shook him loose and took a swing at the tiny beast. But Beau saw it coming and dodged. He circled around, careful to keep his distance but threatening another bite and making too much noise. Gifford made another attempt and missed. Seeing his chance, Beau pounced, seizing Gifford's jeans again and catching a bit of skin in his needle-sharp teeth.

Gifford winced and smacked his leg against the wall trying to knock Beau off. The little dog yelped and released his hold. He hit the ground and took off around the corner, crying and barking. Then Gifford heard the clicking of a latch. He turned to see the man crawling into the doorway on his hands and knees, moaning and trying to find his voice to call for help. Gifford ran up the steps and slid past him into a carpeted den. He raised the ax handle over his head, then sent it down with a grunt. The wood cracked with the force of the blow, and the man was out cold. Gifford dropped his weapon, caught his breath, and listened for the wife.

He heard the TV going upstairs but nothing else. It was safe to finish. He went to the kitchen and searched the counters. There was no knife set. He started pulling drawers and found them on his third try. He chose the longer of two paring knives and went back to the den to complete his work.

If he's on his back, go for the heart. If he's on his stomach, go for the brain stem. Just like I taught you . . .

Gifford lowered himself to one knee and leaned over the man, whose hair was now soaked with blood. A red streak ran across his temple, down his cheek, and to his nose. Gifford knew better than to touch the man's head and risk getting blood on his gloves, but he needed to keep it steady to do the job. He went to the kitchen again and found a hand towel. Came back and used it to hold the head still. He was about to make the thrust when he felt sweat building on his brow. He wiped it with his forearm to keep it from dripping. Then he placed the tip of the blade at the back of the man's head. The place where the skull ended and the backbone began, just like Bishop had taught him. There was a soft spot there between the bones, and Gifford found it.

★ ★ ★

Gifford stepped outside, and Beau was there waiting, ears pinned back and teeth showing. He growled, then jumped forward and started barking. Gifford went down the steps, eager to shut him up, but Beau took off running, stopped about ten yards away, and started barking again.

Despite his frustration, Gifford admired the little dog, respected his bravery and loyalty. If he had been any bigger, he might have been able to put up a real fight. But that hadn't stopped him from trying.

"Sorry, li'l man, but your best friend went and fucked with the wrong people."

Gifford ran past him, crossed the yard, and disappeared into the woods.

13

"We got another one," Braddock said on the phone, and a few minutes later, he pulled up outside Rachel's door.

She climbed into the Tahoe and checked the time on her phone. It was almost 12:45 AM. "What do we know?"

"Not much," he said. "The call went to DCPD."

It took her a second to realize that he was referring to the Dillard City Police Department. "Shit."

"Yep." Braddock tore out of the parking lot with the visor lights flashing red-and-blue strobes through the top of the windshield. "Ted called over there after our meeting, like you suggested. Talked to 'em about how to handle a crime scene. We'll see if it did any good."

"Do they have an investigative unit?"

"No. Just uniformed patrol."

Which was good news.

★ ★ ★

The victim, a thirty-year-old man named Andy Coughlan, lived just inside the city limits, across the river. The drive didn't take long. Braddock parked at the end of a line of patrol cars that stretched around the corner from the house. They got out and jogged the rest of the way. When they reached the end of the driveway, they found the Dillard City Police chief—a wiry man with glasses, a bald head, and a salt-and-pepper mustache—standing behind a barricade of yellow tape. Braddock had said his name was Rich Miller.

"I got four officers on foot searching the woods behind the house," he said to Braddock. "Three sweeping the neighborhood. And Melvin's got four of your units out here too. We've been talking to the neighbors. No one's seen a damn thing. I talked to Ted about getting his cousin to send us a canine unit from Asheville. He says he's working on it, but it'll probably be too late to find a track by the time it gets here."

Rachel counted two other DCPD officers and a sheriff's deputy standing out front. A pair of EMTs were leaning against the side of an ambulance. She asked, "Who's been inside?"

"Just me and"—Miller pointed at one of the EMTs, looked like he was struggling to recall his name—"the fella on the right. Need me to get him over here?"

"No," she said. "We'll talk to him in a little bit. Just you two?"

"Yeah, I got here first." Miller nodded away from the house. "I live just two streets over that way. Never thought something like this would happen so close to home. Anyway, I was the first one here. I mean, Jen was here. That's his wife. Andy's wife . . ." Miller's voice was shaky. He closed his eyes and rubbed his forehead, taking a second to sort through his thoughts. "I got here, and Jen, the victim's wife, met me out front. She was pretty hysterical. I told her to wait there, and I went inside. I found Andy laying facedown in the TV room, feet sticking out the back door. He's got a"—he reached up and cupped the nape of his neck in his hand—"a damn knife in the back of his head. There's also something . . . like an ax handle . . . laying on the floor next to him."

"So just you?" she asked, trying to keep him focused. "None of the other officers?"

He shook his head.

"But the EMT. You said you took him inside. Just one of them?"

"Yeah. Just what's-his-face on the right over there. Made sure the other one waited outside. That's how Ted told me I should do it."

"That's right. You did good, Chief. But I need to ask you something else. Did you touch the victim?"

He nodded. "Yeah, I did. I touched his shoulder. I tapped on it like we learned in first-aid training. Tried talking to him. And then I checked for a pulse on his wrist, but once I got a good look at where that knife was, I knew he was gone."

"Nothing you could do, Chief," Braddock said.

"You all want me to take you inside? Show you the way we came in and out?"

"Let's wait for Detective Fisher," Rachel said.

★ ★ ★

Fisher walked up a few minutes later. Carly was right behind him carrying an evidence collection kit, her camera hanging from her neck. After Braddock relayed what Miller had told them, everyone stood in a circle, and Rachel realized they were waiting for her to take charge.

"All right," she said. "The three of us will go inside. Danny will wait out here. Carly, do you have gloves for us?"

Carly gave them each a pair of individually packaged blue nitrile gloves. As they worked to get them on, Rachel continued to give instructions. "Chief Miller, if you'll show us the way you went in and came out, Detective Fisher will be right behind you. Please make sure you point out anything you happened to touch along the way. Carly, you stay with Shane, and I'll go last. Remember, nobody touches or moves anything without photographing it first."

Miller led them in through the front door. The foyer sat between a dining room and a formal living room, neither of which appeared to get much use. There was a stairway on the right and an arched opening ahead. They moved forward into the kitchen, then turned and entered a small den where the body lay on the floor, just as Miller had described it. He walked around a tan, fabric-upholstered sofa and stopped a few feet from the victim.

"I stayed on this side of him when I checked his pulse," he said. "And I went out the same way I came in."

Fisher made several notes on a Steno pad, and Carly began taking photos.

"Anything else you can think of?" Rachel asked.

Miller shook his head.

"Okay, I'll walk you out."

She escorted him back to the front door and said, "You did a good job here tonight, Chief."

"I don't feel like I did much of anything."

"You preserved the scene. Protected it from contamination."

He stared at the ground for a moment and said, "I suppose."

Rachel thought about everything Braddock had told her during the drive to the house. "Danny said you talked to the victim's wife. She found her husband just before midnight?"

"Around ten till," he said. "She came downstairs to check on him. He was late coming to bed. He usually came up right after his show was over."

"And when was the last time she saw him alive?"

"She said she left him to go upstairs at eleven."

"I see." *Such a narrow window of opportunity*, Rachel thought. "Where is she now?"

He nodded toward the neighbor's house. "Next door."

"Okay. Detective Fisher will want to talk to her. Does anyone else live here?"

"No. Just the two of 'em. And their dog."

"They have a dog?"

"Yeah. A little Chihuahua, I think."

"Where is it?"

He nodded again toward the neighbor's house.

"Okay. Thanks again, Chief." She turned to go inside.

"Miz Carver?"

She stopped and looked at him.

"We're gonna catch this son of a bitch, aren't we?"

There was a plea in his expression. She wanted more than anything to say yes.

When Rachel walked back into the den, Fisher was making a tiny sketch of the room on his pad. Carly was listening to a message on her phone. She hung up and said, "That was Bruce."

Rachel gave her an inquiring look.

"The SBI crime scene specialist," Carly said. "He's on his way. Should be here in about an hour."

"Not that it'll make much of a difference," Fisher said. "This guy . . . whoever the hell he is . . . he's too damn good." He looked at Rachel. "See how he finished the job?" Tapped his pen on the back of his head. "I've read about the military teaching their special ops guys to kill like that."

Rachel nodded. "I've heard of that too."

"Wouldn't surprise me to find out he's some kinda pro."

"Maybe." Rachel thought about both victims. The similarities and the differences. Both were white males in their early thirties. Both were hit on the head, knocked out, so they couldn't put up a fight. Both were stabbed in a way that minimized the transfer of forensic evidence. There were rags at both scenes. The knives were left inside the wounds. But there had been no ax handle left at the first scene. And McGrath had been stabbed in the chest.

"But why change his method?" Carly asked, as if she had been reading Rachel's mind. "If this is such a great way to . . . you know . . . take someone out, why didn't he kill McGrath the same way?"

"Maybe he likes to mix it up," Fisher said. "Maybe he gets bored."

Rachel said, "I think you're right, Shane."

He and Carly both looked surprised.

"I mean about the first part," she said. "This guy is too good." She stepped around the sofa and squatted down next to the body, looked at the broken ax handle, then the rag. Then the knife. "I bet our guy would have preferred to kill both victims this way. He hits them from behind, thinking they'll fall forward and land face-down. Then he severs the brain stem. Very little blood. Victim dies instantly. Only it didn't work out that way the first time. Imagine, he hit McGrath from behind, but McGrath was leaning against the counter. He might've slumped forward, but then he bounced off and landed on his back, face up. The killer would've had to roll him over, and that would've increased his chances of transfer. Blood, fibers, hairs, something . . . so he went to plan B. Not as quick, but just as effective."

Fisher was staring at the body. He looked up at Rachel and said, "I don't know if you know this or not, but it gets a little scary when you start talking like that."

★ ★ ★

Rachel went outside and found Braddock on the phone.

When the call was finished, he said, "That was Ted. I told him we needed some time to get a handle on things before he shows up here and puts everyone on edge. He says he'll wait till just before sunup."

"How about the ADA?" she asked.

"You want him here too?"

"Yeah. I want a warrant for the house. I told Shane and Carly to just focus on the body and whatever's in plain view until we get one."

"You think the wife might be involved?"

"Maybe. You know . . ."

"Right," he said, shaking his head. "Can't rule it out." He called Pritchard back and told him about the warrant. After he hung up, he asked, "How does it look?"

"Clean," she said. "It's definitely our guy."

"So I guess we shouldn't expect to find much in there, huh?"

Rachel turned to look at the house, thought for a moment about the concept in forensic science known as Locard's exchange principle: all contact between a perpetrator and a victim will leave a trace. She said, "I might have an idea about that. How long before the ME gets here?"

Braddock checked his watch. "About twenty minutes or so. Why? What are you thinking?"

"I'm thinking you should call him and tell him to turn around. I want more time with the body before he moves it."

★ ★ ★

The medical examiner agreed to give them a few hours. When Bruce Moore, the SBI crime scene search specialist, arrived, Rachel brought him to the front door where Fisher, Braddock, and Carly were standing.

She huddled them together and said, "Right now, our best chance for collecting any trace evidence from our killer is to process the body while it's still here at the scene. The ME's given you guys some time, so let's use it."

Moore and Carly went inside to get started. Rachel said to Fisher, "You guys have any red crime scene tape?"

"Yeah, I got some in the trunk," he said.

"You might consider using it to tape off the entrances and the area outside by the back door. Creates a second barrier to protect the scene while they're processing it."

He looked around the front yard. "Yeah, I think you're right. We already got too many cops inside the yellow tape."

"What's your next move?" she asked.

"Thought I'd go next door and talk to the wife."

"Good call." She started to walk away.

"Where are you going?" Braddock asked.

"Back to the car to take a nap. Shane's got this under control."

She turned to leave and caught a glimpse of Fisher, who didn't bother to hide the look of pride on his face.

14

Rachel woke with a start, and Braddock looked sorry for tapping on the window. He held up a can of Monster Energy, which was enough to get her out of the Tahoe. It was still dark outside.

"I sent a deputy on a coffee run," he said. "But I thought you might want one of these instead."

"Perfect," she said, cracking it open. "Thank you. Have they found anything?"

"I think so."

She followed him back to the house. Moore, Fisher, and Carly were standing by Moore's Explorer at the end of the driveway. They looked exhausted.

Moore raised his arms over his head to stretch. He yawned and said, "Good call asking the ME to hold off. We found a hair. It was on the back of his shirt over the right shoulder blade. We probably would've lost it if they'd moved him. It looks straighter and thinner than the victim's. At least to me."

"Does it have a follicle on it?" Rachel asked.

He shook his head. "Sorry."

"Damn."

"Does that mean it's no good?" Fisher asked.

"It means the lab won't be able to run nuclear DNA analysis on it," Moore said.

Fisher looked confused. "You can't get DNA from a hair?"

"You can get mitochondrial DNA," he said, "which you can use for exclusion, or for comparison if you have a suspect, but not for CODIS searches. Unless it's for missing persons. Mitochondrial DNA is passed from the mother, so all maternal relatives would have the same profile."

Fisher looked even more confused.

"It means we can't use it to search the databases for a suspect," Rachel said. "But it'll come in handy once we have one."

"Can the state lab run a mitochondrial test?" Braddock asked.

"No," Rachel said. "It'll have to go to the FBI. Assuming it's long enough."

Rachel had read the FBI's *Handbook of Forensic Services* more than once. She knew the hair would need to be at least two centimeters long in order for them to test it.

"It is," Moore said, "but not by much. They'll destroy it when they run the test."

"That won't sound good to a jury," Braddock said.

Rachel remembered that Braddock had a bad history with DNA evidence. It happened during his fourth homicide investigation. The killer had strangled a woman with his bare hands, which left small amounts of his skin on her neck. Those few epithelial cells had provided the lab techs with just enough material to perform what they had called "touch DNA" analysis, a new technique at the time. At the end of a three-month investigation, the case went to trial, and Braddock watched as a talented defense attorney introduced the jury to the concept of secondary transfer. The victim, he claimed, had shaken his client's hand several hours before her murder, leaving some of his skin cells on her fingers and palm. If she had touched her neck at any time between that handshake and the time when she was attacked, his skin cells could have been transferred. Touch DNA was just too sensitive, he had said. He even had a report from the American Academy of Forensic Sciences to bolster his claim. The jury bought it, and the killer walked.

"I'm sure the DA will want to have a say in that decision," Rachel said. "In the meantime, the state lab can still do a microscopic comparison to make sure it didn't come from the victim, the wife, or any of us. You should go ahead and get all the samples you need for elimination."

"Mind if I get a break first?" Moore asked. "I figured now would be a good time to take one, since we're still waiting on the warrant. And I'm starving."

Braddock said, "Go for it. The ME will be here soon anyway."

They dispersed, and Rachel pulled Braddock aside.

"I know you have reservations about DNA," she said, "but when the time comes to make that decision, I think you should push to have the hair sent to the FBI."

He looked skeptical. "I don't know, Rachel. We have one hair, and we want to destroy it on a test that can't give us a definitive ID? I'd feel much better just having it analyzed for comparison."

"Trust me, Danny. You don't want to go to trial without DNA evidence. Juries expect it. And right now is a bad time to be presenting microscopic hair analysis in a murder case. The FBI has come out and admitted that matching a hair to a suspect without DNA is basically junk science."

Braddock's phone rang. He answered it and listened for a moment, then said, "Okay. See you in a few." He put the phone back in his pocket. "Well, like you said, it's going to be up to the lawyers to decide."

"Who was that?"

"Ted. He's on his way here with the ADA. They just got the warrant."

★ ★ ★

The assistant district attorney looked like he had graduated from law school a week ago. After complaining about having to wake the judge up at 5:00 AM, he listened as Braddock summarized everything that had happened at the scene and said he would talk to the district attorney about the hair. Then he left in a hurry to avoid being spotted by a pair of news vans setting up at the end of the street.

Pritchard looked despondent. Braddock said, "Better perk up, boss. Those cameras will be up here in a minute."

"I think *you* should talk to 'em," Pritchard said.

"Oh, I wish I could, but, you know, I can't be tied up in an interview if somebody needs me for something. Or if I get a call . . ."

Pritchard looked at Rachel.

"Not in my job description," she said.

"I quit," he said. "And you're both fired."

15

Gifford woke up to screaming. He jumped out of bed and nearly lost his footing. His left leg tangled in a sweat-soaked sheet. He looked out his bedroom window and tried to guess the time. Sunlight peered through the leaves of a rock oak at the edge of his property, which told him it was midmorning.

Another scream, and he knew it was his mother. Then a man yelled at her.

Gifford untangled his leg and stormed out of his room. "What the fuck is goin' on out here?"

"Get away from me," Gifford's mother yelled at the man hovering over her. She was sitting in her favorite spot on the sofa next to the side table that held her ashtray. The cigarette in her right hand was nearly burnt out. "Get him away from me!"

The man took a step back and looked at Gifford with fear in his eyes.

"The fuck are you doin', Bert?" Gifford asked.

"Throw him out on his ass," his mother yelled.

"He ain't *my* goddamn boyfriend," Gifford yelled back.

"He ain't mine neither," she said. "Not no more."

"Whatever. Y'all need to keep it down while I'm tryin' to sleep."

"I just want my money back," Bert said.

"What money?"

"The money I lent to her."

Gifford's mother lit another cigarette.

"Did he give you money?" he asked her.

Bert said, "She gave it to that worthless brother of yours."

Gifford walked over, looked at his mother, looked back at Bert, and punched him in the mouth, knocking him down. "Say something about my brother again, you sorry-ass motherfucker."

Bert scrambled to his feet, holding a bloody lip, and kept his head down as he ran out the door. Gifford yelled after him, "Let me hear you call him worthless one more time . . ." He turned to his mother. "You know I don't need this kinda bullshit in my house, Momma."

"Kevin needed the money," she said, avoiding his eyes. "It's not like you give him any."

"Jesus Christ," he said. "If only you knew the kinda shit I was doin' for you two."

★ ★ ★

Gifford was lying in bed, staring at the ceiling, when the burner buzzed on his nightstand. He answered it and said, "Hang on." He got up and peeked through the doorway, saw that his mother was still on the sofa watching TV and puffing on a cigarette. He closed the door and said, "All right."

"Everything go okay last night?" Bishop asked.

"Don't you know already?"

"I want to hear it from you."

Gifford swallowed, wished he had a glass of water handy. "Yeah, man. Everything went good. Just like we planned it."

"I don't recall you planning anything."

He started to sweat. Thought about apologizing but couldn't come up with the right way to say it.

"You're sure nothing happened that I need to know about?" Bishop asked.

"Yeah, man. I'm sure. That little dog was a pain in the ass, but other than that—"

"What about the dog?"

"Nothin', man," he said, touching his ankle reflexively. "It just barked a lot. I couldn't shut the little motherfucker up. But it wasn't a problem, all right? I got in, got out. Nobody saw a damn thing."

The line was quiet for nearly a minute, then Bishop said, "All right. Good job. Take it easy for today. I'll call you tomorrow."

Gifford said, "Okay," but the line was already dead.

16

Pritchard was at his desk when Justin Sanford, the special agent in charge of the SBI's Western District office, called.

"I hear you caught a break this morning," Sanford said.

"Yeah? How so?"

"Got a hair off the victim, is what I heard."

"I suppose that's true," he said and kicked his chair into a gentle rock. "Not sure who it belongs to yet."

"Hopefully it won't take the lab too long to get back to you."

"Hopefully not."

"Anyhow, I was just calling to see if you still wanted us to send an investigator your way. I've got an agent that'll be freed up tomorrow."

It seemed like the first good news Pritchard had heard in a long time. He said, "That's great. Send him on."

"You sure? It's okay if you all want to handle this on your own."

"You trying to have a laugh at my expense?"

"No, sir."

"Of course I'm sure." He sat up and leaned forward on his elbows. "Damn, Justin. We were just about begging you to send us help two days ago. And now that we've got another victim . . . why would you even question a thing like that?"

Sanford took a few seconds before he said, "Well, it's just that you've got Rachel Carver running things now, and—"

"Whoa, hang on. What do you mean, *running* things?"

"That's what I was told."

"Danny Braddock is in charge of this investigation. Miss Carver is just here as an advisor."

"An advisor. That's it?"

"That's it."

"Okay," Sanford said in a conciliatory tone. "It's just that . . . you know, things could get complicated with one of our former agents in the mix."

Pritchard understood exactly what he was trying to say. SBI special agents were brought in to assist county or municipal law enforcement agencies that lacked the resources and the expertise to handle difficult cases on their own. Since they were usually more experienced, agents were often expected to take a leadership role in the investigation. The last thing Sanford wanted was to send one of his people into a situation where he might end up butting heads with a former colleague.

"We just hate to have too many cooks in the kitchen," Sanford said. "You know what I mean."

"Yeah," Pritchard said. "I know what you mean. You don't have to worry about that here."

"All right, Sheriff. I appreciate that. My guy will be in touch with Danny first thing in the morning."

Braddock stuck his head in a few minutes later.

"You called, boss?"

"Yeah," Pritchard said. "Come in and have a seat."

Braddock sat down and asked, "Everything all right?"

"Yep. I just wanted to strategize with you for a minute. Where's Rachel?"

"Back at the motel. Hopefully getting some sleep."

"Weren't you gonna put her up over at Shipley's?"

Braddock shrugged. "I tried. She wasn't having it."

Pritchard picked up a pen and tapped it on his desk. A nervous gesture.

"You sure everything's all right, boss?"

He forced a smile. "I just spoke to Sanford on the phone a few minutes ago. Says he's sending an agent our way in the morning."

"That's good news," Braddock said.

"He was a little hesitant at first."

"Why?"

Pritchard looked at him, gave him a moment to figure it out for himself.

"Rachel?"

"He says he's heard that she's running things here."

Braddock laughed. "Does that intimidate him?"

"Maybe. You know how they can be."

"So what did he say exactly? Does he want me to run her out of town?"

"He didn't say anything like that. I think he just wanted some reassurance is all."

"What kind of reassurance?"

"That she understands her role as an advisor. That she'll be able to take a back seat."

Braddock seemed to relax a bit. "Hell, she won't have any problem with that. The only reason she's being so assertive is because I told her that's what I wanted from her. But you don't have to worry, boss. She knows how to play nice with others."

"Well, that's good to know," Pritchard said. "'Cause she can be quite assertive when she wants to be."

17

Rachel's alarm went off at noon. She stepped out of bed onto a crumpled fast-food bag and decided that she needed some exercise. She wanted to be on a mat, training jiu-jitsu, but the nearest school was thirty miles away and only held classes in the evenings. So she slipped on a pair of shorts, a sports bra, and a T-shirt and went for a run.

The air was cool and dry, and the sun felt good on her face. She took the road heading away from town, running on the edge of the asphalt. The river appeared occasionally through breaks in the trees, but the sound of flowing water was ever present. After a quarter mile, her heart rate was in the target range, and her mind began to drift. It almost felt like meditation, until the questions barged in.

Who is this killer, and what is his motive?
Is he finished, or is he just getting started?
Is there a connection between the victims?

There was an ugly truth about hunting a killer: the more people he murdered, the better the chances were of catching him. Finding a link that tied McGrath and Coughlan together might be the best hope for discovering a person with motive to kill them. If it existed, that connection was likely to be something nefarious. Something the victims would have taken steps to hide. For the moment, Rachel was betting on drugs, but only time could tell what they would find.

Rachel came to a bend, and the view opened up for several miles to the west. She stopped to catch her breath and took in the scenery, tried to imagine the killer planning last night's murder. The Coughlan residence was situated at the edge of a neighborhood. High-density housing with lots of potential witnesses.

The best way to get in and out without being seen would have been through the woods behind the house. But with Jen Coughlan awake upstairs, it was only a matter of time before she discovered her husband dead on the floor. Rachel was betting that the killer wouldn't have wanted to risk trekking through the woods for very long, knowing that the police would soon be searching for him. He would've wanted a vehicle nearby. A quick getaway before they could respond.

As her eyes swept the tree-covered mountains and the foothills below them, she thought about trying to find her way through that terrain in the dark. How easy it would be for someone who didn't know the area to get lost. Then she thought about the roads cutting through the rugged landscape and how few there were to choose from.

After her run, Rachel stretched out on the motel room floor to cool down. Then she showered, got dressed, and tried to reach Braddock on the phone. When he didn't pick up, she hopped in her Camry and left for the sheriff's office. A hunger pang hit her on the way, so she stopped at a gas station and bought one of the prepackaged chicken salad sandwiches that had yet to expire. She pulled into the office parking lot and finished eating in the car before she went inside.

Braddock was in his office. "Sorry I missed you," he said as soon as she walked in. "Ted and I were on the phone with the DA when you called."

"How'd that go?"

He shrugged. "You get any sleep?"

"Yep," she said. "Just enough to recharge. Even went for a run."

"Lucky you."

"Gave me some time to think about our killer."

"Come up with anything good?"

"Maybe. Not sure if it'll amount to much, though. Did they finish processing the house?"

"Yeah. Nothing to report there."

"That figures. What's Shane up to now?"

Braddock stood up and said, "Come on. You'll get a kick out of this."

She followed him to the conference room where Fisher and Melissa Howard, the deputy assigned to help index the case file, were huddled in front of a laptop. There were pages of notes, sketches, photographs, and canvass questionnaires spread out across the table.

Fisher looked up and said, "Hey, Chief, Rachel. We've just about got our spreadsheet knocked out. Next we're gonna work on sorting through all these pictures. I'm thinking we can make a grid layout of the crime scenes and then number the photos according to what coordinates they belong to. Carly took so many of 'em, I figured it would help us to know what we're lookin' at."

Braddock leaned toward Rachel and said, "I think you created a monster."

For the first time in her career, Rachel worried that she had overemphasized the importance of organization. "I think that's a great idea," she said, "but I'm surprised to see you doing it now."

"Why?" Fisher asked.

"Well . . . I thought you'd be busy trying to learn as much as you can about the victims. Looking for a connection between them."

He gave Braddock a perplexed look.

Braddock said, "There was a little development while you were at the motel. SBI is sending us an investigator tomorrow. Ted thinks it's best if we take some time to get our paperwork in order before he gets here."

"I see." And Rachel understood the subtext as well. Pritchard was eager to put the investigation in the SBI's hands, and he didn't want his detectives making any mistakes the day before they arrived.

Fisher turned his attention back to the computer screen, and Braddock said, "Let's take a walk."

They went outside, and he led her down a sidewalk toward the corner of the building. Once they were far enough away from the entrance, he said, "I don't really like the idea of us sitting on our asses while we wait for this guy to show up, but Ted and the DA are both in agreement. Apparently you've done too good of a job convincing them that this case is going to hinge on the victimology. They don't want us conducting any interviews without SBI being involved. So that thing you were telling me about a few minutes ago . . . the thing you thought of while you were running . . . any chance it's something we can look into without talking to anyone who knew the victims?"

"Did your patrol captain know either one of them?"

"If he did, he hasn't said anything to me about it."

"Let's go talk to him."

Curtis's office was next door to Braddock's. He was sitting behind his desk looking over an arrest report when they walked in.

"Anything interesting?" Braddock asked as he closed the door.

"Drunk driver," Curtis said, scratching his chin. "What are you all conspiring about?"

"Best to let her explain."

"We were hoping you could help us with something," Rachel said.

Curtis laid the report on his desk and leaned back in his chair. "All right."

"Last night, you helped coordinate the search with the city police?"

"Yes, ma'am."

"I was thinking the killer had to park somewhere close by, but not in the neighborhood or he would've risked someone seeing his car."

Curtis's mustache tilted with a half smile. "Makes sense."

"And I figure he probably used the woods behind the house as cover for his approach and escape."

He seemed to study her for a moment, then he glanced at Braddock, sat forward, and began working the mouse on his desktop. He made a few clicks and spun his monitor so Rachel could see the screen. It was a satellite image from Google Maps. An overhead view of the town surrounded by an ocean of undulating green.

"We were thinking the same thing," Curtis said. He zoomed in on the neighborhood and pointed the cursor at a tiny rectangle. "This is the house. We had deputies going all through the woods behind it this morning. They found a little valley that makes kind of a path through here." The cursor moved across the screen and stopped at a spot on a winding two-lane road. "Comes to an end right here at Peachtree Creek Drive."

"You think he parked his car there?"

"Not there. At least not without blocking part of the lane. The shoulder's not wide enough to park anything bigger than a bicycle. The nearest spot with enough room for a car is about three hundred yards away. We think that's probably the best bet. But it's mostly gravel, so we didn't find any tracks there. We also had deputies canvassing all the houses in that area, looking for anyone who might've seen a strange vehicle parked on the road last night. So far, nothing."

"I don't think he would've wanted to walk along the edge of that road for three hundred yards," she said. "He seems too careful to take a chance on someone spotting him or his car. Mind if I take a look?"

Curtis slid his chair over, and she took control of the mouse. She zoomed out and scrolled the map, then moved the cursor across the road as if she were extending the path the deputies had discovered. She spotted a line cutting through the trees and zoomed in. It was a faint trail. One that emerged onto a grassy field near a gray road. She followed it to the nearest intersection and said, "Captain, do you know where this is?"

He tilted his head and squinted at the screen. "I'll be damned. As a matter of fact, I think I do."

She looked at Braddock. "Anyone up for a ride?"

18

Braddock slowed the Tahoe once they hit gravel. Curtis, in the passenger seat, craned forward to search for the trail. Rachel was in the back seat looking at her phone, thankful to have a better signal than she'd had at the McGrath crime scene. She watched the blue dot on the Google Maps app and said, "We should be getting close."

Curtis said, "I think . . . yep, that's it. Right up there."

Braddock stopped, and they got out, studying the ground as they approached on foot. The trail was a pair of parallel tracks that stretched into the trees on the right side of the road. The grooves were deep, as if they had been there for years, cut into the soil by truck tires making hundreds of passes.

"Any idea where this goes?" Rachel asked.

"I don't think it goes anywhere," Curtis said. "Looks like an old hunting road. Probably just comes to a dead end in the woods."

"Yeah," Braddock said. "Good money there's a tree stand back there somewhere."

"It's not hunting season now, is it?" she asked.

"Not till September," Curtis said.

She knelt down next to a sandy spot where one of the tracks merged with the gravel. "Then I think I might have just found a partial of our killer's tire tread."

"I'll do you one better," Braddock said, pointing at the ground a few feet away.

Rachel walked over and saw it immediately. A perfect impression, the full width of the tread and nearly two feet long. "Call Carly," she said.

"On it." He was on the phone a moment later.

Rachel turned to Curtis. "Think you can get a deputy out here? Looks like we just found ourselves a crime scene."

Curtis waited by the Tahoe while Rachel and Braddock followed the trail into the woods. The tracks ended just before the path became too narrow for a vehicle to pass. Rachel stopped to look around and said, "I think he parked here."

They walked in circles and searched the ground for a few minutes but didn't find anything. Braddock said, "Let's keep going."

The footpath descended to a valley. Rachel looked at the steep incline in front of them, then at her phone and said, "If you go up to the top of that ridge and turn about forty-five degrees to the east, you'll have a straight shot out to the road. Directly across from where the deputies came out of the woods this morning."

"No shit?" Braddock looked at her phone for a minute and said, "Damn, you're right."

Rachel's eyes traced a path up the hill between staggered boulders and trees. "You'd have to be pretty nimble to hike your way up there in the dark."

"That tells us something."

"Yep."

"You think we'll find anything if we keep going?"

"I doubt it," she said. "But there's only one way to know for sure. Think you can handle it?"

"After you."

They climbed to the ridge, turned, and made their way down to a stream. There were dimples in the bank, a recent disturbance of the wet sand, but the water had washed away any shoe impressions. Both Rachel and Braddock took pictures with their phones, then they hopped across and continued onto the road.

"He was right," Rachel said as she stepped around a bush onto the shoulder. "There's no room to park here. How long did it take us to get this far?"

"Less than ten minutes."

"Would've taken a little longer at night. But that's not a bad tradeoff, considering how secluded that spot is."

"Hell," Braddock said, "we never would have found it."

★ ★ ★

The deputy was at the scene, talking to Curtis, when Rachel and Braddock got back. Carly pulled up a few minutes later. Rachel showed her the tire tread impressions and said, "We need some good pictures of these. Also some soil samples from here"—she pointed down the trail—"and back there where we think he parked. If we get a suspect, the lab can compare the samples to any dirt we find on his tires or his shoes."

"Easy enough," Carly said. She went through her kit and found a scale—a yellow ruler that opened up to an L shape. She laid it down next to the larger tread mark and took several shots. She checked them on the screen to make sure the numbers on the scale were legible, then moved to the smaller impression. After shooting it, she checked the photos and put the scale away. "You want me to cast them?"

"Uh . . . is Bruce on the way?"

"He left to go back to Asheville an hour ago."

Rachel realized that Carly hadn't bothered to call him. "Okay . . . have you ever done one before?"

"Several. In class."

"What kind of material do you have?"

"Dental stone."

"And you have everything else you need? Plastic spray? Oil spray? Reinforcing material?"

Carly nodded and said, "Yep."

Rachel was still hesitant. Making a dental stone cast of a tire tread wasn't the most difficult task in evidence collection, but there was only one chance to get it right. She looked at Braddock and said, "Your call."

"All right, Carly," he said, "show us what you got."

★ ★ ★

While Carly was working, Rachel approached Braddock and said, "That tread is more than ten inches wide, and the pattern looks like an off-road type. Like those big custom wheels you see on full-sized trucks or SUVs with lift kits."

"Yeah," he said. "I think you're right."

"You know what I'm thinking right now?"

"If I did, I wouldn't need you here."

"That hurts my feelings, Danny."

He laughed. "What're you thinking?"

"Cameras."

"Okay."

"I'm thinking we should find every route the killer could've used to get to and from this location. And McGrath's house too. There aren't that many. Then we find a camera on each one of those roads . . . a gas station, an ATM, whatever . . . and we collect the footage from the time frames of the murders. If we're lucky, we'll catch a shot of a big truck driving by."

"Hell yeah," he said. His mouth formed a thin smile. "Now we're getting somewhere."

19

When they got back to the office, Braddock printed out a map and gave it to Fisher.

"I don't know, Chief," Fisher said. "I doubt all these roads are gonna have cameras on 'em."

"Maybe not, but it's all we've got to work with right now," Braddock said. "Hit every place along every route he could've taken, and let's hope you get lucky. Where's Tina?"

"Should be on her way back. She took a late lunch."

"All right. Get her to help you. And ask Melvin to give you a couple of guys too."

Fisher left, and Braddock said, "I don't think he's quite as excited about this latest development as we are."

"I'm sure he's getting pretty tired by now," Rachel said. "Speaking of which . . ."

Braddock yawned and rubbed his eyes. "I'm good. Just need some coffee. Another half gallon or so, and I'll be right as rain." He checked his watch. "We'd better find Ted and give him an update."

Pritchard was in the conference room looking through the crime scene photos. When Braddock told him about the tire tracks and the search for camera footage, he said, "Well, damn. That's a lucky break."

"More like good detective work," Braddock said, glancing at Rachel.

"Right . . . of course." He looked back at the photos. "I hope it helps us find this son of a bitch before he does this to someone else."

Braddock yawned again.

"You should get some rest," Rachel said. "There's not much you can do here right now, anyway."

He shook his head. "We've got a press conference in an hour."

"I can handle that," Pritchard said, looking up. "And she's right. You look like hell. Go home and get some sleep. That's an order."

He stared at the floor for a moment, like he was deciding whether to protest, then he said, "All right. Y'all call me, though, if anything happens."

Rachel followed him outside. A news van was sitting at the curb with its side door open. The cameraman leaned against the fender, smoking a cigarette, while the reporter paced up and down the sidewalk with a phone pressed to her ear.

"Kinda glad I won't be here for that," Braddock said. "What are you gonna do?"

"Go to the motel," she said. "Make some notes. Think a little. See if I can come up with any ideas."

"Call me if you do."

★ ★ ★

Rachel went back to the Fontana Lodge and thought about the killer. She sat on the bed with a notepad and wrote down everything she knew about him.

Or her?

She couldn't rule out the possibility that it was a woman, even though the big truck with the custom wheels suggested a man.

He/she is careful. Disciplined. Has a high degree of self-control. Doesn't display rage toward the victims.

He/she knows the area. Is able to climb and move quickly over difficult terrain, even in the dark.

He/she knows the victims' routines. Might be able to pick locks. Understands forensics.

She stared at her notes for a few minutes, then dropped the pad, fell back on the bed, and closed her eyes. She revisited the crime scenes in her mind and thought about how much the killer had to know about his victims. McGrath was easy. Anyone who went to the Riverside Pub would have known his work schedule, would have known when to catch him coming home alone at night.

Coughlan was a different story. He had worked as the manager of a hardware store and made it home every evening before sundown. According to his wife, he was rarely alone. He had been ambushed while taking the dog outside, which he did every night after watching his favorite show. And his wife had been upstairs, expecting him to come to bed when he was finished. The killer had to have known those details beforehand.

Rachel picked up the pad again.

Does the killer know the victims personally, or is he/she surveilling them to get his/her information? Is Jen Coughlan involved?

She would pass those questions along to Braddock and Fisher. She set the notepad aside and turned on the TV, found a channel playing a marathon of *Saturday Night Live* reruns, and wished she had something strong to drink. After three episodes, her phone rang. It was Braddock.

"Think of anything new?"

"Not really," she said. "Having trouble sleeping?"

"Got about an hour's worth. It'll hold me over till tonight. What are you up to?"

"Nothing. Watching TV."

"Wanna grab a drink?"

"Desperately." She cringed at the admission. "I mean, I'd love to get out of this room. You think it's a good idea?"

"I know a place outside Dillsboro about thirty minutes away. I doubt we'll run into anyone from town."

"Works for me."

"I'll come by and pick you up in a few. I'll be driving my old Explorer this time."

"Afraid to take the sheriff's Tahoe out to a bar?"

"Might not be the best thing to do right now."

★ ★ ★

Ernie's Tap House was a small dive tucked away on a dead-end road. A squat white box surrounded by a dirt parking lot. Rachel and Braddock went in, picked a pair of stools at the bar, and ordered two Bud Lights, draft. The bartender, a stumpy blonde woman in a black tank top, delivered them in frosty mugs, then moved on to the end of the bar to chat with another patron.

Braddock took a sip and said, "Whenever I feel like I need to get away from everyone, this is usually where I end up."

"Nice place."

He laughed and said, "Hey, you take what you can get around here."

"I'm not knocking it."

They finished the first round and ordered another. Halfway through it, Rachel said, "Assuming we don't get our hands on any good video footage in the next few hours, I guess tomorrow will be my last day."

He looked a little sad. "So soon?"

"Not much more I can do here. You guys just have to start working the victims until you can find whatever it was that got them killed."

"And what if we get another one?"

"Well . . . you'll have yourself a brand-new special agent to hold your hand through it, I guess."

"You don't have to leave just because he's coming. If you want to stay on . . ."

She shook her head. "I appreciate it, Danny, but you guys don't really need me anymore. You've got all your ducks in a row now. Keeping me around would just be a waste of money."

He was quiet for a minute, then said, "I'm really glad we got to work together again. I hate to admit it, but it's actually been kind of . . ."

"Fun?"

"I was going to say humbling, but that works too."

"Humbling?" she asked. "What makes you say that?"

He shrugged. "I don't know. Just watching you work. You're really good at what you do, you know."

"I guess I've had a lot of practice."

"That's true, but there's more to it than that. You have a gift."

She was about to brush off the compliment when he said, "That's why I don't get why you quit."

"I told you why," she said, suddenly feeling annoyed. "The day after I turned in my badge."

"I know, but I just don't get it. It was a good shooting. You probably saved that deputy's life."

Her jaw tensed. She stared at her mug and made lines in the melting frost with her fingertips.

"Sorry," he said. "I guess it's none of my business."

20

Fisher was getting discouraged. After a dozen stops, he had yet to find a single working camera pointed at any of the roads marked on his map. Glenda's Kitchen and Country Store had one that captured a bit of the service road out front, but the angle didn't give it a view of the highway beyond. He was ready to give up, to drive home and go to bed, when he spotted a tiny black globe on the corner of the Speedy Mart gas station.

He wheeled the Crown Victoria into the lot and parked in front of the door. He ran inside, spotted a kid behind the register, and said, "Please tell me that camera outside works."

The kid looked wary. He opened his mouth to speak but caught sight of the gun on Fisher's hip and stared at it.

"Detective Fisher, sheriff's office," he said. "I need to know if that camera out there works or not."

"Uh . . . yeah, it works." The kid tipped his head toward a monitor behind the counter.

"Can you show me the footage from last night and early this morning?"

"Uh . . ."

"Come on, son. Wake up. This is important."

"I'd better call my boss."

A couple minutes later, Fisher was on the phone with the owner. "What do you mean, it don't record?"

"I'm sorry, Detective. Damn computers took a dump after a power surge back in . . . hell, I think it was January or . . . might've been . . . no, couldn't have been then. Yeah, proba—"

"I get it," he said. "What you're telling me is, that camera's pretty much worthless."

"Well . . . we can use it to keep an eye on folks out by the pumps and what not. We just can't save any of the footage."

"Uh-huh."

"What was it you were hoping to see, anyway?"

"The road in front of your store. From last night to this morning."

"You lookin' for a particular car?"

"Can't really go into that, sir."

"Huh . . . well, I don't know if it'll help, but that fella across the street . . . the one that owns the liquor store . . . I hear he's got a camera that points our way. You might have better luck over there."

★ ★ ★

"I told that sumbitch, what I do in my store is *my* business," the old man said.

Fisher rubbed his eyes. "Sir—"

"And don't it figure that he'd call you all to come over here and harass me. I told him if he wants to go puttin' up a camera to watch what I do over here, then I can put one up too."

"Sir—"

"What's fair is fair, as far as I'm concerned."

"Yes, sir, but—"

"Tell him he can kiss every bit of my wrinkled ass."

"I just need—"

"Sorry sumbitch oughta know that I ain't gonna sit back and—"

Fisher slammed a fist on the counter, making a stand of whiskey flasks rattle. He took a deep breath and said, "Sir, I couldn't care less about whatever kind of disagreement you might be having with the owner of the Speedy Mart. I'm in the middle of a homicide investigation." He pointed at the camera aimed out the window. "And

I just need to know if I can see the video from last night through early this morning."

The old man cleared his throat and said, "Hell, son, all you had to do was say so."

Fisher followed him to a back office that also doubled as a storage room. The camera feed went to a desktop computer sitting on a tiny desk in the corner. Fisher pushed aside a mop bucket and took a seat in a folding chair. When the screen came to life, he saw the live footage on top, bars of recorded material beneath. The program appeared to save up to five days' worth of video before overwriting the files.

Fisher selected a starting point of 5:00 PM, just to make sure he wouldn't miss anything. Then he highlighted the bar up to 8:00 AM that morning and exported the footage in MPEG format. After it finished, he inserted his thumb drive and copied the file. He opened it to make sure it worked. As soon as he saw the image come to life, he closed it and took out the drive, put it in his pocket, and ran for his car.

★ ★ ★

Sitting at his desk, Fisher opened the file and skipped forward to an hour before the murder. After fifteen minutes, two SUVs, a minivan, and a Ford F-150 on what appeared to be stock wheels had passed by, and he decided to try the time frame after the murder instead. He figured it might make for a narrower window, since the killer would have been eager to make his getaway. He started at 11:15 PM, sat back, and fought to stay awake.

He jumped in his chair when the phone woke him up. He looked at the time on the video—11:58 PM—cursed at himself, and answered the call. "Yeah?"

"I think I found an ATM that might give us something." It was Tina Pratt. "But we'll have to wait till tomorrow to talk to the branch manager. How's it going on your end?"

Fisher grabbed the mouse so he could rewind. "Don't know yet. Found a camera at DC Liquors. Watching it now."

"Hey, that's something. Lucky you."

"Uh-huh . . ." He was sliding the red line backward across the replay bar when something caught his eye. A large, dark mass shooting across the screen. He moved the line forward, saw it shoot across in the other direction, then backed it up again and let it play. "Tina . . . ?"

"Yeah?"

"I gotta go."

21

The jukebox was playing Clint Black. Rachel finished her third mug of Bud Light, ordered another, and decided to open up. "It wasn't the shooting," she said. "Not exactly. It was everything that came afterward."

Braddock had switched to water, since he had to drive. He was spinning ice cubes around with a straw, wearing a perplexed look. "What do you mean?"

"I went after Lauren Bailey because she was the only suspect that made any sense at the time. Her boyfriend was found dead in her car, he was cheating on her, neighbors and friends said they fought all the time . . ."

"But now you think she was innocent?"

She took a large gulp. "After we closed the case, Bailey's friend came forward with all these private messages from Bailey on her Facebook account. Dozens of secret conversations they had been having about their boyfriends. Turns out, Bailey had been cheating too. She had at least two other guys on the side, one of whom she may have been in love with. She also talked about how she couldn't stand sleeping with her boyfriend anymore, but he was helping her pay the bills. Helping to support her son, even though it wasn't his kid."

"So she was better off with him being alive."

"Exactly."

He turned in his barstool to face her. "Then who had motive?"

She gave him a sour smile. "I wish I knew. Like I said, it was case closed as soon as she hit the floor. At least as far as the murder was concerned. Bailey's mother is suing Wake County and the state, so the SBI started another investigation. Looking at me, the detectives, the deputy . . . reviewing all our work."

"Anything come of it?"

"Not yet. They interviewed me right after I quit, but I haven't heard anything about it since. The final report came out yesterday."

"And you haven't had a chance to read it yet?"

"Been kinda busy."

Braddock looked like he was about to say something when his phone rang. He checked the screen and answered it. "Hey, Shane . . . No kidding? . . . All right, we'll be there in thirty minutes."

Rachel downed the last half of her beer.

"Actually," he said, "better give us an hour."

★ ★ ★

After drinking a bottle of water on the way to the office, Rachel needed to visit the restroom. She came out, put a stick of mint-flavored chewing gum in her mouth, and went to the conference room. Braddock and Fisher were watching the video on a laptop.

"And here he comes again," Fisher said.

A second later, Braddock said, "I'll be damned. Rachel, come take a look."

She walked around the table and stood next to him.

Fisher clicked on a video clip. "Okay. This is at eleven-oh-three PM."

The image, playing in black and white, seemed to be from a sensitive low-light camera capable of capturing high-resolution video at night. Within a few seconds, a dark-colored pickup moved across the screen. Fisher selected a new clip and said, "Now this is from eleven fifty-four."

The pickup crossed again going the other direction, this time moving noticeably faster. Fisher stopped the playback, rewound slowly until the truck was in the center, and froze it. He pointed at the oversized wheels and said, "Those look custom to me."

"Me too," Braddock said. "What do you think, Rachel? This our guy?"

"Definitely fits the time frame," she said. "Where was this taken?"

Fisher reached behind the laptop, grabbed his paper map, and held it up. He pointed at a spot with his pen and said, "Right here." Then he touched another spot. "And this is where you guys found the tracks."

"Damn." She patted his shoulder. "Good job, Shane."

"All right," Braddock said. "Let's put out a BOLO for a . . ." He squinted at the screen. "You know what make and model that is?"

Fisher said, "Best I can tell, it's either a GMC Sierra or a Chevy Silverado. The body style looks like the ones they produced from 2003 to 2006."

"Okay. Tell everyone to be on the lookout for one of those. Navy blue or black . . . maybe dark green."

"Roger that," he said.

"And call the DMV"—he glanced at his watch—"as soon as they open up tomorrow. Get them to generate a list of all the trucks registered in this area that fit that description."

"That's gonna be one helluva list, Chief."

"I'm sure it will, but if our guy's local, he'll be on it."

"All right. Let me get with Melvin before he leaves for the day." He stood up, closed the screen, and said, "We got you now, you piece o' shit."

★ ★ ★

Rachel followed Braddock to his office. He dropped into his chair and said, "Say we can identify this asshole by tomorrow, you still gonna take off?"

"Maybe not," she said. "I'd love to be here when you put him in handcuffs."

"That'll be a good feeling."

"Usually is. As long as you're sure you got the right guy."

"We'll have a better chance of making sure we do if you stay around to help."

She smiled. "I'm paid up at the Lodge through tomorrow night, so I guess that leaves you till Saturday morning to find him."

22

Gifford grabbed two handfuls of his brother's shirt and slammed him against the wall.

"I'm tired of your bullshit, Kevin," he said through gritted teeth.

"Get off me." Kevin tried to look defiant, but his voice trembled. "I told you, I ain't got no fuckin' money."

"All that shit you been sellin', and you ain't got no money, huh?"

"I'm tellin' you, man, I'm tapped out."

Gifford let go, looked around his brother's filthy trailer, and said, "So where'd it all go? I know you been sellin'. Don't even try to lie."

Kevin mumbled something.

"What?"

"I said I invested it."

Gifford raised a fist. "Lyin' mother—"

Kevin crumpled to the floor, put his hands up in a plea for mercy. "Come on, man. I swear I ain't lyin'."

"What the fuck do you mean, you invested it?"

"In the business. Me and the boys are lookin' to expand our production. You know what I'm sayin'?"

"You gotta be kiddin' me."

"No, I'm serious. This is for real."

"Oh, it's for real, huh? How real is it gonna be when Bert takes his ass to the cops and tells 'em about your business? 'Cause that's what he'll do if you don't pay him his money, dumbass. It's five hundred bucks. He ain't just gonna let you keep it."

Kevin looked surprised. "But Momma only gave me three hundred."

Gifford thought about that for a second and laughed. "Well don't that figure." He took a deep breath, nudged an empty beer can with the toe of his boot, and said, "Do you ever clean this freakin' pigsty?"

"Whatever, man. It ain't like you got room to talk." Kevin stood up, but he kept his head down and put his hands in his pockets. "I'm sorry, all right? I didn't mean to put you in a bad spot or nothin'."

Gifford went to the door and opened it, stood at the threshold, and said, "I'll cover you one last time, little brother. But this is it. I'm done. After this, you're on your own."

"I'll get you back, man. I pro—"

He slammed the door on his way out, climbed into his truck, and started it. Then he noticed the screen on the burner glowing. He picked it up and read the message: "Stay home. Keep ur truck out of sight. Call u later."

The phone buzzed, and he jumped. "Jesus . . . Hello?"

"Where the hell have you been? Why haven't you been answering?"

"You said I had the day off. You told me you were gonna call tomo—"

"Okay, okay. Fine. Where are you now?"

"I'm at my brother's."

"You have your truck with you?"

"Yeah."

"Can you keep it there? Keep it out of sight?"

"I . . . I guess. Why, what's—"

"The sheriff's office has video of it."

Gifford's face grew warm as fear began to consume him. "Shit. How the hell—"

"Just listen. They don't know it's yours yet."

"*Yet*? What do you . . . ? How long before they do?"

"They're going to run a description of it by the DMV. That'll give them a list of people to start investigating."

"Ah *fuck*, man. They're gonna come lookin' for me. What the hell am I gonna do when they—"

"Calm down, goddammit. You know how many rednecks around here drive that exact same truck? The cops are gonna be sorting through this shit for weeks. In the meantime, there's no reason to advertise the fact that you own one. So keep it out of sight and find something else to drive until I tell you otherwise. Got it?"

"Yeah . . . okay."

"And whenever they do come around asking questions, just tell them you were at home on those nights, and don't say anything else. Don't let them rattle you. They don't have shit. Just a video of you driving by a liquor store at night. That's it."

"You sure about that?"

"Yes. I told you. I have my sources. So keep your head down and stay cool, and everything'll be fine. Remember, you've got people counting on you."

Gifford didn't need the reminder. Bishop's threat was always on his mind.

23

Rachel had reached her limit on fast food, so Braddock took her to Everett's Diner on Main. She ate chicken and dumplings with cole-slaw and collard greens and nursed a headache with a Diet Coke. Braddock pushed slices of chicken-fried steak around on his plate. He looked annoyed.

"Anything you want to get off your chest?" she asked.

"Not really. Just pisses me off that Ted went and tied our hands the way he did. We could've been out talking to people all day."

"He's scared. Probably my fault. Showing up here and nitpick-ing you guys to death. I'm sure he's feeling a little insecure."

Braddock shook his head. "It's not just you. That talk he had with Sanford . . . and then the DA and the press conference . . . He'll be happy when he can tell everyone there's an SBI agent in town." He dropped his fork and sat back. "But I keep wonder-ing if we're gonna wake up tomorrow morning and find another body."

Rachel didn't think that was likely. The murders and the inves-tigation were all over the news. The town was on edge. Sheriff's deputies and DCPD officers were pulling double shifts in an effort to blanket the area with patrol units. And people were talking about loading up their guns and keeping them close by in their homes, just in case some unfortunate soul should be foolish enough to jiggle a door handle.

"I wouldn't worry about that," she said. But it didn't seem to make him feel better. "You need another drink. A real one this time. And I think I could use one too."

Braddock agreed to swing by the liquor store after they left the diner. Rachel went in and bought a bottle of cheap bourbon, carried it out in a brown paper bag. When they got to the motel, she got ice from the machine next to the office, then came back and poured their drinks in a pair of plastic cups. Braddock took a seat at the table and cringed after his first taste.

"Don't worry," Rachel said, dropping onto the foot of the bed, "it gets easier."

He watched her swirl the ice around and take a sip. He said, "You know, if you wanted to talk more about what happened to you, I'd be happy to listen."

She waved a dismissive hand. "I'm fine."

"You sure about that?"

A surge of irritation came over her. She didn't want his pity, even though she liked the fact that he cared. And there was no judgment in his eyes, only concern. She decided to change the subject. "I'd rather talk about you."

He leaned back and eyed her suspiciously, took a drink, and said, "All right, Detective. What is it you want to know?"

"Well . . ." She thought for a second. "Might as well dive right in, I suppose. Are you still single?"

He chuckled. "Unfortunately."

"And why is that?"

"Not many good single women around these parts to choose from."

"Uh-huh."

"What?" He put his hands up. "You've been around here for a couple of days now. You see what I've got to work with."

"I think you've been spending too much time at Ernie's."

"That's definitely true."

She finished her drink and made another while he talked about dating in a tiny mountain town. His stories made her laugh. They took her mind off killers and victims and cases gone bad. By the time she finished her second cup, she was feeling warm and relaxed.

Braddock kept talking. Kept finding things to say. It turned to mumbling when she stood and stepped up to him, confiscated his drink, and set it aside. There may have been a question or a half-hearted protest when she took his hand and coaxed him out of the chair. But he got quiet when she slid her hands across his chest, wrapped them around his back, and pulled him in for a kiss.

24

Friday

Braddock's phone woke them before the sun came up. Rachel fumbled to pick it up from the nightstand and passed it to him. When he answered, the exuberant voice on the other end was loud enough for her to hear.

"Chief Braddock?"

"Yeah . . ."

"Good morning. This is Mike Jensen, SBI."

"Morning."

"Sounds like I caught you at a bad time. Should I call ya back?"

"Nope . . . I'm awake. Just moving a little slow this morning."

"I hear ya, Chief. I hear ya. I have my days too. Trust me when I tell ya."

"Yeah, so you're on the way in from Asheville? What time do you think you'll—"

"Oh, I'm here. At your office, that is. Yeah, been here for about thirty minutes or so. Having a look at the case file, if that's okay?"

Braddock sat up. "Yeah . . . uh . . . sure. Make yourself at home. I'll be right over. I just need about ten . . . twenty minutes."

"Hey, no problem, Chief. See ya soon."

He hung up and dropped the phone, rubbed his face in his hands.

Rachel pulled the covers over her head and said, "I can already tell, I'm not gonna like this guy."

★ ★ ★

Mike Jensen had a young face for a man in his forties, but his hair was completely gray. His navy-blue suit, striped tie, and brown wingtips made him look out of place in the sheriff's office, though he didn't seem to mind. When Rachel and Braddock found him in the conference room, he greeted them with a grin and a round of coffees.

"Thought these might help," he said. "There's sugar and half-and-half too, if ya'd like some."

"Yes on all three for me," Braddock said, shaking his hand. "Thanks."

Rachel held up her half-empty can of Monster Energy and said, "I'm all set. Thank you, though."

Jensen took her hand and said, "It's a pleasure to meet you, Miz Carver. I've heard a lot about ya."

"Please, call me Rachel. And it's nice to meet you too."

Jensen leaned against the conference table and propped a foot on one of the chairs. "I have to say, I'm pretty impressed with how you guys have handled everything so far, especially considering what you've had to work with. And when I say you *guys*—"

Rachel smiled. "I know what you mean. No worries."

"Great. So it looks like we've got some work ahead of us. Why don't we go through everything, and you two can catch me up?"

★ ★ ★

Fisher and Pratt turned up just after sunrise and joined the briefing. Pritchard came in a half hour later. With each new arrival, Jensen jumped out of his seat and introduced himself. To Pritchard, he said, "You've got a heck of a good team here, Sheriff."

"Glad to hear it," he said, pulling up a chair. "'Cause it seems like we're gonna need one."

"Oh, yeah, that's the truth. No doubt about it." Jensen sat down, upended his coffee cup to suck down the last couple of cold drops, and said, "I've dealt with a few of these CSI-type killers before. Ones that've seen too many cop shows and know a bit about forensics. Tricky. Always tricky. I have to say, though, this guy, whoever he is, has done a better job than most. Wouldn't ya say, Rachel?"

She was caught off guard by the question. She cleared her throat and said, "Yes, definitely. Most of them tend to make a lot of mistakes."

He kept his eyes fixed on her, nodding slowly, waiting for her to say more.

"But our killer . . ." she said, "he, or she, is the best I've seen. The most careful, at least. And the most disciplined."

"I agree," Jensen said. "So my suggestion would be for you guys to start working on the victimology. See if you can figure out why someone wanted these gentlemen dead in the first place."

"There's an idea," Braddock muttered under his breath.

"And what are *you* gonna do?" Pritchard asked.

"I'm going to be working a different angle. There's been some talk that these murders could be drug related."

"What kind of talk?"

Rachel said, "That was an idea we had based on the fact that Dean McGrath may have had money problems and worked at a bar."

"A biker bar," Jensen added.

"Which may have given him the opportunity to sell on the side."

Fisher said, "But we don't have any indication that Coughlan was involved in drug dealing."

"No, we don't," Jensen said. "That's for sure. But we can't deny that these killings look a little like low-grade professional hits. The victims may not have been taken out by a sniper or a car bomb, but they certainly have that impersonal feel of someone doing this for money. And if I had to pick one illicit endeavor in this region that would motivate someone to kill someone else, I'd have to bet on drugs."

"Well, I guess that makes sense," Pritchard admitted.

"Perfect. I'm glad we all agree." Jensen stood up and started toward the door. "We've got a few contacts in this area. I'll be hitting them up over the next couple of days. See if they've got anything to say. Oh . . ." He reached in his pocket, withdrew a handful of business cards, and laid them on the table. "In case anyone needs to reach me. I already have all your numbers. I'll swing back around this afternoon to see how you guys are doing."

He walked out, and Pritchard looked around the table and said, "Okay . . . well, I guess you all know what you need to do."

Braddock said to Fisher, "Pick up where you left off yesterday. Start at the houses, talk to the families, friends, neighbors. Let's get phone records, financials . . . Talk to the ADA about getting the warrants." Then to Pratt, "You take the DMV. Once you get the list, let's see how long it is. If you need help, we'll figure it out."

They gathered their notepads and left. When they were out of the room, Pritchard said, "That didn't quite go the way I expected it to. I guess I should have let you all get started yesterday." He was quiet for a moment and looked at Braddock like he was about to apologize, but then his expression changed. "Danny, are those the same clothes you were wearing yesterday?"

25

Rachel treated Braddock to breakfast at the diner. Then they went to his house so he could shower and change. He left his bedroom door open while he was getting undressed, and she couldn't resist going in to help him.

"Think you could play some music?" she asked.

He selected a playlist of country ballads on his phone and plugged it into the speakers on his nightstand. It wasn't her favorite kind of music, but she said, "Turn it up a little. I'd hate for the neighbors to hear us."

"You're a bad girl, you know that?"

He barely got the words out as she shoved him onto the bed and climbed on top of him.

★ ★ ★

Five songs later, she let him go. Braddock stumbled into the bathroom and started a shower. Rachel dressed and went out to the kitchen, looked through the cabinets until she found a glass, and poured some water. She sipped on it as she explored the house. It was a quaint craftsman, needing a few repairs and a fresh coat of paint on the exterior, but it was clean and well maintained inside. The furniture in the living area was plush brown leather, which looked cozy in front of the wood-trimmed fireplace.

There were framed photographs on the mantle. She stepped closer to examine them. One showed Braddock on a boat surrounded by friends holding fishing poles and cans of light beer. The other caught the same group in a bar wearing broad smiles, holding large mugs, and hanging on each other for support.

"Friends from high school."

She turned around, startled. Braddock was pulling on a pair of khakis. His wet towel was draped around his neck.

"Sorry," he said. "The guys in those pictures, we all went to high school together."

"Looks recent," she said.

"Right after I got divorced. They took me on a fishing trip down in the Keys." He walked back into the bedroom to finish dressing and yelled, "That was the first time since our ten-year reunion that we were all able to meet up in the same place."

She looked again at the photos and thought about her own life-long friends. Connections she had made as a kid, still so strong regardless of how far life had pulled them apart.

"Danny . . ."

"Yeah?"

"How many high schools are there around here?"

"Just one," he said. "Lowry County High."

"Has it been around for a while?"

"Oh, yeah. For sure. Looks like it was built in the sixties maybe." He poked his head through the doorway. "Why?"

"Fisher's looking for a recent connection between the victims. Maybe we should start at the other end and work our way forward."

"That's an idea. Hell, they were both living in the area when I moved here. I guess there's a chance they went to the same school. Do we go looking for records?"

"Not sure that'll do us much good. We need to find someone who knew them when they were younger. Someone who could tell us if they were friends or not."

He stared at the floor for a few seconds, then looked at her and said, "You know what? I think I know exactly what we need to do."

"What?"

He gave her a playful smile. "We're going to see the Oracle."

★ ★ ★

"Remember the bartender we talked to the other day?" Braddock asked in the Tahoe on the way over.

"Smiley?"

"Yeah. His real name is Clint Jordan. I don't know where he gets his nickname from, but the Oracle is his mother, Brenda."

"Why do you call her the Oracle?"

"It's not just me. The whole town calls her that. When she was younger, she had a reputation for being the gossip queen of Lowry County. When her friends started having kids, she liked to make predictions about how they would turn out. Things like who would go off to college, who would be good at sports, who would be the first to get pregnant or get some girl pregnant, who would get hooked on drugs . . .

"Was all just a bunch of talk, or so people thought. Eventually, her friends got tired of hearing that she was talking about them and their kids behind their backs. They all disowned her right around the same time her husband ran off with another woman. As I'm sure you can imagine, she didn't take all that too well. She ended up becoming kind of a shut-in. Lives with Smiley on top of this hill we're getting ready to go up."

Rachel leaned forward and saw the green slope rising ahead. A narrow road with half a dozen switchbacks snaked across its face.

"Might need to put it in four-wheel drive just to make it," he said. "Oh, and the reason they call her the Oracle is because a lot of those predictions she made came true."

"Really?"

"Yep. That's what people say, anyway. She's become somewhat of a local legend. It's a good bet that if there's anything worth digging up about the victims, chances are she'll know about it."

The Tahoe's tires skirted the edge of the dirt road, inches away from a sheer drop. They slipped twice during the climb, losing traction for only an instant, but Rachel had to close her eyes and grip the armrest on her door each time. When the road leveled on top of the hill, she breathed a sigh and tried not to think about the fact that they would have to go back down the same way.

"That was a little intense, huh?" Braddock said as he shifted into park.

Rachel stepped out without answering.

The Jordans' cabin was nestled between a pair of ancient oak trees. White paint flaked off the wood siding, and dust covered the windows. Smiley's beat-up Durango sat out front. As they drew near the front door, his stuffy voice called from inside. "Mornin', Deputy Danny."

"Smiley, how are you, bud?" Braddock asked.

He appeared behind the screen door, looking miserable. He opened it and said, "Gettin' by, I guess. What can I do for you?"

"We were hoping to talk to your mom."

He stared at them for a few seconds, then tipped his head inside and said, "Well, come on in."

They followed him through a dark living room and into the kitchen. Brenda Jordan was sitting at a round wooden table smoking a cigarette and watching *Fox News* on a tiny panel TV. She put it on mute, squinted at Braddock, and said, "I know you, Mister Chief Deputy." Then she waved her smoking hand at Rachel. "And I bet I know who you are too."

Braddock said, "Miz Jordan, this is Rachel Carver. She's assisting us with an investigation."

"Nice to meet you, ma'am," Rachel said.

"You two might as well dispense with all the 'miz' and 'ma'am' bullshit. Have a seat and call me Brenda."

Rachel and Braddock sat down at the table. Smiley said, "I'm gonna go take a nap before work." He sneezed on the way to his room.

"You need to be drinkin' your tea if you wanna get some sleep," Brenda yelled after him. There was no response. She looked at Braddock and said, "It's a damn shame that boy had to go and get in trouble for tryin' meth."

"I didn't know about that," he said.

"Yep. Right after he got out of high school. That's why I won't let him buy any allergy medicine." She looked at Rachel. "The state of North Carolina tracks all that shit. They keep an eye on convicted meth heads buyin' decongestant. Last thing I need is the damn SBI or the DEA watchin' my house." She reached up and scratched her scalp at a part that betrayed the gray roots of her auburn-tinted hair. "So what brings the two of you up here? You come to talk to me about Dean and Andy?"

"You knew the victims?" Rachel asked.

"I knew Andy when he was younger. His mom and I were friends. I went to high school with Dean's uncle too."

Rachel took out her Steno pad, flipped it open, and clicked her pen. "We're trying to learn everything we can about them. Especially about any connection there might have been between them. Do you know if they were friends when they were growing up?"

"You could say that. For a little while, anyway. You see, Dean wasn't from around here. He moved here when he was a sophomore." She looked at the ceiling. Her mouth moved silently, like she was trying to work out a math problem. "Might have been the summer before . . . but whenever it was, he moved here to live with his uncle, 'cause he couldn't get along with his stepdad." She mashed the end of her cigarette in a glass ashtray and lit a new one. "And to tell you the truth, he had a hard time gettin' along with a lot of people around here. But the younger kids all looked up to him. Includin' Andy."

"So they met in high school?"

"Yep. I remember Andy's mom tellin' me about it when they started pallin' around together. And I remember thinkin' I was glad they were gonna be graduated by a year when my boy got to high school."

"Why is that? Were they troublemakers?"

"Oh, hell yeah. A bunch of them boys . . . Andy and a few of his friends . . . once they took to hangin' around Dean, they got into all kinds of trouble. I mean, nothin' too bad. They never got arrested or nothin'. Just liked to sneak out and skip school. Get drunk, get high, that sorta thing." She puffed on her cigarette, squinted through the smoke, and let out a raspy cough. "See, Dean's uncle used to buy him beer and give him a little weed every now and then. That made Dean a hero to them boys. They worshiped his ass."

Rachel could see that the mention of marijuana had piqued Braddock's interest. He glanced at her and said, "So Dean got Andy and his buddies into doing drugs?"

"Yeah, if you wanna call it that. Wasn't too big of a deal until they all got busted."

"What happened?" Rachel asked.

"They tried to sneak away one day during lunch to smoke a joint and got caught by the basketball coach. And Dean, high as a kite, told that man to go fuck his own mother." She burst into a laugh that degenerated into a coughing fit. After a minute, she recovered and said, "Well, that shit didn't go over too well in this town. So they sent Dean packin'. He went back to live with his mother over in Franklin or some-damn-where, and them other boys turned into goody goodies for the rest of the school year."

"He moved away . . ." She made a note. "When did that happen?"

"When Dean was a sophomore, I think." Brenda thought for a moment. "Yeah, that was when Andy's mom called me, upset as hell. Dean was a sophomore, and Andy and them other boys were freshmen."

"And that was in?"

"Spring of oh-one."

"Do you know if they kept in touch after Dean moved away?"

"Oh, there ain't no tellin', but I doubt it."

"Why do you say that?" Braddock asked.

"'Cause Andy and his other freshmen friends straightened their asses up. In fact, I remember now . . . they expelled a girl for drugs right around that same time, and that scared the hell out of 'em. But apparently, Dean just kept right on bein' a troublemaker after he moved back in with his momma."

Rachel said, "So McGrath moved away in the spring of 2001 and, as far as you know, didn't have any further contact with Andy Coughlan while he was in high school?"

"As far as I know," Brenda said with a nod.

She wrote it down, then asked, "Do you know when Dean moved back here?"

Brenda turned to stare out the window and thought for a moment. "You know . . . I wanna say it was right around oh-nine or ten. The story was, he went off and found a job over in Hyde County somewhere, workin' as a welder or something." She turned back to Rachel and wore a wicked grin. "Oh, I remember now. He hooked up with his boss's wife. Had an affair goin' for like a year or more. And they kept it real quiet right up until she divorced his ass, then she and Dean got hitched and moved out here. And she got all kinds of money from the split. That's when they bought that house over on the other side of town."

"The house he was just living in?"

"Hell no. I'm talkin' about a big one, right on the edge of town overlookin' the river." She took a final drag of her cigarette, put it out, and lit another. "Tiffany. Her name was Tiffany. Anyway, after they got divorced, he took her to the bank. That's how he got the money to buy that old house off Nineteen. The one he owns now . . . or did own."

"The other day when we were talking to your son, he said he didn't know how Dean managed to afford that house. Are you sure he got the money from his ex-wife?"

"Damn straight I'm sure," she said and waved her hand toward Smiley's room. "That boy don't know nothin' about what goes on in this town."

"I see." Rachel made a few more notes, checked them over, and asked, "In the years since he moved back, do you know if Dean and Andy ever spent time together? Ever reconnected as friends or otherwise?"

Brenda shook her head. "Nothin' that I ever heard about. I mean, hell, it ain't a real big town, though. I'm sure they probably ran into each other at some point."

Rachel turned to Braddock. "I wonder if Coughlan ever went to the Riverside Pub."

"That'd be a good question for Smiley whenever he wakes up."

Brenda yelled, "Clint!" She waited for a second and yelled again. He appeared in the doorway in his boxers, holding a handful of toilet paper to his nose. She said, "They got a question for you."

Rachel asked, "Did Andy Coughlan ever come by the bar where you work?"

He shook his head. "Never saw him there."

"Ever hear about him and Dean hanging around together?"

"No, ma'am."

She looked at Brenda. "Do either of you know if Dean or Andy were involved in drugs recently? Ever hear anything about it?" Back at Smiley, "Or see anything?"

"Sorry, ma'am," he said.

"Buying, selling, using, anything . . . ?"

"Nope," Brenda said. "Trust me, I wish I could help you."

Rachel believed them. Smiley was an open book who answered questions without hesitation, and his mother was even more forth-coming. In fact, she seemed to relish the opportunity to tell a good story.

26

Rachel stood by the takeout window at Lexington Barbecue and watched a stream of motorcycles go by on Main. The air was still cool, and the sky was perfect blue with the sun almost directly overhead. It was a great day to be outside enjoying the weather, but she was destined for a lunch meeting in the conference room at the sheriff's office.

Braddock had his head in the window, ordering enough food for everyone on the team. When he finished, he turned to her and said, "Sorry." He had to raise his voice over the rumbling engines. "I know we just had this the other day, but it's the easiest thing to get for everyone."

"I don't mind," she said. "Who knows when I'll have it again?"

He stared at the ground. "Still leaving tomorrow, huh?"

"I think one more night at the Fontana Lodge is about all I can handle. But, you know, if there was someplace else I could stay . . ."

He smiled and took her hand.

She said, "Didn't you say something about a bed-and-breakfast on the other side of—"

He pulled her close and kissed her. She laughed and backed away.

"Careful, Chief. You're gonna get us in trouble."

He wrapped an arm around her waist and brought her back to him. "I couldn't care less right now."

She pecked him on the cheek and put a finger to his lips. "I think your boss has enough problems. But there's always later."

He grumbled and let her go, his hand brushing her backside as his arm dropped away. He winked and said, "I guess we should try and keep it professional during business hours."

"Mmhmm."

★ ★ ★

In the conference room, Fisher had arranged the paperwork in two lines stretching across the table—one for each victim. Photographs, statements, canvass questionnaires, crime scene sketches, notes . . . He stood a few feet away and scanned them, as if trying to get a better view of the case from a distance.

"How's it going?" Rachel asked.

He rubbed his face roughly in his hands. "Not so good."

Braddock set the bags of food down on the other end of the table and asked, "No luck?"

"Besides that little high school drama Smiley's mom told you about, I can't see anything that puts the two of 'em together. And I haven't found any drugs, neither. Nothing in their houses or their vehicles . . . The families don't know anything. I tried McGrath's friend, Butler, and he wasn't any kind of help. I got a list of Coughlan's friends from his wife. I'll start on them after lunch. Tina's working on the phone records. She should have 'em soon."

"Did she get the list from the DMV?" Rachel asked.

"Yeah. It's not as long as we thought it would be, but it'll still take some time. She and Melvin are gonna start working on it this afternoon. Speak of the devil . . ."

Curtis appeared in the doorway, looked around the room, and said, "I got something you all need to hear about."

"What is it?" Braddock asked.

He stepped in and closed the door. "Do either of you know Jerry Hood?"

Braddock shook his head, but Fisher said, "Yeah, I know him. Used to be a bit of a nuisance. Likes to get in fights. Arrested him for vandalism once."

"That's him," Curtis said. "He came in about an hour ago, real pissed off. Said his daddy, Bert, was assaulted yesterday morning by Dylan Gifford."

"I've definitely heard of *him*," Fisher said. "B and E. Twice. Went to juvie both times."

"Yep. Jerry says his dad had a relationship with Gifford's mother. While they were dating, he lent her some money. Around five hundred dollars or so. Well, apparently, she just broke it off, so Bert figured he'd go back and get what was owed to him. Gifford didn't like that idea. He beat the hell out of Bert and threw him out on his ass. I sent Benny"—he looked at Rachel—"one of our deputies, over to where Bert works to talk to him. He confirmed the story. Looks a little beat up too. So then I sent Benny over to Gifford's house. When he got there, Gifford's mom answered and said he wasn't home. Said he was at his brother's. She gave Benny the address, and he rode over there. He just called me. Nobody's home, but guess what he found parked out beside the brother's trailer?"

Rachel said, "A big truck with custom wheels?"

"A black 2005 GMC Sierra, to be exact. We ran the plate. It's registered to Dylan Gifford." He pulled his phone from his pocket, typed in a password, and touched the e-mail app. "I had Benny take these pictures." He laid the phone on the table for them to see.

"Damn," Fisher said, sliding his finger across the screen to flip through the photos. "Looks pretty close to me."

"Did he get a close-up of the tire tread?" Rachel asked.

"It's the last one," Curtis said.

Fisher swiped the screen until he reached it. As soon as Rachel saw the image, she said, "Holy shit." She grabbed the photos from the line Fisher had made with the Coughlan case file and flipped through them until she found the tire impression. She laid it down next to the phone.

"Jesus," Braddock said. "Looks like a perfect match."

Rachel said, "Captain?"

"Yes, ma'am?"

She handed his phone back to him. "Would you mind e-mailing those photos to Shane, please?" She turned to Fisher. "When you get them, try to print the shot of the tire so it's the same size as the one of the tread impression. We need the comparison to look as convincing as possible." Then to Braddock, "I think we might have enough for a search warrant."

"I'll call the ADA," he said.

"Better call Jensen too."

Fisher went to his desk to get on his computer, and Braddock called the ADA.

Rachel asked Curtis, "Is Jerry still here?"

"No, ma'am. He left about twenty minutes ago."

"Think you could get him to come back?"

"I don't see why not."

"Good. I'd like to have a little chat with him."

27

Jerry Hood's bouncing knee made his chair squeak. He chewed on the tip of his thumb and watched Fisher gather up the paperwork and set it aside. Rachel and Braddock sat down on the other side of the table. Fisher returned with a notepad and a pen and took the seat beside Jerry.

"Can we offer you something to eat?" Rachel asked.

"Nah, I'm all right," Jerry said and scratched the stubble on his jaw. "Smells good, though. I ain't gonna lie. Y'all got that from Lex's, huh? They do it right over there."

He was in his late twenties and had sunken cheeks and a black tattoo climbing his neck. Rachel couldn't make out exactly what it depicted, but there were skulls involved. She said, "Captain Curtis told us your father was assaulted yesterday. By a man named Dylan Gifford?"

"Yeah, that's him. Fuckin' cocksucker. I hate that dude."

"Can you tell us—"

"I wanted to go up there and take care of it myself, but I can't be fightin' no more on account of I got a bad knee and all."

"I understand. Can you tell us how long your dad was dating . . . I'm sorry, what's her name?"

"Linda."

Fisher started to write it down. Jerry leaned toward him and said, "*L-I-N-D-A*."

"Thanks, Jerry," Fisher said.

"No problem, man." He dropped against the seatback and folded his arms. "Yeah, Daddy's been datin' her worthless ass for about two . . . probably more like three years now. Off and on."

"How well have you gotten to know Dylan in that time?" Rachel asked.

"Well enough, I guess. I mean, I don't really *know* him, you know. I don't hang out with the dude or nothin'."

"Why is that?" Fisher asked.

"'Cause he's a asshole. You know what I mean? I ain't got time for fuckheads like Dylan Gifford."

"Have you ever known him to be violent before yesterday's incident with your dad?" Rachel asked.

"Oh, hell yeah. Dude loves to beat up on people. I seen him kick the shit outta this boy one time for callin' his brother a name . . . I think he called him a pussy . . . or maybe it was homo or—"

"We get it," she said. "Do you know if he's ever been involved in anything illegal? Like drugs, for instance?"

"Dylan? Nah. Not since he was a kid. That's his brother's thing."

"What do you mean?" Braddock asked. "What's his brother into?"

"Y'all don't know about Kevin?"

"No," he said. "Mind telling us?"

"Dude's a fuckin' crank dealer, man. I'm surprised y'all ain't heard about him."

Fisher asked, "You're sure he's a dealer? Not just a user?"

"Dealer, user, producer . . . he does it all, man. I mean, he ain't big time or nothin', but he's hooked up with some boys that got a little lab up in the hills outside Whittier."

"And you're sure about this?" Rachel asked.

"Yeah, I'm sure. I wouldn't just go makin' up some shit like that. Hell, he even tried to recruit me to join his little deal last year."

Rachel looked at Braddock. "Did you get ahold of Jensen?"

"He's on his way now," he said.

Jerry's eyes darted between Rachel and the food bags at the end of the table. "Hey, ma'am, on second thought, you think I could get a few of them french fries or somethin'?"

Rachel set Jerry up in Braddock's office with two barbecue sandwiches, a box full of fries, and a Coke from the vending machine. Then she went back to the conference room, where Braddock and Fisher were bringing Pritchard up to speed. Jensen walked in a few minutes later.

"Boy, you guys have been busy," Jensen said, looking a little out of breath. He dropped into a chair and wiped his brow with a handkerchief. "That's good, though. I wasn't getting anywhere on my end."

"Good to see you, Mike," Pritchard said with a smirk. "Glad you could join us."

Jensen smiled back, and it looked sincere. "It's good to see you too, Sheriff. I'll tell ya, it's really starting to heat up out there." He wiped his brow again. "So how are things going with the DA's office?"

Braddock said, "She's on her way here now."

"The DA's coming here herself?"

"Yep. We got some more information since I talked to you last."

"Oh, okay. Let's hear it."

"We think our suspect's brother is a meth dealer. Might be cooking it too. Our informant says Kevin Gifford and a few of his friends have a lab over in Whittier."

Jensen dropped his handkerchief in his lap and folded it, then slid it into his pocket and stared at the table for a moment.

"You think you oughta call Justin?" Pritchard asked.

He nodded, then looked at Rachel and said, "You mind if I speak with you outside for a minute?"

It was the second time that he had caught her completely off guard. "Uh . . . yeah, sure."

She followed him out the door, leaving Braddock, Pritchard, and Fisher looking at each other in confusion.

★ ★ ★

Standing outside, Jensen kept his voice low.

"I hope you know I've got a ton of respect for ya, Rachel."

"I appreciate that," she said. "And you seem—"

"I'm not fishing for a compliment. What I need is your honest opinion about what I just heard."

"You think I won't be honest with you if I'm in the same room with Sheriff Pritchard?"

"It's not that," he said. "I just wanted this little talk to be between you and me." He looked around quickly. "Because, the truth is, I'm skeptical about the whole drug connection. I mean, I don't have a clue why they were killed, but unless I'm missing something, I don't see any indication that McGrath and Coughlan were dealing or even using. And everyone I've talked to today says they've never heard of them. I think your best chance of figuring this thing out is to pick up your suspect for the assault and battery and get warrants for his car and his house."

"That's the plan."

"Right, but now we've got a problem. Your informant's tip about the meth lab complicates things. You know about the drug initiative going on in our district, right?"

"Yeah," she said, not liking where this was going. The SBI had original jurisdiction in drug trafficking cases, and the Western District office's antidrug initiative was particularly aggressive in going after meth operations.

"Well, if my boss thinks these murders are related to drugs, he's going to take this case away from the sheriff. You guys will find yourselves sitting on the sidelines in a heartbeat."

"I get the feeling Sheriff Pritchard wouldn't mind that so much." She thought about how Braddock might react and asked, "What will you guys do with Gifford?"

"If Sanford thinks he's part of his brother's operation, he'll put him under surveillance. He won't move on him until we've located the lab in Whittier and any other players that might be involved."

"Otherwise they might get spooked and burn it down," she said.

He nodded. "But all of that would be a waste of time if there's no link between the drugs and the murders."

"Yeah."

"So what do you think?" he asked. "Aside from the fact that your suspect is related to a dealer, is there anything else connecting the victims to drugs?"

"Nothing," she said. "At this point, nothing at all."

"Okay. Then what would you suggest I do?"

"You sure you want to take advice from a hired hand?"

"If you were still an agent, we wouldn't be having this conversation."

Rachel thought for a moment and said, "If I were in your shoes, I might want to try to verify Jerry Hood's story. Spend some more time talking to my informants and see if they've heard about any new labs over in Whittier. What would that take? A couple of days?"

He looked at his watch. "Let's try twenty-four hours from now." Then he turned and started walking toward the parking lot. "See ya tomorrow."

★ ★ ★

Rachel's instinct was to pull Braddock aside and explain the situation to him, but she knew that would be a mistake. He would be tempted to withhold information from his boss if it meant catching the killer. So she decided to put it all on the table and trust Pritchard to make the right decision.

"We need to forget about the meth lab," she said. "At least for now."

Pritchard looked at Braddock. "What the hell is she talking about?"

"I wish I knew." His eyes were wide with disbelief. "Rachel, what are you talking about? Where's Jensen?"

"He's gone."

"Gone?" Pritchard came out of his seat. "Where the hell did he go? The DA's gonna be here any minute."

"I know," she said. "And when she gets here, you should downplay the drug-dealing brother as much as possible."

He fell back into the chair. "Hell, that's the whole reason she's coming down here. And she expects to see Jensen and, at the very least, have a conference call with Justin—"

"Sheriff, I'm going to suggest that you hold off on calling Sanford until Jensen has a chance to find out what he can about the lab. In fact, it's probably a good idea to make sure that all communication between this office and the SBI regarding this case goes through Jensen."

"What in the goddamn hell—"

Braddock put a hand on Pritchard's shoulder to calm him down, then turned to Fisher and said, "Shane, would you mind giving us a minute, please?"

Fisher stood up, gave Rachel a wary glance, and walked out.

"Okay," Braddock said. "What the hell happened out there?"

"Jensen doesn't believe there's a link between the murders and the brother's supposed meth operation," she said. "He wanted to know what I thought."

"And what did you tell him?"

"I told him that there hasn't been anything in the victimology to point us in that direction."

"So he just left?"

"He's going to check with his informants. See if they've heard of a lab in Whittier."

"Even though he doesn't think there's a connection?" Pritchard asked. "I don't get it."

"He's obligated to check it out," she said. "He can't ignore it . . . and he's doing us a favor."

"How's that?"

"If Sanford hears about the lab, he won't want anyone touching Gifford until SBI can find it and get a handle on everyone who's involved. He'll want to set up a big operation . . . surveillance, informants, undercover agents . . . the kind of thing that could take months."

Braddock said, "Meanwhile, Gifford would be walking around free."

"That's right," she said. "They'll watch him, make sure he doesn't kill anyone else, but any physical evidence that might be in his truck or his house could disappear during that time."

Pritchard asked, "You really think they'll let our best suspect in two homicides stay on the street just so they can hunt down a bunch of redneck tweakers?"

"Happens all the time. If they get it in their heads that the murders are a byproduct of the meth business, shutting it down will be their priority. They'll want to round up everyone in the organization at the same time and play them against each other to see who's willing to make a deal. It's possible they could find someone to testify against Gifford. But all of that assumes the murders and the drugs are related."

"But you don't think they are."

She shrugged. "I'm not saying it's impossible. I'm just saying that we haven't seen any indication of it yet."

"I might buy it if we were just talking about McGrath," Braddock said. "But Coughlan . . . I have a hard time believing he was involved in a meth ring."

"Yeah . . ." Pritchard said. He leaned his head against the seat back and closed his eyes. He looked like he wanted more than anything to be somewhere else. "So, since you and Jensen are on the same page, I assume you all worked out some sort of deal to keep Sanford out of the loop?"

"You have twenty-four hours to arrest Gifford and execute the search warrants. After that, whatever Jensen finds in Whittier, he's going to tell Sanford about it."

"Twenty-four hours . . ."

There was a knock on the door. Pritchard sat up. "Yeah?"

Fisher stuck his head in. "Sorry to bother you, Sheriff, but the district attorney just got here. She's waiting in your office."

"Well, shit," he said. "I guess I'm in trouble now. Bring her back here."

28

While Pritchard, Braddock, and Fisher were meeting with the district attorney, Rachel went to Braddock's office to talk to Jerry.

"I been here for a while now," he said. "How much longer y'all gonna keep me?"

She decided not to tell him that he could leave whenever he wanted. "We really appreciate your help today, Jerry. Can I get you anything?"

He looked around. "Is there somewhere I can smoke in this place?"

"Why don't we go out front?"

Rachel led him outside to the corner of the building where a cigarette-butt receptacle stood by a wooden park bench. He lit a Marlboro and started pacing. She sat down and said, "A deputy tried to find Dylan Gifford at the address you gave Captain Curtis, but he wasn't there. His mother said he was at his brother's trailer. Does he stay there often?"

He shrugged. "Not as far as I know. Daddy said Dylan was always there with Linda whenever he went to go see her. That's why he kept bringin' her back to our house, even though he didn't really like her stayin' over. I think Dylan's the one that actually owns that place he and his momma stay at."

She thought about that while she watched him repeatedly flick the ashes off his cigarette after each drag. It was the compulsive, anxious act of someone under a lot of stress. "You seem pretty nervous, Jerry. Everything okay?"

"Yeah, I'm fine." He shrugged as he said it, and his head jerked to one side. He seemed to realize that he looked the opposite. "You know, I just ain't all that relaxed when I get around too many cops."

"There aren't any out here," she said with a reassuring smile.

"What about you?" he asked through a cloud of smoke. "Ain't you a cop?"

"Not anymore."

He walked over and sat down on the bench beside her. "I guess that ain't the only reason I'm a little wound up. I just don't want none of this shit comin' back on me."

"How would it come back on you?"

"I don't know. That damn Kevin . . . I mean, I ain't afraid of him or nothin'. Like, in a straight-up fight, I'd beat his ass. But . . . you know, I ain't tryin' to get shot while I'm out checkin' the mail or some shit."

"You think he would do that?"

"Ain't no tellin'. Dude likes to act like he's some kinda hillbilly gangster. He's got a damn arsenal up at that trailer of his."

She straightened up and asked, "What about Dylan? Does he keep a lot of guns in his house?"

He looked at her with disbelief. "You're jokin', right?" He laughed. "Girl, this is western Carolina. There ain't a redneck in these hills that don't have at least two or three guns in the house."

★ ★ ★

The district attorney left, and Rachel went into the conference room to find Braddock and Pritchard licking their wounds.

"How'd it go?" she asked.

Pritchard said, "I'd rather not talk about it."

"Was fairly unpleasant," Braddock said. "But she's on board. Fisher is gonna work on the affidavits with the ADA. Hopefully we'll have the warrants in a couple of hours."

"That's good news," she said. "So now let's talk about executing them."

Pritchard shook his head. "Jesus, can I have at least five minutes? I don't think I'm emotionally prepared for that kinda talk right now."

Braddock laughed. "What's on your mind?"

"I was just outside talking to Jerry," she said. "He mentioned that both of the Giffords are pretty well armed. Kevin especially, but either way, whoever goes over there might come up against some significant firepower."

Braddock laced his fingers behind his head. "Well, that adds a wrinkle. Normally we'd call the SBI and ask them to send us one of their special response teams, but now . . . I don't guess we can call Jensen."

"We could," Pritchard said, "but that kinda request would have to go up the chain. Sanford won't sign off without knowing what's going on here, and it doesn't seem like Jensen would be willing to just outright lie to him."

The last part was directed at Rachel, and it almost sounded like a question. She said, "I think he's about as far out on the proverbial limb as he's willing to go."

"Doesn't sound like we have a choice," Braddock said. "We call Jensen and tell him what we need. Let him come clean with Sanford, and let the chips fall where they may. I'm not about to send a bunch of deputies up there to get their asses shot off."

Pritchard chuckled to himself. When Braddock and Rachel looked at him, he said, "I think I might have a third option."

★ ★ ★

Pritchard put Sheriff Lee Harrelson on speakerphone and said, "Cousin, I need to borrow your SWAT team."

"Damn, Tee Pee . . . everything all right? What kind of a mess have you gotten yourself into over there?"

"Nothing a little intercounty cooperation can't take care of."

"Uh-huh."

"I'm working on getting two search warrants and an arrest warrant in connection with these murders. I could really use your help."

"I thought you were working with the SBI on that deal."

"It's complicated, cuz."

"Uh–huh . . . well, all right. I reckon we might be able to help you."

"You sure it's no trouble?"

"Ah hell, Teddy, them boys are always looking for an excuse to dress out."

29

Bishop parked the Wrangler at Newfound Gap and checked his mirrors to make sure they were clear of tourists.

"Tomorrow," he said, "you're going to do the last two."

Gifford was stunned. It took him a moment to collect his thoughts before he said, "You want two of 'em done in one day?"

"Yes. Is that a problem?"

"Well . . . I thought we were never gonna do that. I thought—"

"It doesn't matter what you thought," he growled. "Things have changed, so the plan has to change too."

"I don't know, man. I don't like this shit. Changin' things on me."

"I don't give a damn whether you like it or not. You're going to do what the *fuck* I tell you."

"Don't come at me like that, motherfucker."

His voice was too loud. Bishop looked around and said, "Calm down, goddammit."

"Fuck that. I'll get outta here and take my chances. You can finish this shit on your own. You ain't the only scary son of a bitch I know."

Gifford ran his hands through his hair and stared out the passenger window. His rapid breathing sounded shaky. Bishop held his tongue, trying to keep things from getting out of control. They sat quietly for a minute while he tried to find a better approach to getting what he wanted. It was funny how too much fear could make a man brave. He never expected to hear Gifford stand up for himself.

"Look, Dylan," he said, keeping his voice even, "I know you've been through a lot. And what I'm asking isn't easy, but it's almost over. If you take care of these two tomorrow, you'll be done. I'll be out of your life for good."

"For good?"

"Yes. The only thing you'll have left to do is collect your money. Then you'll never see me again."

Gifford's breathing slowed. "It ain't like I don't want to get it over with . . . I just don't wanna get caught. With the whole town on lockdown and everything . . ."

"I understand. It'll be a little tricky, but I know you can do it."

"You sure about that?"

Bishop nodded. "I've worked out every detail." He let Gifford consider it for a few seconds. Then he said, "What do you say? Shall we go over the plan?"

★ ★ ★

The ride back made Gifford nauseous. He got out of the Wrangler on a side street in Gatlinburg and walked two blocks to the Pancake House. He was eager to get home but needed some food to settle his stomach. The dinner meals on the menu looked good, but he was in the mood for breakfast. When the waiter returned with a pile of eggs, sausage links, and hashed browns, he ate half of it, dropped a ten-dollar bill on the table, and left.

He maneuvered through traffic in his brother's F-250 pickup, making good time until he got stuck behind a line of motorcycles cruising along 441. It was a perfect afternoon for a drive in the Great Smoky Mountains, if only he had been in the right state of mind to enjoy it. He was running late, and the last thing he wanted was to be in another argument. His brother was at a friend's house in Whittier, waiting for Gifford to pick him up. When he arrived an hour and twenty minutes later, Kevin came outside and said, "What the hell, Dylan? Where you been?"

"Sorry," he said, walking around to the passenger side. "Got hung up."

Kevin looked like he wanted to complain a little more but decided it was best not to push his luck. "How long before you can drive your truck again?"

"I don't know."

"You gonna need to use mine any more today?"

"No, just drop me off at the house. If I need to go anywhere, I'll use Momma's."

Kevin turned on the radio as they drove away. Once they were on the expressway, he lowered the volume and said, "You doin' all right? You seem a little upset or somethin'. Even more than usual."

"It's nothin'."

Gifford stared out the window and let the low sun lull him into a daze. He didn't speak again until they turned onto the road near his house. "Listen, Kevin," he said, "I been workin' with this asshole on somethin' kinda messed up . . . It ain't really goin' all that well . . ."

"Why not? What's up?"

"I can't talk about it, all right? Just listen. If somethin' goes bad . . . if you hear about me gettin' into any kinda trouble or gettin' hurt or—"

"Hurt? What the—"

"Let me finish talkin', dammit. If anything happens, you take Momma and get the hell outta here. I'm talkin' like right away. Don't wait around for shit. Just get on the road and go."

"Where am I supposed to take her?"

"I don't know . . . it don't matter, just go. Somewhere out west, maybe. Just get outta here and don't ever come back."

"Dylan . . . what—"

"Don't ask me anymore questions, all right? I can't handle it right now. I need to know you two will be safe. Can you just promise me?"

Kevin parked in Gifford's driveway and said, "I'll get Momma outta here, all right. That much I promise. But if some fool's causin' you trouble, I'm gonna have to come back and smoke his ass. For real. I ain't just leavin' you here to fend for yourself."

Gifford decided that was good enough. He gave his brother a pat on the shoulder and jumped out. "Take care of yourself," he said and closed the door.

★ ★ ★

Just below the ridge to the west, lying behind an outcrop of gneiss rock, a sniper and a spotter from the Buncombe County Sheriff's Office Special Response Team watched through a pair of high-powered scopes as Gifford got out of the truck and went inside the house.

30

Rachel stood at the back of the packed conference room as Lieutenant Brian Davis went over the plan for a second time.

"We unload at the intersection," he said, standing in front of a dry-erase board mounted on the wall. He had drawn a rough sketch of Gifford's house and the surrounding property, complete with trees, roads, and other terrain features. There were also photos of the house, each taken from a different vantage point, taped up beside the board. He looked at his men seated around the table and pointed at a spot on the drawing. "Entry team and north-side perimeter security will stay behind the BearCat as it heads up the road and onto the driveway to this point, then you'll split. Perimeter will circle this way to the back of the residence"—he made an arc with the marker—"while the entry team approaches the front door, moving along the south wall. East-side perimeter security will ride shotgun on the running boards. After the split, the BearCat will haul butt to this point"—he drew an *X* on the board—"where you'll jump off and cover any escape attempt to the east. Overwatch has our approach covered from the west. Lowry County deputies will move in behind us to assist. An ambulance will be parked a half mile down the road, should we need it. And Harris Regional has been notified. Any questions?"

Braddock asked, "How many of you are going inside?"

The entry team leader was holding the shoulder straps of his tactical vest. He spun in his chair to face Braddock and said, "Six of us." He stood, walked to the board, and pointed at the entrance drawn on Gifford's house. "Based on what Mister Hood told us, we expect this door to open up to the main living area, with a kitchen and laundry room to the left, bedrooms and bathrooms down a hallway to the right. Once we enter and control the living room, two men go left to clear the kitchen and laundry, the rest of us go right to clear the bedrooms and baths."

Braddock glanced at Rachel. "Okay. Whatever you guys need to do. I just want everyone to remember that our main goal here is evidence collection. We're hoping to find something in that house that will tie the suspect to two homicides."

"We understand, Chief," Davis said with a smile. His tone was on the edge of patronizing. "And we'll do what we can to keep from disturbing anything we don't need to. But the safety of my team comes first, so we're going to be sticking our noses in every nook and cranny that looks big enough to hide someone. If that's going to be a problem, it's not too late to change your minds about this."

Braddock looked over again and said, "Rachel?"

Everyone turned to her. She thought about the options that had been ruled out. Simply knocking on the door would be too dangerous, they had decided. Surrounding the house and ordering Gifford to come out could turn into a standoff, and they would lose the element of surprise. They had considered a phone ruse, but no one could think of a convincing way to lure him outside without making him suspicious and taking the risk that he might destroy whatever evidence they hoped to collect. The assault had to happen.

She scanned the faces of the team—the twelve operators dressed in tactical gear, the driver of the armored BearCat, Lieutenant Davis, and the handful of deputies that Braddock and Curtis had chosen to back them up on the perimeter—and suddenly felt the weight of her decision. The deal she had made with Jensen could have terrible consequences. If something went wrong, one or more of these men might not make it back alive.

"Safety first," she said. "These guys know what they're doing."

Then she thought about the soil samples Carly had collected and the possibility of finding some of the same soil on Gifford's shoes. Or perhaps on the floor in the house. She said, "Of course, it might help if we get some video of you guys washing your boots off before you load up in the BearCat."

The entry team leader tried to stifle a laugh. He put a hand to his mouth, but it was too late. The rest of the room erupted. They seemed to appreciate that she would be willing introduce a little levity to the situation. She didn't have the heart to tell them she was serious.

The meeting broke up, and the team went outside to double-check their gear, weapons, and communication equipment. Davis walked over to Rachel and Braddock and asked, "Did your informant leave?"

"He's in my office," Braddock said. "Been there all day. I think he's about to go nuts cooped up in there."

"I get the sense that he trusts you the most," Davis said to Rachel.

"He knows I'm not a cop anymore."

"Can you talk him into coming along for the ride? Maybe keep him in the car with you?"

"I can try. You think you'll need him there?"

He shrugged. "You never know. He's the only one we have who's been inside the house. But more importantly, I don't want him talking to anyone until we get the place secure. Considering his father's relationship with the suspect's mother . . . I'd just like to keep him under wraps until it's over. And especially keep him off his phone."

Rachel nodded, and Braddock said, "Well, that'll certainly make the ride more interesting."

★ ★ ★

Rachel stood by the passenger door of the Tahoe and watched Braddock coordinate with the deputies. Jerry was in the back seat, peering through a window. Pritchard was on the sidewalk, looking like he wanted to be more involved, but Braddock had convinced him to stay behind in case they needed any support from the office. Fisher pulled up with the warrants just as the team was loading up. He rolled down his window, took a look at the men climbing into the black armored BearCat, and whistled.

"Hell yeah," he said. "That's what I'm talkin' about. You all ready to get this show on the road?"

Braddock yelled, "Shane, ride with Carly. And where the hell is Tina?"

"Wish I knew, Chief," Fisher said as he rolled up his window. He wheeled into a parking space, then jumped out, ran over, and climbed into Carly's Tahoe.

"Melvin," Braddock said, "you ride with Lieutenant Davis. I'll drive mine over with Rachel and meet you guys at the intersection."

Davis stuck his head out the window of his white Dodge Charger and said, "Chief, I need you and Captain Curtis both to ride with me."

Braddock hesitated for a second, then tossed his keys to Rachel. "Just park at the back of the line and wait for me to call you." She nodded and moved to the driver's side. He started for Davis's car, then stopped and turned back, ran to her window, and said, "Let me have the radio in the cup holder." She handed it to him, and he adjusted the frequency, gave it back, and said, "You'll be able to listen in with this."

Rachel started the engine and watched the line of SUVs and cars fall in behind the BearCat.

"Dang," Jerry said from the back seat. "Y'all ain't playin' around. This is one helluva badass parade."

31

When Pratt had called to check in after lunch, Fisher had said that he was waiting on some guy named Jerry Hood to show up so they could question him. Said Curtis had told him that one of the deputies had found a possible match on the truck. But she had wanted to stay clear of the office, so she told him she would start going through the DMV list anyway.

"Just in case it turns out to be nothing," she had said. "But let me know if anything comes of it, so I'm not out here wasting my time."

After that, she found three of the trucks on her list—none of which matched—before her boyfriend called and asked her to quit early. Asked her to meet him at her place. When she asked him in a playful tone what he had planned, he described things that had her giggling into her phone. She teased him and said he wouldn't do those things, but he promised he would if she'd only give him the chance to prove it.

So she went home to wait for him. He was almost an hour late when he finally came through the door. His apology sounded sincere, so she decided to forgive him. She led him into her room and kissed him, pulled his shirt off, and pushed his pants down. The phone rang, but she ignored it, took him in her hand, and worked him until he was ready to make good on his promise.

An hour later, the phone rang again. Pratt's head was nuzzled against his shoulder, and she didn't want to move. She let it go to voice mail and closed her eyes, started to drift asleep. But another call jarred her awake.

"Dammit," she said, getting to her feet. She stomped out to the kitchen and snatched the phone from the counter just as the ringing stopped. The screen said the calls had come from Fisher. She sighed and called him back.

"Jesus, Tina." He was almost yelling into her ear. "Where the hell have you been?"

"Sorry, my phone died. I've just been running around going through this list. So far—"

"Forget about the damn list. We're moving on a suspect. A whole bunch of us are on the way there now. We're following a damn armored personnel carrier, for cryin' out loud."

"Wait. Slow down . . . what the hell are you talking about?"

"Sheriff Harrelson sent us his SRT guys. They're all loaded up and ready to kick ass. I got the warrants in hand. We're going to bust this sorry sucker's door down. And we've got some other guys going to his brother's house to seize the truck."

"Shit." Pratt pulled open a drawer and pushed the contents around until she found a pen and a pad of sticky notes. She pulled the cap off the pen with her teeth, spit it out, and said, "Give me the address for the brother's house. I'll handle the truck."

She wrote it down and ended the call. Turned to go back to her room and bumped into her boyfriend, giving her a start. He had been standing right behind her.

"God . . ." she said and caught her breath. "I'm sorry, sugar, I love it when you rub up on me like that, but I gotta run. Something big is going down."

He followed her into the room. "What is it? What's going on?"

"We're getting ready to make an arrest." She grabbed her pants from the floor and lay back on the bed to pull them up. "I've been ignoring the damn phone. Danny and Sheriff Pritchard are gonna be pissed at me."

"Then I guess you better get out of here."

She fastened her bra in front, spun it around, and slipped her arms into the shoulder straps, then stopped for a second to look at him. "I'm really sorry I have to run out on you like this."

"Don't be," he said. There was a bit of urgency in his voice. "You don't have to worry about me. I just don't want you to get in trouble."

She pulled on her shirt and stepped into her shoes. "You sure you'll be okay?"

He kissed her. "Get out of here. I'll make sure I lock up."

★ ★ ★

As soon as she went through the door, Bishop was on the burner. He heard the first ring and stepped to the window, lifted a slat on the blinds, and looked out to make sure she was leaving. He saw the door on her Pathfinder close. The lights came on as she started the engine.

32

Rachel parked behind the last patrol car but kept the engine running so they could have air conditioning. She adjusted the volume on the radio and watched the activity up ahead at the intersection. Jerry slid to the middle of the back seat and looked over her shoulder. The sun had fallen behind the nearest ridge, but there was still enough light to see clearly.

"Check 'em out," Jerry said. "They dressed for war."

The team filed out of the BearCat. Eight operators formed a line at the back, holding their AR-15 rifles with the muzzles pointed low and the buttstocks pressed against their shoulders. Another man holding a battering ram jumped out and got in line. Two others hopped onto the running boards and held onto a bar above the door. Several voices checked in over the radio: the entry-team leader, the four men assigned to lead perimeter security, and the operator still in the BearCat with the driver. Lieutenant Davis talked to Braddock, then Curtis, then the three of them were gathering the deputies and giving them orders.

Davis came on the radio and said, "Bradley, how are we looking?"

"LT, Bradley, looking good from up here." Rachel realized she was hearing the spotter on the mountainside west of the property. "No activity outside. You're all clear to go."

"Copy that," Davis said. "All right, everyone, green light. Move up, move up, move up."

The BearCat started at a crawl, turned right, and headed uphill with the line of heavily armed men marching behind. They disappeared around the corner, leaving a pair of deputies to guard the intersection.

★ ★ ★

The phone was ringing, and Gifford's mom was yelling for him to answer it.

"I hear it," he said, rushing out of the bathroom. His hands were wet. He wiped them on his jeans, picked up the phone, and tapped the screen. "Yeah?"

"Run," Bishop said. "Right now. They're coming for you."

★ ★ ★

Jerry was looking through the passenger-side window, trying to get a view of the house.

"Man," he said, "I can't see a damn thing from here."

Rachel was holding the radio close to her ear. The operator in the BearCat said, "Twenty yards to the driveway."

Davis said, "Copy—"

"LT, Bradley, we got something . . . Suspect is on the move. He just ran out the back. He's headed east toward the woods."

"Move, move, move!" Davis yelled.

Rachel and Jerry both looked uphill.

"Entry team . . . shit, take the house. Perimeter teams, move on the suspect."

"He's in the woods now," the spotter said. "We've lost visual. Repeat, we've lost visual."

"Everyone move it, goddammit . . . Is he armed? Bradley, is he armed? Chief Braddock, get some deputies back on the road. See if you can cut him off."

"LT, he did not appear to be armed."

Jerry pressed his forehead to the glass and said, "Oh, shit, I see him." He jumped back and jabbed the window with his finger. "Look, there goes that motherfucker. He's right there."

As soon as Rachel saw him, she put the Tahoe in reverse and spun around, stopped on the opposite shoulder, threw it in drive, and took off after him. "I have a visual on the suspect," she yelled into the radio. "He's moving east on foot."

"Rachel." It was Braddock. "Where are you?"

"Headed downhill. East on Howell Branch—"

"This ain't Howell Branch no more," Jerry said. "That ended back up there."

"Shit. Headed east downhill . . . I don't know . . . the same road we came in on."

"He's turnin'," Jerry said. "Look, there he goes."

She tried to look but almost ran off the road. "Which way?"

"Uh . . . he's goin' left. His left."

"Away from us?"

"Yeah."

She got back on the radio. "Suspect has turned—" The road made a sharp turn to the right, and she was going too fast. She slammed on the brakes and dropped the radio as she took the wheel with both hands.

"Whoa, mother—" Jerry yelled as he was thrown onto the center console. "Dang, woman. You gonna get us killed."

They slid to a stop on the shoulder, missing a tree by less than a foot. She put it in reverse and said, "Can you see him?"

"No. Back up, though. I think I saw a trail."

They ran uphill in reverse until Jerry said, "There. But I don't think this thing can handle it."

She reached down for the radio but couldn't find it. "Screw it," she said and switched over to four-wheel drive. "I guess we'll find out. Hang on."

"Aw, hell no."

They went over the side and slid down a steep slope, losing traction on the sand and rocks beneath them. When they hit the bottom, the ground turned up quickly, sending them airborne for an instant. The Tahoe bounced onto a narrow path meant for dirt bikes and ATVs, and Rachel struggled to keep from losing control.

Jerry held onto her seatback and said, "You just went and lost your damn mind, girl."

Braddock came over the radio. "Rachel, we're headed downhill. Do you still have him?"

"Jerry, find that radio. I think it fell under the seat."

The entry team leader said, "We're going in."

And Davis said, "We're in the woods heading east. Someone talk to me."

"Rachel." Braddock sounded desperate. "Where are you?"

"Jerry?" she said.

Jerry was crouched on the floorboard. "I think I can feel it—"

They hit a bump, and he yelled in pain. Came up holding his forearm.

"Forget it," she said. "Just keep an eye out for him."

They veered around a bend, and Jerry said, "There he is."

Rachel saw him a moment later, running alongside the trail to her left about fifty yards ahead. She floored the accelerator and started to overtake him. They were almost on top of him when he looked back and ran across to the other side and into the woods.

"Find that radio and tell them where we are," she said and planted both feet on the brake pedal. They skidded to a stop. She put it in park, jumped out to run after him, and yelled over her shoulder, "Honk the horn. Keep honking it until they find us."

Gifford was just ahead when she plowed through a pepper vine and caught sight of him. He looked back at the commotion, slipped and fell to one knee. She broke into a sprint, and he got to his feet and started along a path that hugged a rock face. Jerry was yelling something unintelligible. Then she heard the horn and distant, muffled voices over the radio. Rachel's adrenaline pushed her forward just as it seemed Gifford was starting to lose steam. She leapt onto the path and reached out to grab him. At that moment, she thought about her pistol—a black 9mm Glock 19—stored securely inside the gun safe in her apartment three hundred miles away.

Rachel's hand snagged the back of Gifford's T-shirt, and she pulled hard to stop him. He turned around and took a swing at her. It was a wide, arcing punch, and she ducked it easily, then lunged forward and wrapped her arms around his waist, getting a better grip on his shirt.

"Get off me, you fuckin' bitch!" he yelled. He was breathing hard. Frantic and powered by fear.

"It's over, Dylan," she said.

He screamed and rushed forward, and they both went down. Rachel was on her back with Gifford above her. She wrapped her legs around his torso and used her arms to pull his head to her shoulder, making it harder for him to get in a good punch.

"Aw damn, y'all better hurry up and get down here. This shit's gettin' real."

Rachel glanced back and saw Jerry standing at the edge of the path, yelling into the radio.

"Dude's on top of her, man. Should I jump in and help? Let me hit him upside the head with a rock or somethin'."

"Stay back, Jerry," she said.

Gifford was flailing and grunting, trying to hit her and break free, but Rachel had trained to be in this position. She waited until he tried to lift himself up and cock his arm back for a big swing, then she shot her left leg up and hooked it behind his neck. Her right foot kicked at his hip, breaking his posture just enough to bring his head back down. She reached up and pulled her left foot into the crook of her right knee, wrapping his head and arm in a technique that jiu-jitsu practitioners called a triangle choke.

"Dude, he's tryin' to punch her," Jerry said into the radio. "But . . . but hang on, now . . ."

Rachel squeezed her legs and pulled on the back of Gifford's head. His forehead started to turn purple. He tried to stand but lost his footing, then tried to claw at her face in desperation. His fingers found her cheek just as the life went out of them. She held him there for a moment longer, then released her hold and kicked him aside.

"I think he's out," Jerry yelled. "Holy shit, she done judo-choked his ass or somethin'. Dude's out cold."

There were heavy footfalls coming up the path. The rattling of tactical gear as Davis and his men jogged around the rock face.

"Rachel!" Davis shouted. "Are you all right?"

The team approached with their weapons trained on Gifford, who was starting to regain consciousness. They rolled him onto his stomach and bound his wrists behind his back with plastic flex cuffs.

"I'm good," she said between panting breaths. She let her head fall back against the ground. "Just give me a second."

Jerry punched Davis in the arm and said, "Dang, dude. Y'all didn't know this girl was such a badass, did you?"

33

Braddock reached down and helped Rachel up to the road. When she stepped onto the asphalt, the circle of deputies gave her a round of applause. Braddock hugged her and lifted her up, then set her back on her feet and said, "What the hell were you thinking?"

"I wasn't," she said, feeling exhausted. She looked down and saw Davis, Jerry, and a deputy making the climb. The rest of the team had come up earlier, escorting Gifford to a patrol car. The Tahoe was stranded at the bottom of the hill. A truck with a winch had been dispatched to rescue it. "Sorry about that, by the way."

"You could've been killed driving that damn thing down there."

"Crazy, huh?"

They walked up to Gifford's house as the last bit of daylight faded. Flashes of red and blue swept the hillsides. When they got to the driveway, Curtis met them with a crooked smile. He said, "That was quite a performance, young lady. You all right?"

"I'll live," she said.

"Well, good. We got the truck. I called and told my boys to move on it as soon as the shit hit the fan. Tina's over there with 'em now. Wanna guess what she found in the glove box?"

Rachel gave him an impatient look.

"A lock-picking kit," he said. "She also bagged a pair of leather gloves she found under the seat."

"Nice," Braddock said and patted Rachel's shoulder. "This is turning into a good day. And they're bringing the truck in?"

"Yep. Loading it on the flatbed as we speak."

"Did the brother give them any trouble?"

"He put on a bit of a show. Almost gave us enough to arrest him with until Benny gave him what for. That calmed his ass down pretty quick. Oh, that reminds me . . ." He nodded toward a patrol car. "We arrested the mother. Apparently, she threw an ashtray at one of the SRT guys when he came through the door."

Rachel could barely make out Linda Gifford's silhouette in the back of the car.

"Must run in the family," Braddock said.

"Hey, Chief, Rachel." It was Fisher calling from the steps just outside the front door. He was waving at them with blue hands. "Carly's found something. Y'all need to come look at this."

★ ★ ★

Gifford's bedroom smelled like old sweat and mildew, most likely from the soiled laundry that was piled in a corner by the closet. There was a dresser standing against the far wall, dark-stained oak with a missing drawer. A nightstand held empty cans of beer and soda. Carly was in the middle of the floor on her knees, taking pictures of something underneath the bed. She stood when she saw Rachel and Braddock come into the room.

"What did you find?" Rachel asked.

"Have a look," Carly said.

Rachel knelt down, cocked her head to the side, and saw an aluminum baseball bat—a Louisville Slugger.

Braddock leaned over behind her and said, "I'll be damned."

"I haven't touched it yet," Carly said. "I thought about checking it for blood, but I wanted to make sure everyone's okay with that. Bruce can't be here till morning."

Rachel glanced at Braddock and said, "You know what, Carly? I think you can handle it. Danny?"

"I think so too."

"What kind of reagent do you have?" Rachel asked.

"Hemascein," Carly said.

"Right. I remember now. And you have an alternate light source?"

"Yeah. Got a BLUEMAXX in my other kit."

"That'll work. Why don't you get everything you need in here, and we'll videotape the whole procedure."

"Sounds good," Carly said and walked outside.

As soon as she was gone, Fisher asked, "There won't be any blood on it, will there?"

"Probably not," Braddock said. "He didn't rupture McGrath's scalp. But he did handle the bat after he stabbed him, so if any blood got on his hands . . ."

"Oh, yeah," he said. "I didn't think about that."

"It's still a long shot, though," Rachel said. "He was so damn careful . . ." She looked around and thought about how messy Gifford's room looked. "Doesn't this place look out of character?"

"What do you mean?" Fisher asked.

Carly came back in with her kit, and Rachel dismissed the thought.

"Shane, would you mind recording this?"

He took his phone out, opened the camera app, and switched the setting to video. "All right, Carly. You're on."

Carly took everything she needed out of her kits and used one of the lids as a table to mix the solutions. Once she had two spray bottles prepared—one with the Hemascein reagent and another with a hydrogen peroxide solution—she went to the bed and retrieved the Slugger. She laid it on the floor next to her kits and reached for a bottle.

"Why don't you hit it with the light first," Rachel said, "so we can have a negative control."

"Right," Carly said. The muscle in her jaw flexed as she admonished herself for forgetting a step. She picked up the BLUEMAXX, which looked like a flashlight with an orange plastic rectangle attached to the end, and turned it on. "Would someone mind getting the lights for me?"

Braddock flipped the switch on the wall, and the room went dark, save for the bright blue beam from the flashlight and the glow from Fisher's phone screen. Carly passed the beam over the bat, rotating it in her hand to make sure the light hit every square inch of it. "Huh," she said.

"What is it?" Rachel asked.

"I got something here."

She walked over to stand behind Carly, looked through the orange filter, and saw thin white streaks.

"Can't be blood, can it?" Carly asked. "It wouldn't glow with just the light. Has to be saliva, urine, or semen."

"Ain't that a pleasant thought," Fisher said.

Rachel said, "Better get some pictures of it."

Carly put an orange filter over her camera lens. "Would you hold the light for me?"

Rachel took the flashlight, and Carly snapped a few shots. When she finished, she checked the screen on her camera and said, "Okay, I got it. Lights, please."

Braddock hit the switch.

"Do we still want to try for blood?"

"Yeah," Rachel said. "Let's see what we get."

"Boss, would you mind holding it for me? I'll spray a little bit above it. When the mist settles, rotate it some, and I'll spray a little more. Don't let it touch the ground or anything else until I tell you we're done."

"Got it," Braddock said, taking the Slugger. Carly sprayed the Hemascein and the hydrogen peroxide solution a little bit at a time as he spun it in his hands. They waited two minutes to give the chemicals time to react, then Rachel turned out the lights.

Carly shined the flashlight, looked through the orange filter, and said, "We got blood."

Rachel looked and saw that the white streaks were now glowing green. Carly took several photos, instructing Braddock on how to turn the bat so she could shoot it at different angles. When she finished, Rachel turned on the light and said, "So we have blood mixed with something else . . . most likely saliva."

"Those streaks look like he tried to wipe it off," Carly said.

"Hot damn," Fisher said. "That's how the blood got on the dishrag. He used it to wipe the blood off."

"But how did he get blood on it to begin with?" Braddock asked. "There's none on the handle. Do we really think he had it on his hands but only got it on one end?"

Rachel remembered that there had been no blood on the knife handle when she had seen it at the hospital. McGrath had been on his back. The blood had run down toward his shoulder and neck, not up the knife. So how would Gifford get blood on his hands? She closed her eyes and imagined herself approaching McGrath from behind.

She hit him on the head. There was no blood or saliva on the Slugger at that point. She dropped it and went for the knife, knelt down over McGrath, and stabbed him. But she left the knife in his chest. The only way she could get blood on her hands was if she touched a blood-soaked portion of the sweat shirt, but she couldn't think of any reason she would do that. And even if she did, where would the saliva come from?

"I don't think so . . ." Rachel said. She replayed the murder again and tried to think of every possible method of transferring blood. Then she remembered that McGrath's lungs had been cut, and blood had gotten inside them. He might have coughed it up with his last breath, which would explain how it became mixed with saliva. But there would have been droplets on the floor. Perhaps even on Gifford's clothes. And Gifford might have anticipated that. To prevent it, he would have covered McGrath's mouth . . .

"With the dishrag," she said.

"What?" Braddock asked.

"I know what happened. Gifford covered McGrath's mouth with the dishrag to keep him from coughing blood all over the place. Then he used the rag to wipe down the end of the bat."

"Why would he do that if there was no blood on it?"

"He was being too careful," Carly said. "I bet he was worried there might be hair on it from hitting McGrath over the head."

Rachel nodded. "And now we have a theory that accounts for every piece of physical evidence in the case." She pointed at the bat. "You guys should send that thing to the crime lab and see if they can get DNA from it."

"I'll go ahead and bag it."

"Nothing plastic."

Carly looked offended.

"Sorry," Rachel said. "Bad habit." She turned to Braddock. "Think the ADA can get you a warrant to collect a sample of Gifford's DNA?"

"Only one way to find out." He was on the phone a moment later.

34

The sheriff's office had two small interrogation rooms and a separate room for observing them on closed-circuit TV. Rachel and Braddock leaned against a table in the observation room and watched the live feed of Carly swabbing the inside of Gifford's cheek. Fisher was in the corner beneath the camera. A deputy stood in the doorway in case there was trouble. But Gifford sat quietly and didn't protest.

"He looks pretty calm," Braddock said.

Rachel squinted to study his face. The resolution on the screen wasn't great, but she thought she could read his expression. "He's confused. He wants to believe that we can't have anything on him. That he was too careful to leave any evidence. But he can't understand how we found him."

The door opened, and Pritchard came in, glanced at the screen, and asked, "Is he talking?"

"Not yet," Braddock said. "But he signed the waiver after Shane read him his rights. And he didn't complain when Carly took about a hundred pictures of him and swabbed his cheek."

On the screen, Carly picked up her camera and her DNA collection kit and left the room. Fisher said, "All right, Dylan, just sit tight, and I'll be back in a few. You want a soda or something?"

"That's good," Rachel said in a near whisper. "Be polite. Use his first name."

Gifford shook his head, and Fisher walked out, leaving the deputy to watch him.

Pritchard leaned over, shook Rachel's hand, and said, "By the way, that was a helluva job you did out there."

"Thanks, Sheriff. Sorry about the Tahoe."

"Don't worry. We'll just take it out of Danny's check."

"Damn, boss," Braddock said.

Pritchard shrugged. "You gave her the keys."

Fisher came in and said, "I gotta say, he's playin' it pretty cool."

Rachel asked, "How does he look? Nervous? Angry? Dazed?"

"A little dazed, I'd say. There's some defiance in him, though."

"So what's the plan?" Braddock asked Rachel. "Do we go at him old school? Or should we try some of your warm and fuzzy?"

The "old school" method was the Reid technique, a standard for police interrogations since the 1960s. An investigator would confront the suspect with the evidence against him, creating a narrative of the crime without allowing him the chance to deny the allegations. The narrative, or theme, as it was called, was meant to break the suspect down. *Look at all this evidence we have. We know you killed him; the only question is why.* When the suspect appeared to be softening, the investigator would try to minimize the severity of the crime, allowing the suspect to choose a motive that might appear to be more acceptable. *Did you plan to kill him, or was it self-defense? You don't seem like the kind of person who would plan to murder someone.* If it worked, the suspect would grab onto the alternative motive like a lifeline, admitting guilt in the process. It was a good technique for extracting a confession, but if the suspect got defensive from the start, it might not produce any good information at all.

Rachel favored a different approach. She liked to build a rapport with her suspects to put them at ease while encouraging them to talk. They would create their own narratives, and she would listen, ask questions, make notes, all while searching for lies and inconsistencies. When she had collected enough of them, she would challenge their stories. It was like catching them in a snare, and the harder they fought to get free, the worse it got for them. They would dig themselves deeper into a hole until she had them right where she wanted them. But it all depended on her ability to get them talking.

"You know my vote," she said.

"What do you mean by warm and fuzzy?" Fisher asked.

Rachel explained, and Fisher said, "I've read about that. The FBI's been pushing it lately. They learned it from the CIA, didn't they?"

"Yep," Rachel said. "Turns out, it's more effective than waterboarding."

"If I had my choice," Pritchard said, staring at the screen, "I think I'd rather waterboard his sorry ass."

"Me too," Braddock said. "Not sure I'm feeling the whole rapport-building thing right now." He looked at Rachel. "And it's not like we can send you in there."

"Well, I guess it's settled," Pritchard said. "I'll go get the bucket."

"I can try it," Fisher said.

"You serious?" Braddock asked.

"Yeah. I think I can get him talking."

Braddock turned to Rachel. "Give him some pointers, coach."

"You're doing good with your tone," Rachel said. "Keep being polite, and don't rush it. Just get him talking. About anything, doesn't matter what. Try to find something the two of you have in common. Once he gets on a roll, let him talk as long as he wants until there's a natural pause, then take a break and step out. We'll see where it goes from there."

Fisher nodded. "Roger that."

★ ★ ★

Fisher went in and said to the deputy in a low voice, "Would you mind waiting outside for me?"

"Sure thing, Shane," the deputy said and stepped out.

There was a table pushed into the corner. Fisher laid his notepad and pen on it and pulled out a chair. He sat directly in front of Gifford, who stared at the floor with his hands folded in his lap. The plastic restraints had been replaced by steel handcuffs. The chain clinked when he reached up to scratch his forehead.

"You've had quite a night, haven't you, bud?"

No response.

"Wasn't really a good idea to take off running like you did."
Gifford scratched his forehead again.

"You didn't hurt yourself or nothing, did you? I can have a medic take a look at you, if you want."

He shook his head quickly, looking annoyed at the question.

"Okay. No worries." Fisher sat back and thought for a moment, tapped his pen on the table, and said, "Your mom's doing all right. In case you were interested."

Gifford looked into his eyes for the first time. "Why wouldn't my mom be doin' all right? What are you talkin' about?"

"I guess you didn't know—"

"Didn't know what?"

He raised a hand and said, "Take it easy, Dylan. She's fine. She's not hurt or nothing. She just got herself into a little trouble is all."

"What kinda trouble?"

"Well, I hear she threw an ashtray at one of the officers."
Gifford smiled.

Fisher let himself chuckle. "Yeah, I thought that was a little funny too. Lucky for her, she hit him in the chest and not his face, or she'd be in a lot more trouble."

"Wait. Did y'all arrest her?"

"Had to, Dylan. She assaulted a police officer."

"She's in jail?"

"Not yet. She's here right now, but she'll be spending the night there."

"Where's my brother?"

Fisher shrugged. "Home, for all I know. We didn't have any reason to arrest him."

Gifford's eyes grew wide. He seemed to be staring through Fisher. "He won't leave without her."

"Without who? Your mom?"

Gifford's knees began bouncing. He leaned back, looked at the ceiling, and said, "Aw fuck, man. *Fuck . . .*"

"What's the matter, Dylan? Talk to me."

He put his face in his hands. "I can't, man. I can't."

"Come on, bud. What's going on?"

"I ain't sayin' nothin'. Not another fuckin' word."

Gifford kept his face covered and took long, shaky breaths through his mouth.

"You know, Dylan, I can't help you if you won't talk to me." Fisher stood, gathered his pad and pen, and went to the door. "Think about it, all right? I'll be back in a minute."

★ ★ ★

"What the hell do you suppose *that* was all about?" Pritchard asked.

Fisher shrugged. "Sounds to me like he's afraid of something, and it ain't us."

Rachel was watching Gifford on the monitor. "He's afraid that something will happen to his brother if he talks."

"Yeah," Braddock said. "His brother won't leave without his mother? Seems like they had some kind of plan for the two of them to skip town if Dylan got busted."

Pritchard: "Does that mean the brother's involved?"

Braddock: "Maybe."

Rachel: "Or someone else is involved, and Dylan's worried they'll go after his family if he talks."

Pritchard rubbed his eyes. "What the hell kinda mess have we stepped in here?"

Curtis stuck his head through the doorway and said, "Sheriff, we got three news vans setting up out front. They'll be coming through the door any minute now."

"Jesus Christ," he said. "Keep them outside and tell them I'll be out in a minute to make a statement." He turned to Braddock. "Do whatever it is you need to do in order to figure this thing out. I'll be back as soon as I can."

"Will do, boss."

Pritchard left, and Braddock said, "All right, now what?"

"Maybe it's time for a little confrontation," Rachel said. "Let him know what we have on him. See if we can get him to worry more about himself than his brother."

"Want me to do it?" Fisher asked.

"No. Let Danny do it. You're still playing the good cop."

★ ★ ★

Braddock went in and leaned against the table, looked down at Gifford, and said, "I'm sure you've figured this out by now, but you're not just here because you beat the crap out of Bert Hood."

Gifford stared at the floor.

"The woman who was in here earlier . . . the one who scraped the inside of your mouth . . . she was getting your DNA. Right now, she's packing it up to send over to the State Crime Lab. You might think that's no big deal, since you were so careful and all, but that's because you don't realize that you left one of your hairs on Andy Coughlan's body."

Gifford looked up briefly, then leaned back and fixed his eyes on the wall.

"When they match that hair to your DNA . . . well, that's going to be very bad for you, Mister Gifford. And that's not all there is. I can place your truck near the crime scene. I've got video of you driving it to and from the spot where you hid it, and I've got a tread impression that matches your tires. But the crown jewel . . . the thing that's really going to do you in . . . is the baseball bat we found under your bed. It's hard to believe, as careful as you were, that you would wipe it down with a bloody rag."

Gifford looked up. He couldn't hide the panic in his eyes.

"That's right," Braddock said. "We're sending it off to the crime lab too. And I'm willing to bet a shiny new Chevy Tahoe that the blood we found on your Louisville Slugger came from Mister Dean McGrath."

The color drained from Gifford's face. He slumped in the chair and stared into space, looking defeated.

"Now you can sit there and keep quiet if you want to. Doesn't matter one bit to me. Once those test results come back, we'll have more than enough to convict you of two homicides. But if I were you, I'd think real hard about coming clean. 'Cause that's about the only thing you can do right now to make your situation any better. And in case you didn't already know it, the state of North Carolina has reinstituted the death penalty."

★ ★ ★

When Braddock came back to the observation room, Rachel said, "That was a little harsh."

"You think?"

"I almost felt sorry for him."

On the monitor, Fisher entered the interrogation room and sat down. Gifford was bent forward with his elbows on his thighs. He looked like he might get sick.

"I guess you got some bad news, huh?" Fisher said. He scooted his chair closer and matched Gifford's posture, lowered his voice. "Look, Dylan, you have a chance to help yourself. But the clock's ticking, bud. Once those DNA tests come back, I don't know how much I'll be able to do for you."

"Damn," Braddock said, looking surprised. "He's a natural."

"Yeah," Rachel said. "Kid's got talent."

"I know you're worried about your family," Fisher said. "That's because deep down, you're a good guy. Okay? If you weren't, you wouldn't care nothing about them. But you do, and that tells me something about you. It tells me that you got caught up in something you shouldn't have."

Gifford put his face in his hands and started to weep.

"Help me understand, Dylan." He waited while Gifford wiped his eyes. "Talk to me. Tell me how you ended up in this mess."

Gifford sniffed hard, looked at him with a fatalistic smirk, and said, "I already told you, man, I ain't sayin' shit to you." Then he looked at the camera and shouted, "And I want all of you motherfuckers to know I ain't sayin' shit to none of you."

35

"No, ma'am," Pritchard said to the district attorney on speaker-phone. "He hasn't asked for an attorney yet."

Rachel sat on the same side of the conference table as Braddock, Fisher, and Pratt and listened in.

"So right now," the DA said, "we have him on the assault and battery and resisting arrest."

"Yes, ma'am. I'd like to charge him with assaulting an officer too. Miss Carver took a couple of hits trying to get him under control."

"Is she okay?"

"Oh, she'll be fine," Pritchard said, smiling at Rachel. "She's pretty tough, as it turns out."

Braddock nudged her with an elbow, and she winced, suddenly feeling a tender spot on her ribs. She hadn't noticed it during the struggle when the adrenaline had masked the pain.

"That's good. Unfortunately, I don't know if I can sell it, seeing as she was hired as a consultant . . ."

There was another voice in the background. Rachel thought it sounded like the assistant district attorney she had met at the Coughlan crime scene. She couldn't make out what he was saying, but the DA responded, "Maybe . . . what the hell. Okay, Sheriff, let's add that to the charges. How long before we can get the test results back?"

Pritchard looked at Braddock, who answered with a shrug.

"Could be a while," he said. "I filled out a rush request, but it's got to go to Raleigh. Apparently, they don't do DNA at the lab in Asheville."

The DA sighed. "And if we want the hair tested, it has to go to the FBI?"

"Yes, ma'am. I'm afraid so."

Rachel put her hands up by her shoulder and mimed taking a swing with a baseball bat.

Pritchard nodded and said, "But that's a separate deal from the bat. If they can match the blood and saliva we found on it, then we should have enough to charge him in the McGrath murder, right?"

"Oh, absolutely," she said. "And not just McGrath. We'll charge him with both murders. Same MO, or close enough. You can place his truck near the Coughlan scene at the time of the murder. I'm sure the judge will let us hold him without bond until we go to trial for the other charges. As long as we get the test results on the bat back before then, and the FBI can get us the results on the hair before the murder trial, we'll be good as gold."

"I like the sound of that."

When the call ended, Pritchard leaned back in his chair, put his hands behind his head, and said, "I think that was the most pleasant conversation the two of us have ever had."

"Yeah, you got her wrapped around your little finger now, boss," Braddock said.

"Was only a matter of time. Just don't go telling her I said that."

Braddock smiled, and Pritchard got a worried look on his face. "I'm serious, Danny."

★ ★ ★

Braddock asked Curtis for the keys to an unmarked Crown Victoria and waited with Rachel outside his office. He stretched and glanced at his watch and said, "It'll be nice to get home at a decent hour tonight." Then he looked around to make sure no one else was nearby. "I'm thinking a little celebration is in order."

Rachel's mind was preoccupied. "Yeah . . ."

"What's the matter?"

She thought for a moment and said, "I wonder if we shouldn't pay Kevin Gifford a visit."

"Aw, Rachel, come on."

"Seriously," she said. "If he knows something, maybe we can convince him that the best way to help his brother is to talk to us."

"Why don't we have a chat with the mother first? She's the one that lived with him."

"You have her in custody. She's not going anywhere tonight. But after what Dylan said, I'm worried Kevin might take off."

"Dylan said he wouldn't leave without his mother."

"You willing to bet on that? He might try to disappear for a while, then come back to get her when she's out."

"You know, you have this way of making sense that can be really irritating sometimes."

Curtis walked up and dangled a set of keys. Braddock took them and asked him, "You think you can spare a deputy for an hour or so?" He looked at Rachel. "We're not going out there with just the two of us."

36

They parked in the driveway behind the F-250 and looked up toward Kevin's trailer. Colored lights flashed through a window, which Rachel guessed were from a TV. There were no lights on outside, so the approach to the front door would be in the dark.

"Maybe we should call him first," Rachel said.

"Yeah." Braddock had gotten the number from Curtis before they had left the office. He typed it in, pressed call, and stared at the trailer while it rang. After several seconds, he shook his head and said, "Went to voice mail. I'll give it another try."

He called again. As he raised the phone to his ear, Rachel saw movement outside the window beside him. She screamed, "Danny!" just as Kevin put the muzzle of a handgun to the glass.

"What the *fuck* are you doin' here?" Kevin shouted. "Who are you?"

Rachel and Braddock raised their hands. "We're with the sheriff's office," Braddock said.

"Bullshit."

The side of Kevin's face lit up. He recoiled and squinted to look at the light.

"Sheriff's office. Drop your weapon." The deputy was moving up the driveway behind them with his sidearm and his flashlight trained on Kevin. He yelled, "Drop it. Now!"

Kevin took a step back, looked like he might turn on the deputy. Braddock unclicked his seat belt and drew the weapon from his hip, groped for the button to lower the window. Rachel saw Lauren Bailey dying in front of her. "Kevin, don't!" she screamed. "We need your help. We're not here to hurt you."

He took another step back, raised his hand to shield his eyes from the flashlight but kept his gun low.

Braddock got the window down and said, "Lowry County Sheriff's Office, Kevin. Drop the gun. Now."

Rachel heard it hit the ground, saw Kevin move away from it. Then the deputy threw him down and put a knee on his back to pin him. Braddock jumped out to help, and she fell back in her seat and clenched her hands into fists to keep them from shaking.

★ ★ ★

Fisher waited until Gifford had calmed down before he went back in. "All right, Dylan, I just wanted to let you know that your mom's on her way over to the detention center."

Gifford didn't react.

"Okay, then," Fisher said. "I've got a few things to finish up here, and we'll be heading that way ourselves."

He turned to leave, was in the doorway when Gifford said, "Detective?"

"Yeah?"

"Is there any way you can look in on my brother?"

"I might be able to send someone by to check on him, if you give me a good enough reason why I should."

Gifford lowered his head. "I'm just worried about him is all."

"That's not gonna do it, Dylan. You want me to help, you need to give me something." He waited for a few seconds, then said, "Think about it while I'm gone."

He stepped out and went down the hall to the bullpen where the detectives shared an open office space with shift supervisors and the sheriff's administrative assistant. Pratt was at her desk filling out a report. He went over and said, "Hey, Tina, have the chief and Rachel left yet?"

She looked up. "Yeah, about ten minutes ago. They should be there by now."

"Thanks."

He went to his desk, dropped into his chair, and called Braddock.

"Hey, Chief. Any luck finding him?"

"Sitting on top of him right now," Braddock said. He sounded out of breath.

"Did I call at a bad time?"

"Oh, we're just explaining to Gifford junior here that it's not nice to point guns at people."

"Damn. He pulled a gun on you?"

"Yeah. He seems a little high strung at the moment."

Fisher could hear a voice pleading in the background.

"Shut up," Braddock said. "Can't you tell I'm on the phone? Anyway, what's up, Shane?"

"I just wanted to let you know I'm getting ready to carry Dylan over to the jail."

"Okay."

"He asked me if I'd check in on his brother. I didn't tell him you all were headed over there, but . . . he seems pretty worried about him. Wouldn't give me any details, but he's definitely afraid the boy's in danger."

"Yeah, this one seems pretty worried too."

"Well, you watch your back, okay, Chief?"

"I'll do my best."

★ ★ ★

Braddock put his phone away and helped the deputy pull Kevin to a seated position. Rachel walked around the car to stand next to Braddock and asked, "Everything all right?"

"Yeah. That was Shane telling us to be careful. Says Dylan's really worried about his brother."

"Man, this is a bunch of bullshit," Kevin said. His hands were cuffed behind his back, so he tried to use his shoulder to wipe the sand off his face. "I swear I didn't know y'all were cops, man. I was just tryin' to defend myself."

"Defend yourself, huh?" Braddock said. "I hate to tell you this, but pointing a firearm at someone because they're sitting in your driveway doesn't qualify as self-defense, as far as I know. What the hell are you and your brother so afraid of, anyway?"

"I don't know what you're talkin' about, man."

"You don't know? You're out here in the middle of the night about to have a shootout with law enforcement, and you don't know why?"

Rachel squatted down to put herself at Kevin's eye level, pointed a thumb at Braddock, and said, "My friend's not having a very good day. He's been up since before the crack of dawn. Someone went and wrecked his car, which the sheriff expects him to pay for . . ."

"We'll see about that," Braddock muttered.

"And now you go and point a gun at him . . . Just a word to the wise: you might consider toning down the attitude a little."

★ ★ ★

Deputy Melissa Howard pulled her patrol car around to the rear entrance and waited with the engine running. A minute later, Fisher escorted Gifford outside and loaded him in the back, then walked around and dropped into the passenger seat. Howard drove out of the parking lot, headed for the expressway.

Fisher said, "So my boss went over to check on your brother."

Gifford's eyes met Fisher's in the rearview mirror.

"Kevin pulled a gun on him. Now why would he go and do a thing like that?"

Gifford turned to look out the window.

"I have to say, Dylan, it kinda pisses me off that I tried to do you a favor, and my boss almost got shot for it. And you still won't tell me what in the hell is going on?"

Gifford mumbled something, but Fisher couldn't make it out through the plexiglass barrier.

"What's that?" Fisher asked. He turned in his seat to look at him. "Speak up. It's all right. You can talk to me."

"I can't. If I tell you . . ."

"You think if you talk, whoever you're mixed up with is gonna hurt your brother?"

"Or my mom." Gifford closed his eyes, and a tear fell.

★ ★ ★

Rachel looked at Kevin's shiny pistol, presently lying on the hood of the unmarked Crown Victoria, and said, "You're not out here wandering around in the dark with that cannon for no reason. Who are you afraid of?"

"No one. I done told you. I just don't like people drivin' up on my property at night is all."

"We already know you were supposed to skip town with your mother if Dylan got busted. And we think it's because someone might be coming after you. You need to stop holding out on us. Does this have something to do with your operation in Whittier?"

Kevin looked up, confusion and surprise on his face. "What? No . . . it don't . . . I don't know what you're talkin' about, lady."

"You're telling us Dylan isn't involved in your little business?" Braddock asked.

Kevin's eyes moved from Rachel to Braddock and back. "Look, I don't know what business y'all are talkin' about, but it ain't got nothin' to do with Dylan, okay? I don't know what he's gotten himself into."

"Okay," Rachel said, "so you two aren't in it together. That's fine. But he must have given you some idea of who would be coming for you."

"I don't know . . . I mean, he didn't say, exactly."

"What *did* he say?" Braddock asked.

When he hesitated, Rachel said, "Dylan's in a lot of trouble right now. If someone else is involved, he can use that as leverage to help his case. But he's not talking to us. If you want to help him, the best thing you can do is tell us everything you know."

"I'm tellin' you," he said, "I don't know what's goin' on. He just said that if anything happened to him . . . if he got in trouble or got hurt, I was supposed to get Momma and head west."

"That's it?"

He looked into her eyes, held a wary gaze for a moment, and said, "He told me he was workin' with some guy on somethin' that was gettin' jacked up, and I could tell it had him scared. I ain't never seen him like that before. He said he wanted to know that me and Momma would be safe—"

Kevin turned toward a rustling behind him. The deputy shined his flashlight, and Braddock's hand moved to his sidearm. Rachel's eyes followed the deputy's beam as it swept the trees. She glanced back at Kevin and saw that he was staring at her with fear in his eyes. Braddock took a step forward, and there was a commotion about thirty yards away. He drew his pistol just as an owl took flight with a tiny rodent clutched in its talons.

★ ★ ★

"Your family's safe now, Dylan," Fisher said.

Gifford looked at him in the rearview but didn't respond.

"All three of you are gonna be locked up tonight, safe and sound. And if you'll tell us who you're worried about, we can make sure your mom and your brother stay that way whenever they get out."

"What makes you think we'll be safe in jail?" Gifford asked.

Fisher twisted in his seat. "What's that supposed to mean?"

He shook his head but didn't answer.

When they reached the junction, Howard eased to a stop, looked left to check that the lane was clear, and gasped. Her window shattered. Red mist burst from her head and sprayed the plexiglass just as Gifford registered the sound of gunfire and ducked down for cover. Fisher started to reach for the gun on his hip but was struck twice in the chest as the window behind him became a spider's web of cracked glass. He braced his hands against the dash and fought to draw in wheezing breaths.

★ ★ ★

The driver was slumped over. Her foot came off the brake, and the patrol car crept forward into the intersection. Bishop kept the muzzle of his AR-15 on the windows as he jogged around the back to the passenger side. He saw the young detective, Shane Fisher, struggling to breathe and fired two rounds into his temple. Then he looked in the back and saw Gifford lying on his side, looking up at him.

Bishop expected to hear screaming, begging, maybe even cursing, but Gifford stared at him without making a sound. Keeping pace with the car, Bishop aimed the red dot of his sight on Gifford's chest and fired four shots through the window. Then he put the dot on Gifford's contorted face and fired two more. He took a quick look inside to make sure the bullets had found their mark before he turned and ran back to his Nissan Juke hidden in a turnout on the next street over. The patrol car drifted off the road, rolled down an embankment, and struck a tree.

37

Braddock veered onto the shoulder and charged past the news vans and the DCPD patrol car blocking the road. It was another hundred yards to the scene of the shooting, which had been cordoned off with red crime scene tape. The area in front of the tape was teeming with sheriff's deputies and DCPD officers. Braddock parked as close as he could, jumped out, and ran up to Curtis and Pratt. Pritchard was on the far side of the road talking to Chief Miller.

Rachel lagged behind. She searched beyond the crowd into the crime scene and caught a view of Howard's patrol car. Just a part of it. The bumper was barely visible above the shoulder. Then she looked back at the reporters silhouetted by camera lights, and her heart sank. The anxiety was overwhelming. Had she missed something? Should she have seen this coming? Perhaps the deal with Jensen had been a mistake. People were dead, and she couldn't shake the feeling that it was her fault somehow. She scanned the sea of uniforms and wondered how many of them blamed her. There was a voice in her head telling her to go back and hide in the car.

Carly climbed up the embankment holding her camera at her side. She had been taking pictures of the car and the victims. The sight had shaken her. She ducked under the tape to rejoin the others, took a faltering step, and stopped. The camera fell away as she sat down on the grass and started to weep.

Rachel ran up and caught the camera before it slid downhill. She looked down at Carly and tried to find the courage to apologize.

"You have to help us," Carly said. She stood and turned away, taking a second to compose herself. She turned back, wiped her eyes with her forearms, and said, "You have to help us catch the sorry fuckers who did this. You have to stay as long as it takes."

Before Rachel could say anything, Carly took her camera and walked away. Braddock was there a moment later. "Jensen will be here soon," he said. "Sanford's coming too. And Bruce Moore."

"I'm so sorry, Danny," Rachel said.

They stared at the car. It sat on three wheels, pitched on the uneven slope. The front end was crumpled against the large oak that held it from sliding farther downhill. From where Braddock and Rachel were standing, they couldn't see the occupants, but there was a lock of blood-soaked blonde hair stuck to the driver-side door beneath the broken window.

Braddock looked away. "I can't go down there, Rachel. I can't see them like this."

"You don't have to," she said.

"Shane was only twenty-nine years old." He closed his eyes and shook his head. "Had a wife and a little girl . . . And Melissa . . . Jesus . . . she couldn't have been more than twenty-five."

★ ★ ★

Justin Sanford was in a navy-blue windbreaker with "SBI" written in bold white letters across the back. Jensen, still in a suit, met him as he stepped out of his car. Together, they approached Pritchard and spoke to him for several minutes before calling Braddock and Rachel over.

"I'm sorry about the people you lost here, Danny," Sanford said. "Truly."

"Thanks," Braddock said with a solemn nod.

"I also want to say that you and your team"—he glanced at Rachel—"did a hell of a job tracking down this Dylan Gifford and catching him. That was good work. But at this point, it's obvious that we're dealing with some sort of organized criminal activity. So after talking with Sheriff Pritchard, we've decided that the wise course would be for our office to take the lead in the investigation moving forward. Having said that, we're still going to need your help, and no matter what happens, you have my word that we'll keep you in the loop every step of the way."

"I appreciate that."

"It's the least we can do," he said. "Right now, I've got another crime scene search unit on the way. They'll go over every square inch of this place, but as you know, that's gonna take some time. Ordinarily, I'd suggest you go home and try to get some rest, but something tells me I wouldn't be able to drag you outta here with a Mack Truck if I tried."

"You're right about that," Braddock said. "Is there anything else?"

"That's it," Sanford said.

Braddock walked away. As Rachel turned to follow, Sanford said, "Miz Carver? Can I have a word?"

He led her back toward his car, away from the crowd. Her eyes caught Jensen's for a moment, and she thought she saw a look of concern in them.

"I spoke to SAC Penter about you on the way over," Sanford said.

It was the last thing Rachel needed to hear—Sanford had called her former boss at the SBI, *her mentor*, to talk about her involvement in a case that had gone tragically astray.

"He had a lot of good things to say about you. He said you were one of the best investigators he's ever seen."

Were, Rachel thought, wondering how deliberate that choice of words had been.

"Of course, I already knew that," he said. "You had quite the reputation while you were still an agent." He glanced over her shoulder at the crime scene. "On the other hand, he did mention something that I didn't know. He said that you have a tendency to become obsessed with your work. That you have a hard time letting go."

Rachel's hands were starting to shake. She found herself staring at the bridge of his nose, at the pronounced bump where the bone turned to cartilage, just before it swung ever so slightly to the left.

Someone had broken that nose, it appeared, years before. Probably an old wound from his days as a beat cop. She wondered if she should try to straighten it for him.

"I'm not going to have to worry about that here, am I?" he asked.

"No," she said. "It's all yours now."

38

Bishop's cabin was ten miles outside Asheville. He sped through the winding mountain roads, making good time. The black, compact Juke was perfect for negotiating the tight curves at high speed, and the thrill of the ride helped burn off the nervous edge.

He checked his watch as he hit the gravel drive. It was just before 11:00 PM—a new record. Smiling to himself, he passed the Wrangler sitting out front and slowed to a stop inside the detached garage that doubled as his workshop. He turned off the engine and closed the overhead door with the remote before he got out. Then he went to the passenger side of the car to finish the night's work.

The AR-15 was stowed in a slender metal box he had attached to the undercarriage. A hiding spot in case he was ever pulled over for speeding. There was always the chance that a cop would ask to search the interior, and he would cooperate, knowing that his weapon would never be found during a routine traffic stop. He withdrew the rifle and carried it to his workbench, gathered his tools, and began the process of taking it apart.

Once he had the barrel separated and stripped of its accessories, he walked to the corner of the garage and dropped it on the steel plate he had embedded into a section of reinforced concrete. He grabbed the twenty-pound sledgehammer leaning against the wall, heaved it over his head, and slammed it down onto the chamber end of the barrel.

After three blows, he picked it up and examined it, then dropped it again and went to work on the rest of its length. When he was finished, the battered piece of metal could no longer chamber or fire a round, which meant it could never be tested for a match to the bullets and cartridge cases the police would recover from the scene. But there was still more to do.

He wiped the barrel clean of prints and placed it into a form he had built with plywood and two-by-fours. The burner went in next, along with the battery. The SIM card had been discarded on the way home. There was a bag of quick-setting concrete and an empty bucket by the side door. He dumped a third of the bag into the bucket, got some water from the spigot outside, then mixed it with a hand trowel. When the consistency was right, he dumped the mix into the form, encasing the barrel and the phone. It would solidify into a block within an hour, and he would dispose of it first thing Monday morning.

He turned off the light and locked the side door, went to the burn pit behind the cabin, and stripped off his clothes. His shirt, jeans, socks, and boxers all went into the hole on top of a pile of dry pine. He doused the clothes with lighter fluid, lit a book of matches, and threw it in. It took a few minutes of poking around with a stick to burn all the fabric. When it was done, he let the fire settle and went inside.

It was dark and quiet in the cabin. Too quiet. He turned on the TV and switched to one of the local stations. A reporter stood in front of a police car barricading the scene. She was giving a recap of everything she knew, everything the DCPD spokesman had told her. They were waiting for a statement from the State Bureau of Investigation, which they would broadcast live. It was expected in the next ten minutes.

Bishop took a quick shower and came back into the living room to dry off and wait for the statement. A few minutes later, the special agent in charge appeared on the screen. Surrounded by reporters holding outstretched microphones, he patted down his red hair, cleared his throat, and delivered a somber summary of the evening's events. He didn't reveal much, but he promised a lot. Did a good job of sounding confident and reassuring.

A phone rang, and Bishop had to think for a second to remember which of his remaining prepaid burners was set to that tone. He followed the sound to his dresser and answered it, knowing that there was only one person who had the number.

"What the hell happened out there tonight?" his partner asked.

Bishop should have expected the call. He fought the urge to yell as he said, "Had to happen."

"Had to . . . Jesus Christ, this is getting out of hand. This isn't what I wanted."

"No, but it's what you got, so I suggest you come to terms with it real quick."

There was a deep breath, and the man said, "Just tell me you've still got this under control."

"Everything is under control."

Another deep breath.

Bishop said, "If it makes you feel any better, the kid was always going to die."

"Why in the world would that make me feel better?"

"It was inevitable. Part of the plan." He walked over to a window facing out back and watched the flames flickering in the pit. "Even if he had finished the job and gotten away with it, I never would have let him live."

"Loose end, huh?"

"That's right."

"And when all this is over, am I going to be one of your loose ends?"

"Not if you keep your mouth shut."

Bishop ended the call.

★ ★ ★

The reporter was repeating herself, so Bishop turned the TV off, grabbed a beer from the fridge, and went outside to sit by the fire. The flames and the crackling wood were mesmerizing. His eyes felt heavy, and the tension he had been carrying in his neck and shoulders finally started to ease.

Gifford's arrest could have been a disaster had Bishop not acted in time. He only hoped the detectives had not gotten anything during the interrogation. Pratt would tell him as soon as he got her alone. She was always willing to say more than she should, and he was willing to force it out of her if it came to that.

Assuming he was in the clear, Bishop would be free to take out the last two targets on his own. There was no need to get creative or introduce anyone else into the mix. The sheriff's office and the DCPD were already off balance, and the SBI would be spinning their wheels for weeks chasing tweakers.

Gifford had been an effective instrument, even if he hadn't lasted as long as Bishop had wanted. With all the surveillance that Bishop had conducted on the victims—countless hours over the course of several months—there was a good chance that he had been spotted a time or two. But with Gifford carrying out his plans, he had been free to establish alibis for the nights of both murders.

He had been with Pratt during the McGrath killing. When Coughlan had died, he had been busy hitting on a brunette at a bar in Asheville. He knew the bartender, and he had a credit card receipt that showed the time and date. If Gifford had managed to finish the job, Bishop could have retired him, permanently severing any link between himself and the victims. And the brother's meth business would have become the obvious focus for investigators with nothing else to go on. Unfortunately, the cops had found the video of Gifford's truck, bringing his utility to an end a little too early.

Bishop had tried to accelerate the plan to compensate. He had tried to convince Gifford to take out both targets in one night, but that wasn't necessary anymore. He no longer had the luxury of being able to set up an alibi, but he didn't have to worry about anyone else getting caught either. It was all on him now. All he needed was a new plan.

39

Saturday

The SBI search unit recovered fourteen shell casings from the road and the shoulder at the intersection. They took hundreds of photos, collected the broken glass lying on the asphalt, and bagged samples of soil and grass from the embankment where they thought the killer had initiated his ambush. Jensen and Sanford walked the scene and developed a theory about how it all went down. When they were satisfied that they had gathered all the evidence they were likely to find, they decided it was time to bring the car back onto the road. The three occupants were still inside.

A tow truck driver said he couldn't guarantee that he'd be able to pull it up the slope without causing a lot more damage, especially with how it was wedged against the tree. Said there was a chance it could get stuck or, even worse, it might break free and keep rolling downhill. Their best option was to use a crane. Sanford ordered that one be brought out as soon as possible, no matter who they had to wake up to get it done.

Rachel and Braddock had watched it all unfold from behind the tape.

"I don't know how much longer I can stay here," Braddock said. "They're just letting them sit down there . . . I can't take it."

He turned and walked to the car, leaned against the door, and buried his face in his arms on the roof. Rachel rubbed his back. There was nothing she could think to say that would console him, so she didn't try. He looked at her and said, "We fucked up, didn't we?"

She couldn't answer. He stared at her for a moment. Her eyes welled, and she looked away.

Jensen was watching them from the side of the road near the wrecked patrol car. Rachel's eyes met his, and he gave her the same look of concern he had earlier. There was something he wanted to tell her but couldn't with everyone around. A part of her was curious to know what it was, even though it probably didn't matter. Whatever he had to say, it wouldn't change what had happened.

"I'm leaving," Braddock said. "You want to come with me? It's all right if you want to stay."

She shook her head and walked around to the passenger side. "There's no reason for me to be here if you're not."

They got in, and Braddock started the car, took a last look across the road, then put it in gear and wheeled around. A minute later, they were heading into town. The Fontana Lodge appeared on the left. He turned into the parking lot, which was filled with motorcycles, scanned it, and said, "I know you're paid up for the night, but I'd rather you stay at my place. If you still want to."

There was a sad longing in his eyes that said he couldn't handle being alone. Rachel squeezed his hand and said, "Just give me a minute to pack up. I'll follow you."

As she stepped out, he said, "Don't forget that bottle of bourbon. I have a feeling I'm going to need some of it."

While Rachel was packing her suitcase, a text came in from Jensen: "Need to talk. Mind calling when u get a minute?" She wondered if he was feeling guilty about hiding information from his boss. If he was worried that people had died because of it. He might even be afraid of losing his job. But Rachel wasn't in the mood to ease his conscience or reassure him, so she put her phone away and tried not to think about it. She finished packing and loaded her luggage in the Camry.

The drive gave her too much time to think. She was relieved to pull into Braddock's driveway. When she got out, he was standing by the Crown Victoria, looking at his watch. "One fifteen," he said. "We've been up for almost twenty hours now."

"Feeling tired yet?"

"Yeah, but that doesn't mean I'll be able to sleep."

She kissed him on the cheek and held up the bottle. "This should help."

He put on a weak smile. "Yeah . . ."

They went inside. Braddock took down a pair of Old Fashioned glasses from a cupboard next to the fridge and set them on the counter. He stared at them for a moment and said, "I think I need a shower. Just a quick one. I feel . . ."

"Go ahead," she said. "I'll be here."

He shuffled into the bedroom while she filled a glass with ice and poured the first drink. The cubes cracked as bourbon washed over them. She took a sip and spun the ice around. A second later, her phone chimed. She pulled it out of her back pocket, saw it was Jensen, and almost turned it off.

"Damn you, Rachel," she said to herself, unable to ignore the message.

She unlocked the phone and read it: "Really need to talk. Important!"

The shower came on. She glanced at the bedroom door and decided it was best not to mention it, at least not until she knew exactly what Jensen wanted. Braddock had enough on his mind already. She went outside and made the call from the front porch.

"Hey there, Rachel. I'm sorry to bug ya so late. How ya holding up?"

"As good as can be expected. What's going on?"

His voice lowered. "I need to see you. First thing in the morning, if that's possible."

She glanced at the door. "I'm sure Danny and I will be at the office first thing—"

"Without Danny," he said.

"Well . . . Mike, the sheriff's office hired me. I don't think it's a good idea for us to meet without them being involved."

Voices were shouting in the background. Jensen said, "Shoot. Hang on." Then he was yelling at someone, and there was beeping, like the alert signal a large truck would make when moving in reverse. "The crane just showed up. I gotta go. Think about it, okay? If you change your mind, send me a text, and I'll meet you anywhere you want."

The line went dead. Rachel went back inside, grabbed her glass of bourbon, and downed it. It was almost too much to swallow without gagging. She shook her head to ward off the aftertaste and poured a refill. Then she filled the other glass and carried them to the bedroom. The shower was running, but Braddock was sprawled across the bed, still wearing his clothes. He was sound asleep.

She turned off the water, went back to the living area, and settled into the sofa to sip on her drink. The room was dead silent, no distractions. She started thinking. Questions poured in. Anxiety and a rush of emotions came with them. She tamped it all down, not wanting to give in and let herself feel the pain and the guilt. There was a TV on a stand next to the fireplace. She jumped up and grabbed the remote control from the coffee table, turned it on, but kept the volume low. It was tuned to CNN.

"Can't handle this right now," she whispered.

She flipped through the channels, looking for something mindless. Found a sitcom as she finished her glass and moved on to Braddock's. A buzz kicked in, and she started to relax. She laughed at the show, forgetting for a moment everything that had happened just a few hours earlier. But it didn't last. Fisher's baby face, with its soft features and the ridiculous mustache he was barely capable of growing, appeared in her mind.

Like a lot of young men she had worked with, he had started out cocky and headstrong, but that was only because he had wanted more than anything to be good at his job. For three days, she had watched him work, watched him absorb every ounce of information she had given him. And he had demonstrated real potential, the makings of a great detective. That was over now.

Rachel took out her phone and typed Jensen a text. She wanted to meet. She would let him know where in the morning. His response came quickly. "Sounds good." She set the phone aside, took another sip, and allowed herself to cry.

40

Rachel woke on the sofa. She sat up and rubbed her eyes, stretched her arms over her head.

"Morning," Braddock said from the kitchen. "Coffee?"

She stood up and stumbled, took a moment to steady herself. "No, thanks. What time is it?"

"A little after eight," he said, pushing scrambled eggs around a pan with a spatula. "You sleep okay?"

"Yeah, I think so."

He nodded in the direction of the Old Fashioned glasses sitting on the counter. "Sorry I couldn't join you last night."

"It's okay. You needed the rest."

"I wish I had more to offer you." He scooped the eggs onto two plates. "I don't usually make breakfast."

She smiled and said, "It looks great."

They ate in silence. Rachel felt numb, almost in a daze. Braddock stared at the table until they were both finished. Then he stood, carried the dishes to the sink, and said, "The county commission is having an emergency meeting in about an hour. I'm sure they want to grill Ted about everything that happened yesterday. I need to be there." He rinsed the plates quickly and set them at the bottom of the sink, turned to face her, but kept his eyes on the floor. "We're gonna need to sort through all this mess . . . write some kind of official report. Ted wanted me to ask you if you'd consider staying around for another day or two to help us out with it."

"Sure," she said. "I can do that."

He nodded. "I booked you a room over at Shipley's Bed-and-Breakfast. It's the best place to stay in town."

"Oh . . . okay." She couldn't hide the disappointment in her voice.

He finally looked into her eyes. "Things are just so screwed up right now. And, let's face it, you'll probably be leaving soon anyway."

"Right. I understand." She stood, thought for a moment, and decided not to argue. "I think I'll go ahead and take off. Get over there and get settled in. Try to clean up before the meeting, if you think you'll need me there."

"It's up to you. No rush, though. If you can't make it, I'll see you at the office later."

She slipped on her shoes and picked up her phone from the coffee table, took a quick look around, and realized she hadn't brought anything else in with her. Braddock was watching from the kitchen. He looked like he was trying to think of something to say, so she hurried out the door, dropped into the Camry, and drove away.

★ ★ ★

Dorothy Shipley was only the second black person Rachel had met since she had arrived in Dillard City—the other being an officer with the DCPD.

"Welcome, young lady," Shipley said at the door. "You come inside and make yourself at home."

She was in her sixties and was a little overweight, wore a constant smile, and never let Rachel say a word.

"It's just you here, I'm afraid. The plumbing's gone bad in the other room. These old houses . . . Did you know this is the oldest house in all of Dillard City?"

Rachel didn't know that, though she didn't get a chance to say so.

"I've spent ten years fixing or replacing just about every bit of this place." Shipley waved her arms in broad arcs. "Every *bit* of it." She leaned toward Rachel, and her voice lowered in pitch.

"Course, I don't do plumbing, now. I'll call somebody else for that mess, you know."

She led Rachel on a tour through the two-story Victorian, pointing out the various improvements and restorations she had made through the years. On the stairs, Shipley stopped halfway up and spent several minutes describing how she had stripped and sanded, then stained and varnished the mahogany balustrade. "Can you believe some fool would go and paint up all this gorgeous wood? Lord have mercy."

When Rachel finally got to her room, she closed the door, hoping for a few minutes of silence. Though she couldn't help but smile when Shipley knocked on the door and said, "Whenever you get ready, now, you come on downstairs to the kitchen and let me fix you up a plate. I got fresh biscuits. They just came out of the oven."

"Thank you, Mrs. Shipley. I'll be down in just a few."

The floorboards creaked as Shipley made her way through the hall and down the stairs. Rachel unpacked her suitcase, set aside her plastic bag filled with dirty clothes, and went for a shower. The hot water ran out a little too fast, but it was probably for the best, since she could have stayed in all day. She dressed and brushed her hair and didn't mind that it was still wet when she went down to the kitchen.

Shipley had a pile of warm biscuits on a plate, covered with a white napkin. When Rachel came in, she pulled back a corner and said, "You've got to have yourself one of these."

Rachel took one and had a bite. "Wow," she said. "That's really good." And she wasn't just being polite. She eyed the plate. "May I have another one?"

Shipley's voice went falsetto as she said, "Of course you can, child. Have as many as you want. Can I fix you up a little sausage gravy to go with it? Won't take but a minute."

"Oh, thank you, but I actually ate before I came here. And I have to get going soon."

"Well, okay." She sat down at the table. "I'll leave these out, though, in case you want one later on whenever you get back. I suppose you'll be gone for a while."

"Probably. It could turn out to be a busy day."

Shipley studied her for a moment and said, "I'm sure it will, with all this craziness. Such a shame about those poor folks last night."

"Yeah."

"And if you don't mind me saying so, it's a shame you and Danny didn't work out either."

"Um . . . I'm sorry?"

Shipley laughed. "Child, this town is too small for us ladies not to notice when a young single man like Danny Braddock takes an interest in someone. Especially when she's not from around here."

"I don't . . . Really? The whole town knows?"

"You must be kidding." She waved a dismissive hand. "Of course we do."

Rachel turned a little red. She finished her first biscuit, wrapped the second in a paper napkin, and said, "I guess I'd better get going. Thanks again, Mrs. Shipley."

Shipley straightened. In a formal tone, she said, "It's been my pleasure."

Rachel smiled and turned to leave, got to the kitchen door, and stopped. She turned back and said, "Mrs. Shipley, did you know Dean McGrath or Andy Coughlan?"

"I sure did," she said. "Dean kept to himself after his wife left him, but I'd see him around every now and again. I knew Andy a lot better."

"Really? How so?"

"Well, you see, my husband was his accountant."

"Was?"

"Yes. Terry passed a little more than three years ago."

"I'm sorry to hear that."

"Lord knows, I do miss him so. Every day."

Rachel waited a moment, then said, "I know this may be difficult to talk about, but do you think there's any chance that Mister Coughlan might have been involved in anything illegal?"

"Illegal? Like what?"

"Drugs maybe?"

Shipley looked at her like she was crazy. "I'd sooner believe the sheriff was a crack dealer."

Rachel thought about that for a second and said, "Okay. Thanks again, Mrs. Shipley. I'll be back later this evening."

"You take care of yourself, Miss Rachel." She rose from her chair. "It's not safe out there. Not anymore."

41

The commission's meeting room was in the Lowry County Court-house, a tan, one-story brick building with an overpowering red metal roof. Rachel saw a crowd gathered out front as she turned into the parking lot. The people looked tense. Some were arguing.

Rachel parked away from the entrance and considered skipping the inquisition altogether. She sent Jensen a text saying that she was available to meet and waited for a response. After five minutes without a reply, she decided to go inside. She got out and headed for the front at a brisk walk. When she reached the crowd, she kept her head down and marched past them quickly. They murmured after her as she went through the door.

A pair of deputies stood in the lobby. Rachel didn't know them, but they both seemed to recognize her immediately. The one to her right pointed at a security checkpoint set up in front of a door. She whispered a thanks as she walked by him, took her phone and keys out of her pockets. Her phone case had slots for her ID, credit cards, and a small amount of cash. She slipped her driver's license out and showed it to the security officer, then put everything on the conveyor belt and stepped through the metal detector.

Once she cleared the checkpoint, she walked into a long hall. Braddock, Curtis, and Pritchard were huddled together next to a door about halfway down, talking in low voices. They stopped when Braddock saw her approaching.

"Hey," he said. "You get settled in at Shipley's?"

"Yes, thank you," she said. "It's a nice place."

"Much better than the Fontana, I'm sure," Curtis said.

"Dorothy's a sweet woman," Pritchard said, shifting his weight from one foot to the other. He wiped a bead of sweat from his forehead. "She and her husband bought that place about ten years ago. She was a school teacher before that. Second grade. Taught my oldest before she retired. Damn shame about her husband. He died of a heart attack a couple years back."

"Damn shame," Curtis said.

They stood there quietly for several minutes before the door opened and a young man in a gray suit leaned out and said, "They're ready for you, Sheriff."

Rachel's phone chimed as they started to enter. The message was from Jensen. He wanted to meet right away. She could choose where.

Braddock lingered in the doorway. "You coming?"

"Um . . . actually, if you don't need me, I should probably return this call." She raised her phone quickly.

He glanced inside. "Go ahead. You don't need to be here for this."

Outside, Rachel slipped past the crowd and sent a message telling Jensen to meet her at Everett's Diner. Then she hopped in her car and hurried over. When Jensen finally came through the door fifteen minutes later, Rachel was in a booth sipping on a Mountain Dew. She waved to get his attention.

"Hey there," he said, sliding into the seat. "This isn't exactly what I had in mind when I said first thing in the morning."

"Ever hear the saying about gift horses and teeth?" she asked, sounding a little annoyed. "You're lucky I'm here at all."

The server came by, and Jensen ordered a coffee, black. Rachel thought a piece of warm apple pie sounded good, so she asked for one of those with a little vanilla ice cream on the side. When they were alone again, she said, "So?"

"I wanted to give you a heads-up. Last night, Sanford got a call from the assistant director. He wants us to start an investigation into the sheriff's office. To see if we can find any issues with how the case was managed. Issues that may have contributed to the shooting."

"That figures," she said, shaking her head in frustration. "Shouldn't surprise us, though."

He looked around. "It's going to be a witch hunt. I think someone's got it in for the sheriff."

Rachel thought about the commission meeting and said, "Yeah, there's a lot of that going around at the moment. Anything else?"

"Sanford says we need to take a hard look at your involvement. What role you may have had in pushing for Dylan Gifford's arrest without consulting the SBI special agent assigned to the case."

"Kind of puts you in a tricky spot, doesn't it?"

He stared at his hands folded on the table but didn't answer. Just as Rachel had suspected, he was searching for reassurance, but she wasn't in the mood to give it.

The server dropped off a cup of coffee and said, "Your pie should be out in just a minute, hon."

When she walked away, Rachel asked, "Any word on the meth lab?"

Jensen cleared his throat and said, "I talked to one of our informants who says he knows Kevin Gifford. Says he's bought from him in the past."

"And?"

He looked around again. "It's nothing. A tiny operation. So small . . . it's no wonder we've never heard of it. They have a little travel trailer up in the woods on some property that belongs to one of Kevin's friends. Actually belongs to the kid's father, but regardless, they only cook once every three months or so. If that. My informant says there's about five of them working together. But he could only name three, and he says he only bought from them when he was having supply issues. Says all their regular buyers are small time."

"How small?"

"Barely more than personal use."

Rachel sighed. "So what's your next move?"

"We take down the lab." He grabbed four packets of sugar from the caddy at the end of the table, tore them open, and dumped them into his coffee all at once. "I just spent an hour on a conference call with Sanford and two guys from Special Services. You wouldn't believe what we're planning to put on these kids. Surveillance teams, undercover agents . . . I'll tell ya, no matter how small their operation may be, the media's going to treat them like rock stars when we get through with them."

"You just told me they don't make more than a handful of meth four times a year."

"That's true," he said. "Can't deny that. But Sanford thinks they're trying to expand. He thinks they might have hooked up with an outlaw biker group operating north of Asheville. Apparently, they've been known to finance smaller operations like Kevin's. Oh . . . and those shell casings we picked up last night . . . five-point-five-six. The exact type of ammunition you'd need if you were planning to ambush someone with an AR-15. Know who happens to have one of those registered in his name?"

"Kevin?"

"You got it."

"We had him in custody at the time of the shooting."

"You've never lent anything to a friend before?"

Rachel rubbed her eyes with her fingertips. "You really think Kevin would conspire to take out his own brother?"

"People do crazy things for money."

She studied him for a moment and said, "You're a good soldier, Mike."

He smiled. "Thank you, Rachel."

"It wasn't a compliment."

★ ★ ★

Braddock sat next to Curtis on a bench in the front row. Ahead and to his right, Pritchard stood behind a lectern, sweating and answering questions with a shaky voice. The chairman had closed the meeting to the public, so the rest of the aisles were empty.

The other commissioners had taken turns asking about the shooting. The tone had remained civil until Lawton Jones had started his barrage. He wanted to know why Pritchard had ignored his warnings about the threat posed by motorcycle gangs. Why he had not consulted with the SBI before arresting Dylan Gifford. Why he hadn't asked for their assistance on the raid, and why he had asked for his cousin's help instead. Had he deliberately kept them out of the loop so he could claim full credit for the arrest?

Pritchard did a good job of keeping his cool. Braddock was impressed. It wasn't until Jones asked his last question that he saw his boss's anger flare.

"Does it even bother you, Sheriff, that two of your deputies have died on your watch?"

"I swear to God, Lawton," Pritchard growled, "I'm gonna walk up there and beat your miserable fat ass, you sorry—"

"Sheriff Pritchard!" the chairman shouted.

Pritchard gripped the edges of the lectern and looked away. The muscles in his jaw worked as he gnashed his teeth. Braddock felt sorry for him, even a little responsible. Maybe he shouldn't have insisted on hiring Rachel in the first place. They could have just waited for the SBI to take the case over and avoided all this mess. And maybe Fisher and Howard would still be alive.

★ ★ ★

After she left the diner, Rachel took a walk through town, stopping in the middle of the Everly Street Bridge to watch the river rush by beneath her. She thought about everything Jensen had said and felt a surge of frustration. Sanford was all but obsessed with Kevin Gifford's meth operation, and Jensen was going along with it, even though there wasn't a shred of evidence linking it to McGrath or Coughlan. At least, none that they had found.

She wondered if she was being closed-minded. After all, it had only been a few days. Perhaps there *was* a connection yet to be discovered. Maybe Jensen was doing the right thing by falling in line behind his boss. If so, then she had been too hard on him.

She looked up, spun slowly in a circle, and took in the town. There wasn't much to see. Braddock had said there were only two thousand residents, and Dillard City was the largest in the county. People in this area knew each other. They knew details about each other's personal lives, their secrets. Rachel had only been there since Wednesday, but Shipley had said the whole town already knew about her and Braddock.

Shipley had also said that she knew Coughlan. Had known him for years and could never believe that he would be involved in making or selling drugs. "I'd sooner believe the sheriff was a crack dealer," she had said. It just didn't make sense.

★ ★ ★

A half hour later, Rachel arrived at the office. She went inside looking for Braddock but couldn't find him. In the bullpen, Pratt was at her desk, staring blankly at a report. When Rachel approached, she looked up with puffy red eyes.

"I'm sorry to bother you, Tina," Rachel said in a soft voice. "Do you know if Danny's still at the courthouse?"

Pratt shook her head. "He and Sheriff Pritchard went to go meet up with those SBI agents. They're going back to all the crime scenes to look at"—she shrugged—"whatever it is they want to look at."

"I see. Thanks." Rachel stepped away, took out her phone, and called Braddock. It only rang twice before it went to voice mail, which told her that he had pressed ignore to dismiss her call. She felt a pang of rejection.

"He mentioned you might be coming by to write a report about your involvement in the case," Pratt said and tipped her head toward the conference room. "The files are in there on the table, if you want to get started."

"Oh . . . Yeah," she said, trying to hide her embarrassment. "Perfect. That's exactly what I needed. Thanks again."

She went in and sat down at the table, opened her briefcase, and took out her laptop. As it powered up, she found herself fixating on the fact that Braddock had not asked her to join them. He hadn't even called to tell her what he was doing. It was one thing if Sanford, or even Pritchard, had wanted to exclude her, but to be sidelined by Braddock was something else entirely. She hated feeling the sting that came with that thought.

When she couldn't force it out of her mind, the sadness turned to anger. She opened the files, took out her Steno pad, and started reviewing her notes. It would take her a few hours to finish her report, and she would stay for a few more in case there were any questions about it. Then she would say good-bye and treat herself to a nice dinner, maybe a few drinks, and a good night's sleep. In the morning, she would get up and get on the road. It was time to go home.

42

Bishop peeked around the tree and saw the man step out of the back door of the American Shooters Gun Shop and Range.

After nine years in the Marine Corps, a back injury had left the man with a medical discharge, a slight limp, and little else to do but sell guns to civilians. Most of the customers had taken to calling him Gunny, which he seemed to like, even though he had never earned the rank of gunnery sergeant. His wife addressed him as staff sergeant when she was feeling playful, and he seemed to like that too.

Staff Sergeant Mark Newfield. *Target number three.*

It was a clear afternoon, and the sun was shining directly in Newfield's face as he crossed the back lot—just as Bishop had planned it. Newfield was on his lunch break, heading to the shady spot where he always parked his car. When he stepped out of the direct sunlight, Bishop took his chance before Newfield's eyes had time to adjust. "Hey there, Gunny," he said.

"Hey," Newfield said, digging in his pocket for his keys and straining to see the person who had called his name.

Bishop raised the .45 and fired. Newfield grunted and coughed and staggered. He fell against his car door and struggled to draw a breath. And Bishop fired again. And again. And Newfield dropped face first to the pavement.

Bishop laid the gun at the base of the broad oak tree he had chosen to hide him from the security camera near the back door and started jogging. The best thing about using a stolen gun was that it could be left at the scene. There was nothing at all tying it to Bishop. It was a shame to leave the sound suppressor, though. Bishop had made it himself, and it had performed quite well. The shots were still pretty loud for anyone standing nearby, but they sounded more like small firecrackers than .45-caliber rounds. The customers and the other clerks in the gun store, buffered by layers of sound-dampening insulation meant to keep the noise from the range to a minimum, probably hadn't heard a thing.

Bishop made it through the grove in a few seconds, emerging at the eastern edge of the Haywood Mall's expansive parking lot. He slowed to a walk as he hit the asphalt. Kept his stride even and controlled his breathing as he removed his gloves and stuffed them into his pockets. He slowed a bit more as he pretended to check his phone. Anyone who happened to see him wouldn't say that he looked like he was in a hurry. When he got to the Juke, he slid in, started it, and drove away as if he had just finished a day of shopping. He even had a new shirt in a Dillard's bag sitting in the passenger seat, just in case.

Three down, Bishop thought as he turned out of the lot and headed north.

There was no reason he couldn't finish in the next couple of days. Months of planning, preparing, and studying his targets were paying off. The hiccup with Gifford had required a little course correction, but he was back on track. He smiled as he crossed the border into North Carolina.

One to go.

43

Braddock came into the conference room as Rachel was putting the finishing touches on her report. He stood just inside the doorway, waiting for her to look up. She kept her eyes on the screen and pretended not to notice him. After a minute, he said, "Hey, I just wanted to let you know I'm back if you need anything."

"Thanks," she said. "I'm fine."

He approached the table. "We're trying to plan a memorial service for Shane and Melissa. It'll probably be on Tuesday. You think you could hang around till then?"

"No," she said flatly. An instant later, she regretted it, glanced up, and said, "I was planning to go home tomorrow, but I can come back, if you think it's a good idea."

"It's up to you." He pulled out a chair and sat down, wanted for something more to say. "Ted and I just took Sanford and Jensen back through all the crime scenes. Felt like a waste of time, really."

"Is that why you didn't want me to go along?"

He didn't answer, let her work for another minute, then said, "Apparently, the shell casings they found last night look like they might have come from an AR-15."

"Hmm. I bet Kevin owns one of those."

"Yeah, as a matter of fact, he does."

"Sounds like case closed."

He stared at her for a few seconds, but she kept her attention focused on her computer.

"I guess you want to be left alone," he said.

He stood and started to leave, stopped at the door, then closed it and said, "How did you expect me to handle this, Rachel?"

She looked at him. "Handle what?"

"Us. What did you expect me to do?"

"Are you sure you want to get into this right now?"

"Might as well."

He was getting angry. She closed her laptop and stared at the table, afraid of what she might say if she were forced to answer.

"Did you want me to fall for you and then just sit here and wave good-bye as you leave to go back home? Or did you want to try to have some kind of long distance relationship? 'Cause that's not gonna work unless you're willing to move here at some point in the near future. I'm sure as hell not going back to Raleigh."

"I don't know what I wanted," she said. "I know I didn't want it to end like it did this morning. But I'm a big girl. I can live with that. What really bothers me is that I feel like I'm being shunned, and I can't help but wonder if it's because you blame me for Shane and Melissa."

He sat down again, leaned forward, and rested his elbows on his knees. "Of course I don't blame you. We all wanted to move on Gifford. We made that decision together."

"And we were right," she said, indignation creeping into her voice.

"Rachel—"

"We were right, Danny."

"Stop saying that." He glared at her. "Two of my people are dead. We ignored what Jerry Hood told us, and it got them killed."

"That's bullshit."

"Sanford and Jensen think—"

"I know what Sanford and Jensen think!" she yelled. "They're wrong."

He stood up, said, "Good-bye, Rachel," and walked out the door.

★ ★ ★

Rachel finished her report and e-mailed it to Braddock and Pritchard. Then she stormed out of the building, got in the Camry, and sped out of the parking lot. She considered packing up and going home right then, but she had promised to stay around until morning. There was always the chance that Pritchard or Braddock might need her to come in and discuss her report. She had given them until 10:00 AM, then she would be gone.

As she pulled up to Shipley's, she saw a white DCPD Explorer sitting in the driveway. She parked next to it and went inside. In the salon off to the left of the entry hall, Chief Miller was sitting in one of the armchairs that flanked the fireplace. Shipley came out of the kitchen with a smile, clasped her hands together, and said, "Well hello there, Miss Rachel. How has your day been?"

Rachel replied with a weary smile. "Could've been better."

Shipley's face formed an exaggerated frown. "I'm sorry to hear that." She stepped close, glanced into the salon, and whispered, "Have you met Chief Miller?"

"Yes, I have."

"Well, I hope you don't mind, but he insisted on waiting for you. He's been sitting in there for almost forty minutes now. Said it was real important that he talk to you."

"Okay. Thank you, Mrs. Shipley."

Miller stood up as Rachel walked in to greet him. "It's good to see you again, Miss Carver."

"What can I do for you, Chief?"

"I just wanted to have a quick chat with you before you left town." He sat back down and beckoned her to take the other arm-chair. When she was seated, he asked, "Have you ever lived in a small town like this before?"

She shook her head. "No."

"I moved here from Atlanta about eighteen years ago," he said. "I love it. It's quiet. Peaceful. Everyone gets along"—he rocked his head from side to side—"for the most part, anyway. Coming from a big city, that was a nice change. And it was safe. At least until a few days ago. I'm sure you can imagine how much of a shock this whole episode has been for this community."

Rachel nodded solemnly.

"Did you know that the Gifford boys and I are somewhat related?"

She tilted her head with curiosity. "No, I didn't. How so?"

"My wife's cousin is married to their uncle."

"I see. Did you know Dylan very well?"

"Not really. But I tried to keep tabs on the boy. Did my best to make sure he was staying out of trouble. Now I hear he and Kevin might have been mixed up with a bunch of drug dealers out of Asheville."

"That's one theory," she said.

"You don't sound convinced."

She shrugged. "It's in the SBI's hands now. Doesn't really matter what I think."

"Well, I don't buy it." He studied her for a long moment, then said, "I take it you've met Lawton Jones?"

"I have."

"Would it surprise you to know that he happens to share the SBI's opinion about this case? That the Gifford boys have somehow partnered up with a big-time biker gang to expand their little meth-making operation?"

"No, it wouldn't," she said, recalling the night she met Jones.

Miller leaned forward in his chair, hesitated for a second, then said, "I'm going to be straight with you, Miss Carver. I think Lawton went to Justin Sanford and sold him on the idea. And I think Sanford is going along with it so Lawton doesn't kill him in the media. They're playing politics with this case. And did you know that Sanford helped spearhead the SBI's antidrug initiative in this area? How good do you think it'll make him look if he can figure out a way to pin these murders on a meth ring?"

"Those are some harsh accusations."

"You disagree?"

Rachel chuckled. "Even if I didn't, the sheriff's office is no longer on the case, which means neither am I."

"Something tells me you could make do just fine without any help from the sheriff's office."

Rachel almost came out of her seat. "Are you suggesting that I continue the investigation on my own?"

"I was hoping you would consider it."

She could hardly believe what she was hearing. "Look, Chief, as much as I'd love to stick around and see this thing through to the end, I've already been warned to stay away. Sanford made it abundantly clear that he doesn't want me anywhere near this case. Besides, Sheriff Pritchard isn't going to pay me to satisfy my own curiosity."

Miller seemed to consider that. He scratched his chin and asked, "Are you planning to leave town tonight?"

"Tomorrow morning," she said.

"Good. Think it over. We'll talk again in the morning. If money's really an issue, then I'll pay you to satisfy *my* curiosity."

"And Sanford?"

"If what I've heard about you is true, I doubt you'll let a guy like him scare you all the way back to Raleigh."

44

Rachel went upstairs to her room and dropped onto the bed, closed her eyes, and allowed herself a short nap. When she woke, her stomach was growling. She took a shower and put on a fresh pair of jeans and a T-shirt, left the blazer lying on a chair in a corner, and went downstairs.

Shipley was in the kitchen, humming to herself and cutting vegetables for what looked like the makings of a stew. She sang, "Good evening," when Rachel came through the door.

"Evening," Rachel said. "I think I'm going to go out for a bit. Walk the town. Maybe grab some dinner."

"Do you think you'll be out late?"

"I doubt it, but I have the key you gave me if I change my mind."

"Well, I sleep pretty soundly," Shipley said, "so you come and go as you please, and don't worry about waking me up whenever you decide to come in. But I do hope you won't be out too late, Miss Rachel. It's not safe out there."

★ ★ ★

It was a quiet half-mile walk through town to get to Everett's Diner. Rachel strolled past the storefronts on Everly and crossed the bridge. The sun was peering up the valley, setting the water alight with a swath of orange flame. It disappeared when she reached the southern bank and stepped in the shadow of an old pharmacy at

202 | J. R. Backlund

the corner of Main. The temperature plummeted, and Rachel realized she had made a mistake leaving her jacket behind.

She walked into the diner rubbing her arms. The hostess said, "Welcome back," and beckoned Rachel to follow her. Half of the tables were occupied. Eyes tracked them as they passed by. Rachel ignored the glances, settled into her seat, and examined the menu, which was easy to do with a hunger pang focusing her attention. When the server arrived, she ordered the meatloaf with mashed potatoes, collard greens, and a Mountain Dew. Then she sat back and played solitaire on her phone while she waited.

The bell rang on the door. Rachel looked up to see Carly standing next to the hostess stand, scanning the tables. When their eyes met, Carly marched over and dropped into the booth facing her. "I hear you're leaving," she said.

Rachel put her phone down. She decided not to mention the fact that she was considering Miller's offer. "There's not much more I can do here, Carly."

"Really? 'Cause I also heard you've been asked to stay."

"There really aren't any secrets in this town, are there?"

"So?" Carly was agitated. She sat stiffly with her arms crossed. "Are you going to stay here and help solve this thing? Or are you just going to tuck your tail between your legs and run?"

"And who exactly would I be helping?" Rachel asked, letting irritation sneak into her voice. "As far as I can tell, I'd be working alone."

Carly looked away, thought for a second, and said, "I'd help you."

The server dropped off Rachel's food and asked them if they wanted to order anything else. Carly shook her head quickly, and the woman shuffled off for the kitchen.

Rachel looked at the mound of gravy-covered food and said, "You want some of this? I probably won't be able to eat it all."

"No, thanks. I can't eat right now."

"Seems like all I can do lately," she said, driving a fork into the mass. After several bites, she took a break and said, "You have a job, Carly. If the sheriff or Danny finds out you're working with me on a case they've handed over to the state, you'd lose it. Simple as that."

"You say that like you're actually thinking about it."

She swallowed a mouthful of mashed potatoes and said, "I haven't decided yet."

Carly was quiet while Rachel ate the rest of her meal. After the server brought the check, she said, "I hear you like to have a drink every now and then."

"Is there anything you haven't heard about me?" Rachel asked.

"Let me buy you one."

Rachel opened her phone case and took out a credit card, but Carly snatched the check, stood up, and walked over to pay the server with cash. She came back and said, "Come on. You at least owe me a little time for buying you dinner."

"I was just going to bill the sheriff's office for it."

Carly glanced back at the kitchen. "Oh . . . Whatever, let's go."

★ ★ ★

A country singer strummed an acoustic guitar in a corner of the Riverside Pub. His tiny PA system could barely contend with the boisterous crowd of bikers in bandanas and leather vests. Rachel and Carly squeezed into a space at the bar and waved Smiley over for a round of drinks.

"You look a lot better," Rachel said. She repeated herself when he turned his ear toward her.

"Got a friend been slippin' me some fexo-somethin'-or-other," he said. "Ain't sneezed one time all day. Momma thinks it's the damn tea finally kickin' in."

He gave them a pair of Bud Lights in bottles and moved down the bar. Carly drained half of hers in her first gulp.

"Woah," Rachel said. "Take it easy. I don't want to have to carry you out of here."

"Better get him to come back. I'm going to need another one in a minute."

By the time she was near the bottom of her third beer, Carly's eyes looked glassy. She leaned in close and said, "I slept with him once."

Rachel was shocked. "Smiley?"

"What . . . ? No. Shane."

"Oh." She didn't know what else to say.

"He was sweet. Didn't always show it, but . . ." Her eyes welled. "I miss him. I miss them both. I didn't even know Melissa hardly . . ." She upended the bottle, set it down, and slid off her stool. "I gotta pee."

Carly wiped her eyes and disappeared into the crowd. Rachel took out her phone and opened her e-mail. She scrolled down until she found the message from Bryce Parker, the reporter. She had ignored it long enough, she decided. At the bottom, there was an attachment. It was a scan of the SBI's report on the Lauren Bailey investigation. She opened it and started reading.

Carly came back and hopped up on her stool, waved Smiley down for another beer. She wanted a shot too. Tequila. The good kind. Something clear. "You want one?" she asked.

Rachel shook her head, kept her eyes on the screen as she scanned the document. There were photos and pages of interview transcripts, a summary. It found no fault with any of the officials involved. The sheriff. The detectives. The deputy. Rachel . . . all in the clear. The investigation had been proper and thorough, conducted in accordance with standard practices and procedures. A four-month-long review, and they had found nothing new. Case closed.

"On second thought," Rachel said, "I will take one of those."

45

Bishop watched the routine through his scope.

It had been another long day for the man who owned a tree nursery on the edge of town. He got home after dark, exhausted, having just finished his last delivery. He took a shower, which got most of the dirt off, then went to the kitchen to make a pair of roast beef sandwiches. He wrapped them in a paper towel and went out to the family room and fell into his plush recliner where he ate dinner every night. He sipped on a Miller High Life and flipped through satellite TV channels. Usually, he looked for a boxing match. Tonight, he got as far as a rerun of an old college basketball game before he fell asleep.

Caleb Rucker. *Target number four.*

Perched on a ridge behind Rucker's house, on the other side of a narrow valley, Bishop was at just the right elevation to see through the window. The perfect spot to execute the latest version of his plan. But it wouldn't happen tonight. There was still work to be done.

If the task had fallen to Gifford, the plan would have been for him to pick the lock on the back door, to be inside when Rucker came home. He would have hidden in the spare bedroom, waited until he heard Rucker snoring, which happened every evening. Sometimes Rucker would sleep there through the night. Sometimes he would wake shortly after midnight and relocate to his bed. Gifford would have caught him still in the recliner. Would have hit him with the baseball bat, then gone to work on him with a kitchen knife.

But Gifford was no longer part of the equation. And that method now came with too much risk. When thinking about his plan of attack, Bishop had considered it. The bat and the knife had proven to be such an effective combination. But the SBI crime scene tech had found a hair on Coughlan. Gifford's hair. Bishop wouldn't chance that. If it was just that amateur Cherokee girl at the sheriff's office, he'd walk over there now and sneak in. He'd take care of Rucker tonight. It just wasn't that easy anymore.

There was too much heat on this case now that the SBI had taken over. They weren't looking for Bishop, and they hadn't bothered to connect the victims yet, but they would be all over another murder. Especially one with the same MO. Bishop didn't want to get within a hundred yards of Rucker's house. So he had spent the day searching for the right spot. The perfect vantage point with a level trajectory. And not very far away for someone who was a decent shot with a rifle.

Bishop slid the scope into his backpack and went over the ridge. He worked his way downhill until he reached the trail that led to his car, then turned on his flashlight. He strolled along happily, satisfied that he had settled on a good plan. It was almost over. He would finish the job tomorrow night. If he were being less careful, he might have hummed a tune to match his mood. Something upbeat. Like "Piece of Mind" or "More Than a Feeling." He always liked Boston.

46

Standing in the parking lot outside the pub, Rachel said, "You're in no shape to be driving."

Carly looked at her silver Civic, then at the keys in her hand. She held them out and said, "You drive."

Rachel chuckled. "I'm not much better."

"Shit."

"Can you walk home?"

"Too far," Carly said.

"Want me to call a cab?"

"You really think we have taxis in this town?"

Rachel looked around. "Didn't think about that."

Carly took a deep breath and steadied herself. Her eyelids were half closed. "You're staying at Shipley's, right?"

"Yeah."

"Can I just sleep with you?"

"Uh . . ."

Carly laughed, lost her balance, and fell against her car. She slid down to the pavement, gasping and hiccupping. Tears ran down her cheeks as she tried to stifle the giggling. "I . . . I meant . . . can I . . . can I stay in your room . . . ?"

Rachel was getting annoyed. "Come on," she said, helping Carly to her feet. "It's cold out here, and we've got like a mile walk ahead of us."

Carly was quiet on the way back to Shipley's, looked like she might have been fighting nausea. Rachel was thinking about her conversation with Miller. About Jones and Sanford steering the investigation toward Kevin and his little ring of meth-making friends.

Politics, she thought. The same reason she had been forced to give up the Lauren Bailey case. It had been easier than admitting the truth. That Bailey was probably innocent of killing her boyfriend, but she had pointed a gun at a deputy, forcing Rachel to shoot her. How could Bailey's family ever accept that?

They couldn't. But that was a poor justification for closing the case. For letting the real killer go unpunished. Rachel had never wanted to drop it—she had been forced to. Now she found herself in the same situation again.

Jones and Sanford had made up their minds about what, and who, was behind the murders. To them, drugs made the most sense, regardless of the victimology. The hit on Gifford, taking out two cops, seemed too brazen to be anything less than organized crime. And in this part of the country, crank-dealing biker gangs were the most likely candidates.

Like Miller, Rachel didn't buy it. Not without a connection to Gifford's victims. She wished she could convince Braddock and Pritchard, but they wouldn't listen. Not yet. Braddock was racked with guilt, and Pritchard was happy to be rid of the case. She didn't blame him for wanting to wash his hands of it. He was in over his head. Had been from the moment McGrath had turned up dead. Rachel understood that, but it didn't mean she had to walk away.

Fisher and Howard. Coughlan and McGrath. They deserved better. And Rachel owed it to herself to see it through to the end. To finish what she had started, even if it meant doing it alone.

When they got to Shipley's, it was quiet inside, and most of the lights were out. They tiptoed upstairs to Rachel's room. Carly dropped spread-eagle across the bed and asked, "Where are you gonna sleep?"

"It's a king," Rachel said.

"Yeah, but I don't feel like moving."

"You know, Carly, it'd be a shame if I had to choke you out and drag your ass downstairs to sleep on the front porch. It's mighty chilly out there."

"Good point."

Carly pushed herself back to her feet. She approached Rachel, leaned in, and kissed her gently on the corner of her mouth.

Warm breath swept across Rachel's cheek. She closed her eyes and wished for just a moment that she could change who she was long enough to enjoy the sensation. It felt good to be desired.

Carly pressed forward for another kiss, but Rachel stepped back and said, "I'm sorry, but I—"

"Oh . . . don't be." Carly backed away, her face turning red. "I'm the one who should be sorry. I don't know what I was thinking. I just . . . I'm gonna go."

"Wait," Rachel said. "You don't have to leave. I'm not upset."

Carly had her hand on the doorknob. "You're not?"

"No. I'm really flattered, actually."

"Really?"

"Yeah. And I want you to stay, if you want. But as a friend." Rachel thought for a second and said, "You know, I've never said that to a woman before."

Carly laughed. "That's okay. I've never done this before either."

"What, sleep with a woman?"

"Oh, no. I do that all the time. I've just never gotten drunk and hit on a straight woman before. Not that I'm trying to make excuses, but this whole thing with Shane and Melissa . . . it's got me pretty messed up. My plan tonight was to try to talk you into staying, not get drunk and make a pass at you."

"Well, if it makes you feel any better, I've decided to stay."

"Yeah?"

Rachel nodded.

"In that case . . ." Carly looked at the bed. "I think I'm gonna pass out now."

47

Sunday

Rachel and Carly crept down the stairs, hoping Shipley wouldn't hear them. When they hit the last step, a voice called from the salon, "Good morning." It was Miller, seated in one of the armchairs next to the fireplace. Shipley was at one end of a sofa, dressed in what looked like her best church clothes. A white blouse with a purple skirt suit and matching hat. She leaned forward to look Carly up and down, sat back, and said, "My word . . ."

Rachel realized she had been hunched over, as if that had somehow made her quieter. She straightened, cleared her throat, and said, "Good morning, Chief. Mrs. Shipley."

She walked into the room with Carly trailing a few paces behind. "I should go," she whispered.

Rachel shook her head. "It's okay."

"Is it?" Miller asked. "Considering what we're here to talk about?"

"It's fine," Rachel said.

"Mmm-hmph," Shipley said with a thin smile. "Well, I believe that coffee should be just about ready by now. Would either of you like some?"

"Sure," Carly said. "Thank you."

Rachel smiled and shook her head. They sat down on a love seat as Shipley stood and went to the kitchen.

Miller asked, "Have you given any more thought to what we talked about yesterday?"

"I'm staying," Rachel said. "I'm going to keep working it. At least until I run out of ideas."

"So you have some?" Miller asked. "Ideas, I mean."

"A couple."

Shipley came back in the room carrying a tray with three cups of coffee, four spoons, a creamer, and a bowl of sugar cubes. She set the tray on the table and said, "You all help yourselves now. Fix it up however you like. That's half-and-half in there, but I have milk if anyone wants some."

After they each got a cup and sat back down, Rachel said, "McGrath and Coughlan were friends in high school. So far, it's the only thing I know of that connects them. That's where I'm going to start."

"High school?" Shipley wore a skeptical smirk. "Has anyone considered the possibility that the Gifford boy was just a bad seed? Lord have mercy, I hate to speak ill of the departed, but maybe he was picking people at random. That child had some serious anger issues, you know. One of the worst students I ever had."

"That doesn't explain the shooting," Carly said.

"Well, maybe that didn't have anything to do with Dean and Andy at all," she said. "Maybe Dylan just knew too much about his brother's other activities. People are saying he's been dealing drugs and all. Could be, whoever his partners are, they just killed poor Dylan to keep him quiet."

Rachel shook her head. "I don't think so. Dylan and Kevin were both scared that someone was coming for them, but Kevin didn't know who. Whoever else is involved in this, I don't think they have anything to do with Kevin's business."

"Hmph." Shipley didn't look convinced.

"Sounds like you've got somewhere to start, at least," Miller said. "What can I do to help?"

"Nothing," Rachel said. "It's best if I handle this on my own. If I need help, I know where to find it."

"Fair enough. But if anybody asks, you're working for me. Plain and simple. And I'm paying you the same as Ted was."

She was about to protest, but he said, "No arguing about it, either, or I'll run you outta town myself."

"Okay," Rachel said. "Thank you, Chief."

"And you can stay here for free as long as you need to," Shipley said.

"Oh, no, Mrs. Shipley, I—"

Shipley raised a hand to stop her. "Child, don't even think of trying to tell me otherwise. Andy was my friend. If there's anything I can do to help, then by God, I will."

There was no use in arguing. Rachel smiled. "Thank you."

Miller checked his watch and stood up. "Well, Dorothy, I guess we have Sunday services to get to."

"Yes sir, we do," she said, rising to her feet.

"Thank you again for the coffee." He turned to Rachel. "Good luck, Miss Carver. I have a feeling you're going to need it."

★ ★ ★

"So what can I do to help?" Carly asked.

Rachel was driving her back to her car at the Riverside Pub. She turned onto Main and asked, "Are you off today?"

"Yep."

"Then go home and get some rest. Tomorrow, go back to work and don't tell anyone that you were at that meeting. If I need anything, I'll let you know."

She pulled into the parking lot and stopped behind Carly's car.

"If you say so." Carly opened the door but hesitated to get out. "I feel like I should be doing *something*."

"I know," she said. "It sucks, but we have to be patient. It's going to take me some time to figure this thing out."

"You know, when we had that first meeting, and you were telling us about how victimology would probably be the thing to break the case open"—Carly's eyes were fixed, staring into space through the windshield—"I wanted to prove you wrong. I wanted it to be some piece of physical evidence. Something I could process and bag and hold up at the trial and say, 'Look what I found.' And I was so excited when I saw that goddamn bat. It didn't even occur to me at the time that I never would have found it had you not led us right to it. You've been right every step of the way." She looked at Rachel. "And you're right about this too."

"Let's hope so," Rachel said.

"What're you gonna do now?"

"I'm going to see the Oracle."

Carly stared at her for a moment, then asked, "Did you think that was going to sound cool when you said it? 'Cause it really didn't."

"Get out."

★ ★ ★

The Camry started to lose traction halfway up the hill. Rachel found a relatively level spot near a switchback, kicked in the parking brake, and hiked the rest of the way. Ten minutes later, she was panting and knocking on Brenda Jordan's screen door.

Brenda padded out of the kitchen wearing a blue house coat, holding her hand up to shield her eyes from the sun. "Is that you, Miss Rachel Carver?" she asked, her voice muffled by the cigarette bouncing between her lips.

"Hi, Miz Jordan."

"I'll be damned. What's got you up here all by your lonesome this early in the mornin'?"

Rachel checked her phone. It was 8:15. "Is it too early? I can come back later."

Brenda opened the screen and waved her in. "Hell no, you already made the trip. Come on in." She led her through the living room. "And I done told you about that 'Miz Jordan' crap. Call me Brenda. I mean that."

They sat down at the kitchen table. "Clint's in there sleepin', so we can't be partyin' hard or nothin'." She let out a raspy laugh. "But you want a soda or somethin'? I got Orange Fanta and some Diet Rites in the fridge."

"I'm fine, thank you," Rachel said. She took out her pen and Steno pad. "I wanted to go over a few things with you regarding the conversation we had the other day. Maybe ask a few follow-up questions, if you don't mind."

"Sure. Have at it."

"I'm curious about the incident you told us about. The one that happened when Dean and Andy were in high school. When they got in trouble for smoking marijuana."

"Uh-huh."

"Can you tell me any more about that?"

Brenda tapped her cigarette on the ashtray. "I can try. Course I just know what I heard from Andy's mom."

"I understand," she said. "Just trying to get as much background information as I can."

"You might be better off talkin' to her. Course I think she lives over in Hoke County somewhere now."

"I might do that. But maybe you can tell me what you remember first."

"Well . . ." She looked at the ceiling. "From what I remember, there was four or five of them boys that got busted. All the teachers were real hush-hush about it. Like they were afraid to say too much. I asked my old English teacher, Mrs. Reynolds, about it at the time. She had gone on to become an assistant principal by then . . . but we were always pretty tight, her and me, even after I graduated. Anyway, she got all tight-lipped and wouldn't say a word. Even got kinda pissy with me just for askin'. Was the first time I can ever remember her gettin' mad at me for anything."

"Really?" Rachel made a note of that.

"Yeah, but hell, that just made it worse. Everyone was talkin' about it. Speculatin' on what had happened. Before you know it, Dean was movin' back to live with his momma, and some other girl got expelled. I think she might have been the one to give 'em the joint."

"I thought you said Dean got it from his uncle."

"Yeah . . ." Brenda looked out the window, trying to sort through her memories. "That's true. I'm tryin' to think . . . Maybe she got busted for somethin' else . . . No, I'm sure it was drugs."

"Hmph. Why don't we get back to Dean and his friends for a minute?"

Brenda was lost in thought. She shook it off and said, "Yeah, anyway, they all got in trouble for it. The basketball coach, Mister Grisley . . . God, what a name . . ." She laughed and coughed. "He busted their asses out in the woods behind the school."

"And, as far as you know, he and Andy stopped hanging out together after that?"

"Yep." She put out her cigarette and lit another. "As far as I know."

It wasn't much, but it was the only connection Rachel had. She needed to know more. "Can you tell me who the other boys were?"

"I think it was Caleb and this other boy named Martin, if I remember right. They were always together, the four of 'em."

She wrote the names down. "Caleb and Martin."

"I think so, yeah."

"Would you happen to remember their last names?"

"Oh, yeah, Caleb's. Caleb Rucker. He still lives around here. Owns a tree nursery over on the west side of town."

"And Martin?"

Brenda closed her eyes and tilted her head back. "Martin, Martin, Martin . . . I'm almost positive that was his *first* name." She looked back at Rachel. "But hell, for the life of me, I can't remember his last. He left outta here as soon as he graduated. Never came back, as far as I know."

"I see." She made a final note. "I appreciate your help, Brenda."

"That's it?"

"That's it."

"Well, that wasn't much. I hope it helps you get whoever shot them deputies."

"Oh, that's up to the SBI at this point. I'm just getting as much follow-up information as I can. For the reports and all."

"I bet you got a bunch of 'em."

She nodded. "Yeah. Better get to them. Thanks again."

"Hell, anytime." They stood and walked out to the living room. "By the way, I noticed you were breathin' kinda heavy when you got here, and I don't see a car. Did it break down on you or somethin'?"

"No. Unfortunately, it wouldn't make it up the hill."

"Up the hill?" Brenda pointed out the screen door. "You mean you came up the front?"

"Yeah . . ."

She laughed. "Damn, girl, that trail ain't meant for you to be drivin' up. The main road is out back. Lets out on the expressway just a half mile from here."

"Huh," Rachel said, looking out at the mountains. "Doesn't that figure?"

48

The phone was ringing in Bishop's Bluetooth earpiece as he worked on his AR-15. He had a new barrel in place, a longer one, meant for greater accuracy and higher muzzle velocity. He tightened the nut that held it secure, then installed the gas tube with a low-profile block.

"Hey," Pratt said when she answered. She sounded groggy and stuffy, as if she had cried herself to sleep last night.

"Hey there, pretty lady. Just thought I'd check in on you. How you holding up?"

"Okay, I guess. Missed you last night."

"Yeah, sorry about that. Wish I could've been there for you."

"Tough night at work?"

"Aren't they all?" He slid the free-floating handguard into place. It was free floating because its only connection was to the upper receiver. It didn't touch the barrel, which meant it wouldn't interfere with the natural flexing of the metal as the bullet travelled through it. That was supposed to make the rifle more accurate. Bishop trusted that, even though he didn't know for sure that it helped.

"Yeah," Pratt said with a sigh.

"So listen, I was thinking . . . since you're off tomorrow, maybe we could get away for a couple of hours. Maybe go for a picnic at Lake Fontana or something."

"Mmm, that sounds perfect. Can't we go today?"

"Sorry, sweetness," he said, tilting his head to get a better view as he threaded the first of six screws. "I've got too much work to do today. But if I really bust my butt, I think I can take off all tomorrow *and* Tuesday morning."

"Really?"

"Yep."

"So . . . ?" She sounded hesitant to ask. "Does that mean you might be staying the night?"

"Would you be okay with that?"

"Oh, God, sugar, you know I'd love it."

He chuckled, reached for the hex key to tighten the screws. "Good. I was worried you might be getting tired of me."

"Never," she said.

"All right. It's a date then. I'd better get back to work. I'll call you a little later when I get a break. See how you're doing."

"Okay." She sounded giddy. "Work hard. I'll be waiting for you."

He pressed the button on his earpiece to end the call, confident that he was in the clear. At least as far as the sheriff's office was concerned. The SBI was another matter, but there was no way to know what they were up to. He had to trust that he had done everything right, that he had left them with nothing to go on. They were grasping at straws. Shaking familiar trees, hoping some meth-head bikers would fall out.

He finished tightening the last screw, then reassembled the rest of the rifle. Once everything was in order, he popped the magazine in place and loaded it into the hidden compartment under the Juke's passenger door. Then he put his tools away, hit the button to open the garage door, and climbed in the car. He had a spot in mind fifteen miles to the north. A secluded place where he could finish his preparations.

★ ★ ★

The dirt road came to an end at a rotted pine log. Bishop parked and got out. In the back seat, there was a thin sheet of plywood with a reactive target stapled to it. The twelve-inch card had a black bull's-eye over a fluorescent backing. When a bullet struck it, the black material surrounding the hole would break away, leaving a highly visible ring that could be seen from a distance.

Bishop took out the target and set off for the drop, a steep escarpment lining the south side of a valley. When he reached the edge, he turned and climbed down along the cuts in the face, taking his time to ensure good footing with each step.

When he got to the bottom, he jogged to the soggy stream bed, hopped over, and hiked up the north side until he found a sandy patch. He propped the target up in front of it, looking back across to guess at a good spot for a matching elevation. Then he went back for the rifle.

The weapon fell into his hand as he opened the compartment. He looked around to make sure the area was clear and then went back to the ledge. He climbed about halfway down, which put him level with the target on the other side, and leaned against a boulder. A pair of foam earplugs sat in his pocket. He scanned the valley as he took them out, rolled them in his fingers, and stuffed them into his ears. Satisfied that he was alone, he drew back on the charging handle and let it go, put the bull's-eye in the crosshairs of his scope, and squeezed off a round.

The pop sounded dull, but he knew it was resonating and echoing along the valley. He pulled the plug from his left ear and listened for several seconds. There was no sound of anyone nearby. Looking again at the target, he saw the fluorescent-green circle the bullet had left in its wake. It was to the right of center and a little high. He took a dime from his pocket and made three clicks on the windage adjustment on his scope, two on the elevation. He stuffed the plug back in his ear, lined up another shot, and fired.

The fresh green hole was just right of center. He made another click on the windage screw, sighted the target, and fired. The bullet struck center, and he smiled. He took a breath, braced the stock against his shoulder again, and sent a volley. One round after another, as quickly as he could without sacrificing accuracy.

He fell into the rhythm easily. Had practiced it many times before. He didn't bother to time it now, but he knew, at this range, he could make ten hits on target in less than eight seconds. And that was good enough.

He clicked on the safety, collected the shell casings, and went back to the Juke. He stowed the rifle under the car then made the climb down to retrieve the target, taking a second to smile at the fluorescent-green rings. A few minutes later, he emerged from the woods and tossed it into the back seat. Then he jumped in, started the engine, and sped away.

49

It took more than ten minutes of slow going, mostly working the brake pedal, for Rachel to negotiate her way down the trail in reverse. A cool droplet of sweat ran down her side as she hit level ground. She sighed and shifted into drive and turned onto the expressway, heading west back into town. She stopped at a gas station to buy a sandwich and an energy drink and ate in the parking lot, leaning against the back of her car and thinking about her conversation with Brenda.

She had no new details about McGrath or Coughlan, but she did have two new names. One of those men still lived in the area. Perhaps he knew of a more recent connection between them, something that didn't date back to when they were all teenagers. But if he did, why had he not come forward to say so? Perhaps that connection, whatever it was, seemed inconsequential to him, not worth mentioning. Or perhaps it was something he wanted to keep secret.

She balled up the wrapper with the last bit of her sandwich and tossed it in the trash. Dropped in the Camry and continued west on Main, like Brenda had told her, looking for Rucker's Tree Nursery ahead on the left. It appeared in a large clearing half a mile past the edge of town. She turned into the gravel lot and parked in front of a chain link fence.

A gate in the center opened to a path that split the yard between shrubs and flowers on one side and saplings on the other. Rachel followed the path to an old office trailer, ascended the shaky, weather-worn wooden steps, and poked her head inside. A large barrel-chested man in khaki shorts and a green sweat shirt was accepting money from an elderly woman.

"Just hang on a minute, ma'am, and I'll get you some change."

"Oh, you keep that," she said.

"You sure, ma'am?" he asked, scratching a sun-spotted patch of leathery skin on his forehead. What was left of his sandy hair danced around his ears as he sat down in front of a tiny fan on his desk. "I got it right here."

"Of course I'm sure. I couldn't have loaded all that myself. I just hope my lazy grandson will be there to help when I get home."

She smiled at Rachel as she walked out. He stood and came to the door and said, "Well, if he don't, you just call and let me know, and I'll come by this evenin' and help you myself."

The old woman glanced back and waved, then continued down the path.

"Mornin', ma'am," he said to Rachel, as if noticing her there for the first time. "How can I help you?"

"Mister Caleb Rucker?" she asked in her most official-sounding voice.

"Yeah?" he said with a wary look. "That's me."

★ ★ ★

Rucker led Rachel through an aisle of dogwoods toward a pop-up canopy.

"I ain't talked to Dean since high school," he said.

They stepped into the shade where a small fountain spilled over a pile of stacked stones into a plastic pond. Rucker eased himself onto one end of a concrete bench and kept his eyes on the water. Rachel sat down beside him and asked, "How about Andy Coughlan?"

He shrugged. "Once in a while, whenever I saw him around town. Jen used to drag him over here every spring to pick out a new bunch of annuals. I guess they would've been comin' by soon if he was still . . . you know . . ."

"Would you know if the two of them kept in touch over the years? Or maybe reconnected when Dean moved back to town?"

"Oh, I wouldn't know nothin' about that, I'm afraid. Could be, but I kinda doubt it."

"What makes you say that?"

He scratched his forehead and said, "Hell, I don't know. Just wouldn't think they would is all."

Rachel studied him for a moment. "I heard about an incident that happened when you were in the ninth grade."

Rucker shifted, looking agitated. "Yeah?"

"Yeah. An incident involving drugs."

He scratched his forehead again.

"Mind telling me about it?" she asked.

"Ain't much to tell, really. Got caught smokin' a joint is all."

"I heard Dean moved away after that. Was it just because you guys got in trouble?"

"Pretty much. They was threatenin' to arrest him over it. Said he had to get outta town if he wanted to stay outta jail. He had to move back in with his mom and everything."

"Seems pretty harsh for smoking a joint."

"Well . . ." he looked at his feet. "Yeah."

"Was there something else?" she asked.

He shrugged and used the toe of his hiking shoe to shape a tiny mound of yellow sand.

"Mister Rucker?" She waited until he looked at her. "There's something else, isn't there? There's more to the story?"

"Yeah, I guess there is."

He didn't volunteer, so Rachel asked, "It was you and Andy and Dean? You went out into the woods behind the school during your lunch break?"

He nodded. "Yeah."

"What about your other friend? Martin?"

His brow furrowed. "I don't know no Martin. You mean Mark?"

Rachel pulled the Steno pad from her jacket pocket and flipped it open. She drew a line through Martin and wrote a correction. "Okay . . . Mark. He was there too?"

"Yeah, he was there."

"Anyone else?"

He looked away.

"This is important," she said. "Mister Rucker?"

He was chewing on his lip. He rocked his head to one side and said, "Yeah, there was someone else. Andy's girlfriend."

Rachel recalled Brenda's comments about a girl being expelled. "Is she the one who gave you guys the joint?"

"No," he said, shaking his head quickly. "Dean got it from his uncle. He always had some for us."

"Okay. So you four boys and Andy's girlfriend. What was her name?"

"Jamie."

"Jamie," she said, writing it down.

"Yeah, Jamie Moody."

"Okay. So tell me what happened. The five of you snuck out together? Off into the woods to get high? No big deal, right?"

He shook his head. "Yeah . . . I mean no, no big deal. Not at first."

"But then . . . ?"

"Andy and Jamie started makin' out," he said. "And then Dean got in on it. You know, he started kissin' on Jamie too."

"What did Andy do?"

"Nothin'. I mean, he was kinda eggin' her on to do it. She wasn't really into it at first. He had to talk her into it." He kicked the mound over. "Then, all of a sudden, Dean told us to keep a look out, and the three of 'em went off deeper into the woods. And they was back there for a while until Coach Grisley showed up."

"What happened then?"

"We were supposed to yell out to warn 'em, but Mark and I was too busy puffin' on that joint. It was just a tiny roach by then, but coach caught us with it red-handed. He was like, 'What in the hell is goin' on here?' Then he heard Dean and Andy and Jamie scramblin' to get dressed and went after 'em. And all the while, Mark was holdin' onto that roach like a dumbass."

He chuckled. Rachel wanted to laugh too, but she sensed that there was real pain behind his story.

He said, "Imagine . . . Coach walks up and finds us like that . . . Dean and Andy and Jamie screwin' . . . me and Mark high as hell. He drug our asses straight down to the principal's office."

"How much trouble did you all get in?"

"Me and Andy and Mark, we all got suspended for a week. Our parents came in and begged 'em not to do any worse. Said we'd straighten up and stay outta trouble, and we did. But Dean was known as kind of a troublemaker already. They looked at it like he was the instigator, gettin' us started on drugs and all. So, like I was sayin', he had to leave town to keep from goin' to jail."

"And Jamie?"

"They were real tough on her. Coach tried to make her sound like she was a little whore or somethin', performin' sex acts for drugs and what not. They expelled her for good."

Rachel was jotting down the details. She looked up and asked, "Does she still live around here?"

He shook his head. "Ain't seen her since around that time. Maybe just once or twice after that, then she and her mom moved away."

"Were her parents divorced?"

"I don't know about all that. I just know Andy said her dad didn't live with her."

He raised his head up and looked past Rachel. There was a man standing by the door to the trailer, looking around for help.

Rucker said, "I'll be right back," and walked over to meet him.

Rachel took the opportunity to finish writing the story. Sex and drugs and ruined friendships. It was interesting, but it didn't help much. At least not yet. Perhaps there were more layers to uncover. She had a few people left she could try to talk to about it, but she doubted there was a motive for murder hiding in there.

She walked back toward the office and spotted Rucker in the parking lot, helping his customer load a pair of small maple trees into the bed of a pickup. When they were finished, Rucker accepted

226 I J. R. Backlund

a handful of bills and shook the man's hand, then came back to the trailer to drop the cash in a lockbox.

"Gonna be a good day," he said, smiling.

"That's great," Rachel said, leaning against the doorjamb. "I don't want to take up too much of it. Just a couple more questions, if you don't mind?"

His expression soured. "Yeah, sure. I guess."

"Did you know Dylan Gifford by any chance?"

"I heard of him. Met his mom a couple times. She come around with Bert Hood once or twice."

"How do you know Bert?"

"We went to high school with his boy, Jerry. He was a couple years behind us."

"I see." She considered that for a moment. "Can you think of any reason why Dylan would want to kill Andy or Dean?"

"No, ma'am. I really can't."

"Do you know if Andy or Dean were into drugs recently? Or anything else illegal?"

"No, ma'am. Not as far as I know."

So little to go on, she thought, but it was all she had. "Do you happen to know where Jamie Moody lives now?"

"Sorry," he said, shaking his head.

"How about Mark?"

"Nope. Sorry."

"Okay, well . . ." She glanced over her notes. "Thanks for all your help . . . Oh, before I forget, do you remember Mark's last name?"

"Newfield," he said.

"Newfield," she repeated as she wrote it down. "Thanks again."

Rachel went to her car and fell into the driver's seat, wondering if she was wasting her time. It was a normal thought when a lead seemed to be heading nowhere, but persistence had solved more tough cases than she could count. Especially ones that depended on victimology. Studying the lives of the deceased, learning intimate details about them through second- or even third-hand accounts. Collecting stories from people who knew the victims, but never quite knew them well enough. They offered up parts and pieces that Rachel had to assemble. A patchwork that could never be completely sewn up but might, nevertheless, reveal a mosaic if she worked hard and got lucky.

She took out her phone and opened the web browser, typed "Mark Newfield," and pressed the search button. The results appeared a moment later. A banker on LinkedIn, an insurance agent on Facebook, an orthopedic surgeon at some clinic in Knoxville, and dozens more, but none that stood out as the man she was looking for. She could spend hours, perhaps even days searching the Internet trying to track him. Even longer if she went looking for public records on her own.

As a private citizen, she was handicapped. There were services she could pay to do the work for her, companies that had websites designed for investigative searches. But they were expensive, and she would have to go through the trouble of setting up accounts with them. She could call Miller and ask for his help, or perhaps even Carly for that matter, but there was another option she wanted to try first. One that would let her kill two birds with one stone. It had been on her mind since she had read the SBI report. Last night, sitting at the bar, making up her mind about whether she would stay in town, another thought had struck her. It was time to set the record straight about Lauren Bailey.

50

"Hi, Rachel, can you hear me?" Bryce Parker asked when he answered the call. He sounded like he was standing in a hurricane.

"Yeah, I can hear you. Barely."

"Sorry, I'm at the beach. It's windy out here. What's up?"

"I need your help with something."

"Okay . . ." he said cautiously. "What kind of help are we talking about?"

"Remember the other day when I told you I was out of town?"

"Say that again. Where?"

"Out of town," she said louder.

"Okay. Yeah?"

"I'm in Dillard City working on a case for the local police department. I'm in a bit of a time crunch, though, and I'm running around like a chicken with its head cut off. Anyway, I was wondering if you could help me do some research on a couple of names."

"Uh . . . well, you know, Rachel, I'm out of town too, actually. I'm off for the weekend and—"

"I didn't know reporters took days off."

He let out a quick laugh. "Yeah, sure feels that way sometimes. But look, I'm really—"

"I have something I can offer you in return," she said.

"Yeah? What's that?"

"Lauren Bailey. The report you sent me. I'd be willing to talk to you about it."

"I already wrote that story, Rachel. Afraid I couldn't wait on you. Posted it Thursday morning."

"Posted it," she said. "By that, you mean you put it up on the website, but it didn't make the print edition?"

"Wasn't much of a story there."

"There will be when you hear what I have to say."

He was quiet for several seconds. Rachel heard distorted wind battering his phone. Then he said, "Give me a couple minutes. I'll call you back."

It took him five. "Had to run back to my car," he said. The background was quiet. "Just let me grab a pen . . . Okay, I'm ready."

"Let's not get ahead of ourselves. I need to find two people, fast. All I have are their names, ages, what town they grew up in, and what high school they went to."

"And I'd be doing you a huge favor by getting that for you. On my day off, no less. So let's hear what you have to say, and if it's as good as you're telling me it is, then I'll be more than happy to help you."

"Then put the pen away, 'cause right now we're off the record. Agreed?"

"Okay. Off the record."

"Lauren Bailey was innocent. She didn't kill her boyfriend."

"You're serious right now?" he asked after a moment.

"Yes."

"How . . . Wait, what makes you think she didn't do it? I mean, is there evidence or . . . ?"

"Settle down, scoop. One thing at a time. I mentioned I'm on a time crunch, didn't I?"

"Yeah, you did."

"So? Do we have a deal?"

"Give me the names."

★ ★ ★

Parker called back from his hotel room forty-five minutes later. Rachel was sitting in the gas station parking lot, sipping on a fresh can of Monster Energy and searching the Internet for more information on Rucker.

"That was fast," she said.

"Well, I started with Moody first. You're not going to like it."

"What did you find?"

"An obituary and an article in the *Johnson City Tribune*," he said. "Looks like she killed herself, February of last year."

"Shit."

"Yeah, sorry. The article mentions her mother, Clarissa Moody, if that helps. I did a quick search on her. Found an address in Tennessee just outside Johnson City."

She put him on speaker and opened the map app on her phone. "Let me have it."

He read it to her, and she typed it in. When the route appeared on the screen, she said, "Got it. It's not too far from here." She shifted into drive. "I'm headed there now."

"All right. I'll get started on Mark Newfield."

★ ★ ★

Two hours and twenty minutes later, Rachel parked by the curb in front of a brick ranch house partially hidden by overgrown shrubs. She got out and looked around at the neighborhood. Most of the houses were in a similar state. Old and poorly maintained. Their yards were littered with old appliances and dilapidated cars.

On her way to the front door, a voice called out, "Ain't nobody home right now."

Rachel searched and found a white-haired woman in a rocking chair beneath the neighbor's carport. She walked over and said, "Good morning."

"Mornin'." The woman's sandals scuffed the sandy concrete as she advanced and receded in the rocker. Her bottom lip puffed out, loaded with dipping tobacco. Her right hand held a Milwaukee's Best can, the top of which had been cut off. There were brown drips running down from the edge. "You lookin' for Terry?"

"Actually, I'm looking for Miz Clarissa Moody."

"Uh-huh." She put the can to her chin and spit, wiped the excess from her bottom lip with her finger, and said, "Well, she ain't around, neither."

"Would you happen to know where I could find her?"

"She's at work, I assume."

"And where's that, if you don't mind me asking?"

The woman looked her up and down, suspicion in her eyes. "You a debt collector or somethin'?"

Rachel forced a smile, pretended to look embarrassed. "Oh, no, ma'am. I work for Lowry County High School. I'm here to talk to Miz Moody about her daughter, Jamie. You see, we're coming up on the school's fifty-year anniversary, and we wanted to make a little memorial for those students who've, you know, passed on. I was hoping to see if I could get some photos for the slideshow."

The woman put a few cycles on the rocker while she contemplated that, then dropped another deposit in the can, wiped the residue off her lip, and said, "Well, all right. I guess she wouldn't mind that."

★ ★ ★

Clarissa Moody was working the chicken fryer at the Cash Saver grocery store. Rachel stepped up to the deli counter and asked the man in the hairnet if she could talk to her. Moody walked over a couple minutes later and asked, "How can I help you, ma'am?"

She looked gaunt and tired, but not as old as Rachel had expected. She must have gotten pregnant while she was still a teenager.

"Hi, Miz Moody. I'm sorry to bother you at work, but I'm working as a consultant with the Dillard City Police Department. I have a few questions about your daughter, Jamie. You think you might be able to spare a minute or two?"

Moody took a step back and looked away, thinking. She appeared to be on the verge of asking Rachel to leave, but then she glanced at the clock on the wall and said, "I go on break in twenty minutes. I'll meet you out back."

She came out a few minutes early, pulling off a pair of clear poly gloves and dropping them in a trash bin. She put a stick of red chewing gum in her mouth and stood by the door, watching Rachel apprehensively.

"You say you're working with the police department in Dillard?"

"Yes, ma'am," Rachel said. "Chief Miller hired me to consult on an investigation."

"I don't know who that is. It's been a long time since I lived there."

"About fifteen years, right?"

"Uh-huh. What did you say your name was?"

"Rachel Carver."

"And what is it you want to ask me about my daughter?"

"I don't know if you've heard, ma'am, but there've been a couple of murders recently in and around Dillard City."

Moody leaned against the wall and folded her arms. "I haven't heard about it, no. But I don't watch the news much anymore."

"I can't blame you for that."

"Who was it that got killed?"

"Two men," Rachel said. "Men your daughter knew in high school."

After Rachel finished explaining why she was there, Moody went inside for a minute. When she came back, she was holding a cigarette and a lighter. She led Rachel to the designated smoking area, which was a metal picnic table situated by a dumpster full of rotting food.

"Sorry," Moody said. "I'm trying to quit, but you showing up here ain't helping."

"I understand."

She lit the cigarette, pulled a long drag, and closed her eyes. "As far as I know, Jamie hadn't talked to any of them boys since we moved away. I mean, damn, I haven't even heard any of their names since the whole thing happened."

"Is it possible your daughter kept in touch with either of them without you knowing about it?" Rachel asked.

"Anything's possible. Especially with Facebook and all. But I never heard her talk about either of 'em."

"Did you and Jamie talk often?"

Moody shrugged. "Depends, I guess. Off and on. We could fight like cats and dogs sometimes, you know. Not see each other for months on end. Then she'd show up at the house, usually needing money. My boyfriend, Terry . . . he was always trying to keep the peace between us, but . . ."

Her voice was getting shaky, and her eyes were turning red. She rubbed the skin beneath them and said, "Damn."

Rachel gave her a second, then asked, "Do the names Dylan or Kevin Gifford mean anything to you?"

"No . . ." She stared at the table, searching her memory. After a moment, she shook her head. "No, can't say I've ever heard of 'em before."

Rachel thought for a moment. It was starting to feel like a dead end. "Do you mind if I ask . . . about your daughter's passing?"

"What about it?"

"Do you know why she did it?"

Moody stared at the cigarette in her hand, rolled it between her thumb and forefinger. "She didn't leave a note, if that's what you're asking."

"I'm sorry, Miz Moody. I can't imagine how difficult—"

"Stop," she said, her voice cracking. "I don't want to hear that shit no more. You know how many people have said that to me?"

Rachel stayed quiet, expecting Moody to stand up and walk away, but she sniffed hard, took another drag, and said, "Jamie was a troubled girl. Always. I don't know why or what I done to make her that way. Maybe it's because I worked too much or because her dad and I never got along. Maybe it was because she drank too much, and it messed with her mind . . . I just don't know."

She threw the cigarette butt on the ground and stamped it out.

Rachel recalled what Rucker had said about Jamie's father not living with her. She asked, "Did Jamie know her father?"

Moody was wiping a tear from her cheek. She laughed and said, "Oh, yeah. She got along with him a lot better than she did with me. I guess it's easier when you don't have to be the full-time parent. Jamie and him were thick as thieves. I tried to keep her from going to see him, but she didn't blame him for nothing."

"What would she have blamed him for?"

"For not being there when we needed him," she said indignantly. "When it mattered. Before that whole thing happened at the high school, I wanted to get her out of there. I wanted to send her to a private school. A good Christian one where she'd get some discipline. Some morals. That's all she needed. She was smart, you know. Smarter than me. She could've gone to college. But he wouldn't help me pay for it. Not one bit."

"Wouldn't or couldn't? Private school can be kind of expensive, right?"

Moody's eyes narrowed. "What, you think he couldn't have afforded it?"

Rachel suddenly regretted asking the question. "Sorry, I guess it's not really relevant to—"

"Let me tell you something. That man owns half the land in Western North Carolina. If he wasn't so damn tight with all his money, Jamie could've had a chance at a decent life." She was crying, wiping her cheeks with her sleeves. "And he used to try and tell me I was after him for his money, but I didn't want anything from that sorry sack of . . . I just wanted him to do what was right by that baby girl."

She stood from the table and turned away, sobbing. Paced in a circle as she wiped her eyes and tried to steady her breathing.

Rachel felt a shock of realization. She tried to keep her voice even as she asked, "Miz Moody, who was Jamie's father?"

★ ★ ★

Rachel had been heading south on I-26 for nearly an hour, processing what she had learned from Moody, when she remembered that her phone was still on silent. She had turned the ringer off to keep it from interrupting her interview. She took it out of her pocket and checked the notifications. Parker had left a voice mail and two text messages. She slid her thumb across the screen to call him back.

"Rachel?" he said quickly after the first ring.

"Hey," she said. "I found Moody's mother. You wouldn't believe what she told me. I'm on my way back—"

"Rachel," he said, talking over her. "Rachel, listen to me. He's dead."

"Who? Newfield?"

"Yes."

"How?"

"He was shot. Yesterday. He walked out the back door of the gun range where he worked, went to his car, and took three in the chest. In broad daylight."

"Holy shit." She felt panic rising within her.

"I know, right? It's crazy. What the hell are you working on up there?"

"I'll call you back."

She hung up and scrolled through her contacts until she found Braddock's number. Held her thumb over it but took a second to reconsider. She wasn't ready to talk to him yet. She needed a clearer picture, a better understanding of what was happening. A theory that made all the pieces fit. In the meantime, she had to protect Caleb Rucker.

She decided to call Miller instead. When he answered, she gave him enough details to convince him that Rucker was in danger.

"He's the last one, Chief. And I'm willing to bet whoever's behind this is coming for him next."

"Jesus Christ," he said. "You sure about this? I mean, McGrath, Coughlan, the Moody woman, and now this Newfeld guy . . . all dead because of some sex thing they got in trouble for back in high school?"

"New*field*," she said. "I don't have the why yet. I'm still trying to figure that out. All I know is that three of the five people who were there when it happened have all been murdered in the past week. Moody supposedly killed herself, but who knows what really happened. Rucker's the only one left. So either he's the mastermind of all this or he's next on someone's list."

He sighed, and the line went quiet for several seconds. "Well, shit," he said finally. "I guess we'd better make sure Caleb gets through the day without getting shot."

"You should bring him into the station."

"I was thinking I could just send a unit over to babysit him."

"After what happened the other night?"

"Damn. I knew you were going to say that. All right, I'll try to bring him in. I can't force him, though. If he don't want to come along, I can't make him."

"You have to try," she said.

"Yeah . . . okay, I'll go over there and talk to him myself. But at some point, this had better start making a lot more sense."

"I know, Chief. I'm working on it."

Rachel weaved through the light traffic that was accumulating on the outskirts of Asheville, grateful that it was a Sunday.

"Hey," Parker said. "What's going on?"

"Had to make a call." She hit the brake on a downhill turn, barely keeping the wheels off the shoulder. "I know I'm pushing my luck here . . . *Shit*." She jerked the wheel to avoid hitting a motorcycle that suddenly appeared in the right lane. "Where in the fucking hell did *you* come from?"

"Say what?"

"Nothing. Sorry. Look, I know I'm asking a lot. More than we agreed on, but—"

"Yeah, yeah," he said. "Just promise me an exclusive on whatever you're working on."

"You got it."

"Great. What do you need?"

"I've got another name for you," she said. "I need you to tell me everything you can about this guy. His personal info, his family, his business deals, his political activities, any criminal history, anything he's been in the news for . . ." She checked the map on her phone. "And I need it within the next hour and a half."

"That's a tall order," he said. "I'll do what I can. What's the name?"

"Lawton Jones."

51

Dorothy Shipley was standing at the counter in the Main Street Pharmacy when her neighbor came through the door, spotted her, and scurried over.

"Dorothy," she said, barely able to contain her excitement. "Dorothy, you have to hear this."

"Geraldine," Shipley said, "what in the world are you so worked up about?"

Geraldine was a tiny woman who was prone to fits of anxiety. She treated them with some kind of all-natural herbal medication that she ordered online, which never explained why she made so many trips to the pharmacist. Shipley suspected she was supplementing her treatments with valium and the occasional glass of white wine. But she appeared stone sober as she took a breath and said, "I think Chief Miller just arrested Caleb Rucker."

"Arrested Caleb? For what?"

"Well, how am I supposed to know that?" she asked with a look of irritation.

"Okay, girl. Calm down and tell me what happened."

"I'm sorry . . ." she said, touching Shipley's forearm. "You know how I get."

"Mmhmm."

"Anyhow, I was over at the nursery looking for some violets to replace my geraniums that died last year . . . you know, the ones I had around the fountain by the guest room . . . I was hoping to get four or five of them planted today, but no sooner had I started looking than Chief Miller came up in that big SUV of his, got out, and walked straight up into Caleb's office trailer. A couple minutes later, here they come together. They walked right by me without saying a word. And Chief Miller went and loaded Caleb in the back seat and drove off."

"Just like that?"

"Just like that."

"And didn't say anything to you?"

"Nope," she said. "Didn't say nothing to nobody. There was two or three other people there too. Standing around, not knowing *what* to do. We all just left after a while."

"My word," Shipley said. "I wonder . . ."

"Wonder what?"

She lowered her voice. "Well, you know that detective woman the sheriff hired?"

"Yeah," Geraldine said, leaning in close.

"She's working for the chief now."

"How do you know that?"

"I'm letting her stay at my house. She and the chief met in my living room first thing this morning."

"Really?"

"Yes, ma'am. I just hope . . . Lord, I hate to even say it . . . I just hope Caleb didn't have anything to do with all that mess."

"Hmm. You know, I always—" She looked over Shipley's shoulder, cleared her throat, and said, "Well, hi there, Commissioner."

Shipley turned, surprised to see Lawton Jones standing a few feet away, holding a large bottle of antacids.

"Geraldine, Dorothy . . ." He looked lost, as if he'd forgotten where he was or how he'd gotten there.

"You feeling okay, Commissioner?" Shipley asked.

"Uh . . . yeah. Sorry to interrupt, but . . . Caleb . . . was he in cuffs?"

"Beg your pardon?" Geraldine asked.

"Handcuffs," he snapped. "Was he in handcuffs?"

"Oh . . . No, he wasn't, come to think of it."

Jones started for the door. Halfway there, he realized he was still carrying the bottle. He set it on a shelf at the end of the cosmetics aisle and hurried out.

"Now wasn't that plain odd?" Geraldine asked after he was gone.

"It sure was."

The pharmacist stepped up to the counter and said, "Here you go, Miz Dorothy." He handed her a bag containing her blood pressure medication. "Any questions for me?"

"No, sir," she said. "I believe I'll be just fine."

He smiled and wished her a good day. She said bye to Geraldine as she turned to leave, promised to call if she learned anything more about the situation. On the drive home, she decided she would pray. She would ask the Lord to forgive Rucker for his sins, whatever they might have been. *After all,* she thought, *what else is a good Christian to do?*

★ ★ ★

Bishop raised his head above the ridge and spotted the back of the house. It looked closer than he had remembered. Almost too close. But he was in the right spot, nice and level with a line of sight directly into the window by Rucker's recliner.

He rolled up his backpack and laid it in front of him. Then he pushed down on its center, brought his rifle up, and set the handguard on the indentation he had made. He checked his watch. Rucker would be at work for at least two more hours. Perhaps even longer if he had deliveries to make. But Bishop had been too restless to sit at home.

He lay prone on the rise and pulled the rifle against his shoulder, looked through the scope, and found the window. The glass pane was just a couple of feet from the recliner, he judged. Given his position, a bullet would strike it at a near ninety-degree angle. Any change in its trajectory from impacting the glass would be minor, if it happened at all. And he would send enough of them downrange to ensure that it wouldn't matter if the first one went a little astray.

He made a slight adjustment on the eyepiece ring, then laid the rifle on its side and backed down the slope until he could stand. He rose to a crouch, careful to keep his head below the ridge, and went over to a flat spot at the base of a sugar maple. He sat with his back against the mold-covered trunk and looked up at the branches. New buds were pushing from the tips. They looked like they could break open any day now.

The burner buzzed in his jacket pocket. He stood and jogged downhill, wanting to put more space between himself and the house. Not that it mattered—Rucker lived in a remote spot, four miles outside of town and a quarter mile from the nearest neighbor.

"What is it?" Bishop whispered into his hands cupped around the phone's mic.

"We're in trouble," Jones said. "It's over."

He sounded scared.

"What are you talking about?"

"That Carver bitch has figured it out. She's working for Chief Miller now. And he's gone and picked up Rucker and taken him into protective custody."

"When the fuck did that happen?"

"Just now."

"How did you find out? Did they question you?"

"What? No, I heard about it from Geraldine and Dorothy at the goddamn pharmacy, for Christ's sake."

"All right," he said, fighting the urge to shout into the phone, "just settle down, and we'll figure this out."

He looked up at the ridge, felt a rush of fear. Could the DCPD be on their way here now? There was no way to know. He had to get moving.

"Are you at home?" he asked.

"Almost," Jones said.

"Just stay there and keep cool. I'll call you back."

He ended the call and stuffed the phone in his jacket, sprinted up the hill and grabbed the rifle and the backpack. He took a quick look around, saw nothing, but felt no sense of relief as he descended the slope and jogged the trail back to his car.

★ ★ ★

When Jones got home, he rushed inside and went straight for the single malt on the top shelf of his liquor cabinet. It felt a little safer to be in his house, though he couldn't figure out why. It didn't matter when all was said and done. If the cops came for him, it would be the first place they would look. Not that he had any designs on running. That had never been an option for him.

Revenge came with a cost. He had known that from the beginning, had been willing to pay the price. At least when he had conceived it, when he'd sworn that he was willing to do whatever it took to see it through to the end. But he had hired Bishop for the job. He realized now that had been a mistake.

The phone rang as he finished his first shot. He poured a refill and answered.

Bishop sounded like he was driving fast. "Are you home yet?"

"Yes."

"Are there any cops there trying to arrest you?"

"No . . . What?" He went to the window by the front door and looked out at the driveway. "No, there's no one here."

"Then take it easy. There's nothing to worry about yet."

"Yeah . . ." He took a mouthful of scotch, swallowed hard, and said, "Okay."

"We don't have any idea what they're talking to Rucker about. Even if they figured out how he fits into it, that doesn't mean they know a damn thing about us."

"Right. Wait . . . Oh, *shit*."

A white sedan eased to a stop on the road by the mailbox. Jones recognized it instantly.

"She's here," he said.

"Who?"

"Who do you think, you fuckin' asshole? The Carver woman. She just pulled up out front. What do I do?"

"Invite her in," Bishop said. "I'm almost there."

"What?"

There was no answer.

"Hello?" Jones yelled. He checked the screen and saw that it was black.

Outside, the car crept forward onto the driveway.

52

"I'm just getting started," Parker said. "I haven't found out much about his personal life or his politics, but he's into all kinds of businesses. A lot more than just real estate."

Rachel was riding the brake down Jones's driveway. She stopped a short distance from the walkway to the front door and shifted into park. "Has he ever been arrested?"

"Not as far as I can tell, but, you know, real research takes time."

"Yeah. Okay. Thanks, Bryce."

"Want me to keep digging?"

"You don't mind?"

"Are you kidding?" he asked. "I feel like I'm helping you solve a real mystery."

"I'd be lying if I said I couldn't use the help."

"Count me in."

Rachel let him get back to work. She slipped her phone into her jacket pocket as she stepped out and took in the elevation of Jones's massive log home. It rose two stories toward steeply pitched gables. The ground sloped away from the driveway on the southern end, exposing a third story encased in stacked stones. A mansion clinging proudly to the mountainside.

She went to the front door and rang the bell. He answered a few seconds later. His face was red and moist. He held a whiskey tumbler in his left hand. A thin coat of whatever he was drinking lined the bottom.

"Afternoon, Miss Carver." He didn't seem surprised to see her. "Come in."

She stepped inside and followed him to the kitchen where he refilled his glass.

"Can I offer you a drink?" he asked with his back to her.

"I'm fine, thanks."

"I hope you don't mind if I have one without you. I'm starting a little earlier than normal today."

There was an edge to his voice. He was struggling to hide it, trying too hard to keep his cool. Rachel suddenly felt vulnerable. An alarm went off in the back of her mind, a distant voice yelling the word *danger.*

"Not at all," she said.

It had been a mistake to follow him inside. Alone. Unarmed. Jones was guilty. She didn't understand the motive yet, but she was certain of it. His demeanor told her everything.

"This house is amazing." She took a quick look around the kitchen. There was a large island separating them. To her left, a wall of floor-to-ceiling windows offered an expansive view of the valley to the west. To her right, cabinets, a gas range with eight burners, a pair of ovens stacked on top of each other, a knife block sitting on the counter near the corner. She stepped closer to the knives, pretending to admire the stone countertops.

"I'd die for a kitchen like this."

He laughed uncomfortably, and she smiled.

"I'm sorry to bother you on a Sunday," she said, "but I'm trying to finish up some reports for the sheriff. I just have a couple of questions for you."

"Reports, huh?"

"Yes, sir," she said with a nod. "Definitely not my favorite part of the job."

He took a sip, dribbled some on his chin. "And what kind of questions would you have for me?"

"I hate to bring this up, since there's probably nothing to it, but I was hoping you could tell me about a woman named Jamie Moody."

Jones stared at his drink for a moment, then he downed the contents and went back for more. Rachel watched his hands out of the corner of her eye, making sure they didn't reach into a drawer and return with a gun.

"Do you recognize that name, Commissioner?"

He didn't answer.

"See, the trickiest part of this investigation," she said, "has been trying to figure out what the victims had in common. So far, I've only found one thing—they were friends for a little while back in high school. There were actually four of them that spent a lot of time together. Dean McGrath and Andy Coughlan . . ."

Jones's hand shook as he lifted the tumbler.

"Mark Newfield . . ."

He sucked in a shot, started pouring another while trying to swallow what was still in his mouth.

"Caleb Rucker . . . I hear they were the best of pals. Right up until they all got in trouble for sneaking away during their lunch break one day. Apparently, that was the last time they were all together. And Jamie Moody was with them." She watched him lean against the counter and close his eyes. "You know about that incident, don't you, Commissioner? Jamie was your daughter, wasn't she?"

Slowly, he turned to face her. His shoulders slumped. He looked sad and weary.

"She was a good girl," he said. "Those boys ruined her. They got her high and they . . ."

★ ★ ★

Bishop crested the ridge in a sprint, then followed it to an outcrop where the back of the house stood in full view. He raised his rifle and searched through the scope, found Jones and the woman in the kitchen. He sat down, propped his elbow on his knee, and kept his eye in the scope as he got on the burner. Jones answered a moment later.

Bishop heard him say, "Excuse me, I need to take this. Hello?"

"I can see you."

"All right." Jones turned away from her. "What do you think?"

The woman was watching him closely, but for all she knew, Jones was on a business call. He could be discussing any number of mundane topics that had nothing to do with whether she would die within the next few minutes.

"You tell me," Bishop said. "If she's questioning you, then she's getting a little too close to the truth, wouldn't you say?"

"I agree."

"Maybe it's time for her little journey to come to an end."

"All right. If you think that's best."

"I could wait for her to leave and follow her out. Take her down while she's on the road."

"Uh-huh."

"Or I could find out where she's staying and take her in her sleep."

"Right," Jones said, glancing back. It looked like an involuntary action. "I uh . . . I know where that is, if you need that information."

"Hmm." He adjusted his grip on the handguard, put the crosshairs on her chest. "Of course, I could just take her out right now. That would be the safest bet, don't you think?"

"Well . . ." He cleared his throat. "I'm not sure. Maybe one of the other two options might be—"

"Out of curiosity, do you think she knows who I am?"

"I don't think . . ." he glanced at her again. "I really don't see how that's possible."

"Good-bye, Lawton."

★ ★ ★

Jones put the phone in his pocket and said, "I'm sorry, Miss Carver."

There was a snap at one of the windows. Rachel saw a long crack form in the glass. Jones grunted. Then there was another snap, and another. Shards broke away from the window pane. Jones grunted again and dropped the tumbler. It shattered and spread across the tile floor.

He looked out the broken window in disbelief. Rachel seized him by his shirt and yanked him down onto his back. A zip and a thud as a bullet passed over them and struck a cabinet door a few feet away. The sound of gunfire echoed through the valley outside. Lying facedown, she spun and clawed her way toward the island, dragging Jones with all her strength.

"Come on, goddammit," she screamed. "Move!"

He kicked hard, slid a couple of feet, then wheezed as another bullet found him. He tried to kick again, but his foot slipped. He was losing strength.

Rachel made it behind the island. She sat up, braced her foot against a cabinet, and pulled with both hands. Another zip and a crack, and she felt a sting in her neck as the edge of the countertop exploded behind her. Jones's shirt ripped, and she fell backward. She reached again, grabbed two handfuls of fabric, and pulled him to cover.

She spun around and lay flat on her back with her head next to his. "Hang on. I'm calling for help."

He coughed. Warm droplets of blood rained on her. She pulled her phone out and dialed 9-1-1 with shaky hands. When the dispatcher answered, Rachel yelled at her to send help, then yelled at Jones to stay with her, then yelled back at the dispatcher, who was trying to keep Rachel calm.

Jones was looking weaker by the second. He was losing consciousness. A word formed in his mouth. He blurted it out in a sudden burst of energy that quickly faded. But he repeated the word as many times as he could manage while his life drained away. The last two were barely a whisper.

"*Bishop . . . Bishop . . .*"

53

Lying on the kitchen floor, staring into Jones's dead eyes, Rachel had plenty of time to think. It had taken more than three hours for the SBI Special Response Team to arrive. An army of deputies had secured the front. Braddock had tried to push past them to get to her, but Jensen had talked him down. Rachel had helped over the phone. Jones was dead, and she was in a safe spot, hiding behind the island. There was no reason for him to go inside until they were certain the sniper was no longer a threat.

So Rachel waited while Jensen's team combed the wilderness behind the house. And she thought about Jamie Moody.

Those boys ruined her, Jones had said.

Was it really that simple? She took out her Steno pad and flipped to the notes from her interview with Clarissa Moody. Across the top, she had written Moody's number in case she had any follow-up questions. She called it twice before Moody answered.

"I don't know if you've heard yet," Rachel said. "But there's been a shooting at Lawton Jones's house. I'm here now."

"A what? Damn . . . is he okay?"

She looked at Jones's gray face. "We can't say yet. There's a SWAT team searching for the shooter. An ambulance is here. Things are a little crazy right now."

"I don't know what to say. I mean, I never wanted anything bad to happen to Lawton . . . Is it the same one who killed them other people?"

"I need to ask you for a favor, Miz Moody."

"Oh . . . Okay, what is it?"

"Would you tell me more about your daughter?"

"What about her?"

"Everything you can. Starting from the moment she was expelled from Lowry County High."

It wasn't a pleasant story. Moody told it matter-of-factly, crying occasionally but never quite breaking down. Jamie had been a good student until the ninth grade. Then she started skipping classes, sneaking out at night, disappearing on the weekends. At that time, Jones and Moody were barely speaking, even though he was spending his weekends with Jamie. When Moody had begged him for the money to send her a private school, he had refused. Then came the joint-smoking incident.

Moody moved Jamie to Knoxville and put her in a new school. But things only got worse after that. By the time she was seventeen, Jamie had been arrested three times: underage drinking, drug possession, and shoplifting. She spent three months in juvie hall, as Moody called it. Got out just before her eighteenth birthday, but she never came home. When Moody saw her a year later, she was hanging on the arm of a middle-aged biker, a man who eventually got sent away for selling cocaine to an undercover cop.

The story went on. Years of bad relationships, alcohol and drug abuse, trouble with the law . . . "She hit bottom two years ago," Moody said. "She came home and sat down with me and said, 'I need help, Momma. I can't live like this no more.' So I got her some help. At the church, there was this group. They had AA meetings and all. I got her in it, and they helped her a lot. They really did. Got her a job. Got her a little apartment. But then . . .'"

Rachel heard her exhale. It sounded like she was smoking a cigarette.

"What happened?"

"She started hanging around that old crowd again. Then she started borrowing money from me. I knew she was getting back into trouble, but I just couldn't say anything to straighten her out. She would just tell me, 'Oh, Momma, I told you I'm all better now.

There ain't nothing to worry about.' I really wanted to believe that."

"Was she seeing her dad regularly?" Rachel asked.

"Oh, yeah. She made trips over to see him all the time. They spent a lot of time together, right up until about a month before she died."

"What happened?"

"I think he got mad at her over money. She was always asking him for more, and, you know, he was always kind of tight with it."

"And when was the last time *you* talked to him?"

"The day she died. I called him and told him. It was the first time I'd spoken to him since we moved away from there."

"How did he react?"

"Hmph. Like a self-righteous asshole."

"How so?"

She sniffed, took a second, and said, "He yelled at me. Said it was my fault she had turned out the way she did."

"Why did he think it was your fault?"

"'Cause I didn't stop her from hanging around them boys she got in trouble with. He said they'd raped her that day behind the school, and I hadn't done nothing to prevent it. I told him that they hadn't raped her, it was just sex, but he wouldn't hear it. He kept saying I didn't do enough to protect her. But I told him that was bullshit. I told him it was his fault as much as it was mine."

★ ★ ★

By the time Rachel hung up with Moody, the sun had set. She brought up Parker's number, and the screen cast a pallid glow over Jones's body. It held her gaze while she listened to the phone ring. The eyes and mouth were half open, fixed in that moment of agony just before death.

Rachel felt a shudder and looked away. She didn't want to think about how close she had come to dying. Had the shooter been aiming for both of them? Was she alive because she had simply gotten lucky? She felt tears welling in her eyes. She felt weak, and that made her angry. For the first time in her life, she wanted to kill someone.

As a professional investigator, she had always managed to keep her emotions in check. She had never allowed herself to hate a suspect. She had never thought of doing anything more than finding the evidence needed to make an arrest and get a conviction. But this time was different. Whoever the shooter was, she wouldn't be satisfied by watching him go to prison. She wanted him dead.

When Parker answered, Rachel asked, "Find anything interesting?"

"Not really," he said with a yawn.

"Can you tell me anything about his personal life?"

"Yeah, a little. He's had two divorces, as far as I can tell, both of which made the local papers. Those small-town reporters are fascinated by rich people. Anyway, that's about all there is. It doesn't look like he has any children. I mean, other than Jamie."

"Makes sense," she said. "Can I add something to your search?"

"Sure. What is it?"

"Something Jones said to me. I didn't get a chance to ask him what he was talking about. He said the word 'Bishop.'"

"Bishop . . ." he repeated as if he was writing it.

"Yeah."

"That's it? He didn't say anything else?"

"Kind of a long story."

Parker laughed. "Okay. I'll look into it."

★ ★ ★

Rachel lay in the dark, stared at the ceiling, and tried to put it all together.

Had Jones had been unable to cope with his daughter's suicide? Maybe.

Perhaps the guilt had been too much for him to handle, so he had projected, found someone else to blame. He had traced the roots of Jamie's self-destructive behavior back to her ninth-grade year. Coughlan, McGrath, Newfield, and Rucker were his scapegoats. In his mind, *they* had been responsible for Jamie's life going down the drain. *They* were to blame for her death.

His only daughter. Divorced and nearly fifty, he might never have another. Guilt had turned to rage. When he could no longer contain it, he used his best weapon to take action: his money. Jones had hired a killer. Someone vicious and resourceful. Smart and careful. Someone who was capable of manipulating people and getting them to do his dirty work. Someone who was ruthless enough to take out anyone who got in his way. Someone who knew when it was time to cut his losses and eliminate anything or anyone that might lead back to him.

Like he had done with Gifford . . . and now Jones.

It wasn't impossible, but it felt like a stretch. Guilt wasn't the most plausible motive for hiring a professional killer. There had to be more. Had Jones actually believed that the victims had raped his daughter? Had he known something that no one else seemed to know about the incident? If so, he was taking it to his grave.

54

Bishop finished pounding on the rifle barrel, dropped it into the form with the burner and its battery, and dumped the concrete mix over it all. Then he stripped, burned his clothes, and went inside to check the TV. His work had made the twenty-four-hour news networks. He couldn't help but smile, even though he knew it was nothing to be proud of.

When the anchor switched to another story, he got on the phone and called Pratt. After several rings, it went to voice mail. She called him back a few minutes later.

"Hey. I had to go to my car. I can't talk for long."

"That's okay," he said, sounding relieved. "I'm just happy to hear your voice. I'm watching the news and . . . My God, what the hell's going on over there?"

"I don't know," she said. "This is crazy. Nobody seems to have a clue what's happening. The SBI is all over this place. I've never seen anything like it before. I think they're getting ready to go inside. Yeah, I'd better go."

"Okay. Stay safe and call me whenever you get a chance."

"I will. I miss you."

As the call ended, he chuckled to himself, thinking about how ridiculous he had sounded. He flipped through the channels in search of more news coverage. When nothing appeared, he stared blankly at the TV and considered his future.

As payment for his services, Jones had provided the financial backing for Bishop to start a security company. That had been the deal. A reasonable price, considering what Jones had asked him to do. And Bishop had been paid in full. It didn't matter that one of the men was still alive. Not anymore.

The business was doing well. It had grown rapidly in its first eleven months. Jones had also hired Bishop to provide security guards for several of his residential developments, and other developers had been quick to follow suit. Bishop was presently on track to become the largest security service provider in Western North Carolina within another year.

But Jones had remained a silent partner, supplying the additional capital that had allowed the company to expand so quickly. Now that he was gone, Bishop had to figure out how to handle Jones's stake in the partnership. There were provisions for dealing with his untimely death in their agreement, but it was all written in legalese. Bishop would have to consult his lawyer about it once enough time had passed. Until then, he would play the distraught friend and business associate. He would attend the memorial service, shake hands, and look somber. Act like he didn't know how he could continue without Jones's guidance.

The man was more than a partner, he would say. *More than just a friend. He was a mentor.*

Bishop laughed at that thought.

With nothing to watch, he went for a shower, came back ten minutes later, grabbed a beer from the fridge, and dropped onto the sofa. The local news was breaking in on a commercial. The scene behind the reporter showed deputies blocking a road. The entrance to Jones's driveway was barely visible in the distance. At the bottom of the screen, the ticker said, "SBI HUNTS FOR SNIPER."

The anchor and the reporter went back and forth, trading questions for speculation. They promised the full story at 11:00. And Bishop thought, *If only they knew.*

55

Rachel heard Braddock and Jensen rush through the door, calling her name. The beams from their flashlights struck her a few seconds later. Braddock said, "Oh, shit," when he saw her. He started to move forward, but Jensen grabbed him.

"Hang on," he said and went searching for a light.

Rachel stood and stretched, felt her shirt and her hair sticking to her back. "They didn't find him, did they?"

The lights above the island came on, and Braddock's eyes went from Rachel's head to her feet. "You sure you weren't hit?"

There was urgency in his voice.

"I'm fine," she said, looking down. She had been lying in a pool of Jones's blood.

"Let's get you out of here," Jensen said.

Braddock reached out for her. She didn't need his hand, but she took it anyway.

Outside, deputies crowded the driveway. An ambulance backed in, and a pair of EMTs jumped out and rushed over. They wrapped her in a blanket and pelted her with questions. Once they were convinced that she could do without medical attention, they followed Jensen and Pratt inside to make Jones's death official.

Braddock led Rachel away from the crowd, found a short rock retaining wall to serve as a bench, and guided her to it. He sat beside her, rubbed her back, and stared at the ground in front of their feet.

"Are you okay?" he asked. "I mean, I know you're not hurt, but . . ."

She leaned in and nudged him gently with her shoulder. "I'm good."

"You're tougher than I am. I'd be freaking out right now, if I were you."

She laughed, heard her voice quiver. "I think it hasn't quite hit me yet." She looked at him and smiled nervously.

He pulled her close and held her for a moment. Then he let go and said, "Looks like you've got a couple of visitors."

Carly jogged over and wrapped her arms around Rachel. "I should've known better than to let you do this on your own."

Pritchard marched up, waited until Carly backed away, and said, "You gave us all a good scare, Miss Carver. Glad to see you made it out in one piece."

"Thanks, Sheriff."

"Course, when the call came in, the first thing I wondered was what the hell you were doing here in the first place." He glanced at Carly. "I guess it didn't take you very long to find another job, did it?"

Rachel opened her mouth to speak, but he held up his hand and said, "I'm glad you're all right. That's all that matters. We'll talk about the rest later. Right now, I've got to think about what I'm going to say to those vultures up the street. I'm getting tired of seeing myself on the damn television every night."

He hurried off to talk to a group of deputies. Braddock looked at Carly and said, "Carly, would you mind giving us a minute?"

She hesitated, said, "Sure," and walked away.

"I guess I should apologize for not hearing you out yesterday."

"Don't," Rachel said. "There's no need for that."

"Yeah, well . . . obviously, you were right. Jensen knows it too. He feels like a total jackass, and those are *his* words, not mine." He leaned close and lowered his voice. "I was talking to him about it while we were waiting to get in there. He told me they're all over Kevin Gifford's buddies, but they had no indication that this was coming. Nothing. And not a peep about it from any of them since it happened. Seems like the only one who knows what's going on around here is you."

"It was Jones," she said. "He was behind it all."

Braddock's eyes went wide.

Rachel was about to explain when her phone rang. She checked the screen, saw that it was Parker, and said, "Give me a sec."

When she answered, Parker yelled, "What the shit, Rachel?"

"I guess you've heard the news."

"Yeah, and I've just got one question for you: What the shit, Rachel?"

She couldn't help but laugh.

"Oh, I'm glad you think this is funny. Meanwhile, I'm going out of my mind thinking I might've given you some piece of information that could've gotten you killed and . . . You're all right, aren't you?"

"Yes," she said in a reassuring tone. "I'm perfectly fine."

"Good, then I don't have to feel guilty about yelling at you."

"Listen, Bryce, I appreciate you calling, but I've got a lot going on here . . ."

"Hang on, I got something for you."

"What is it?"

"The name you asked me to look up. Bishop? I think I found him. Looking at him right now, actually. Derek Bishop."

"Tell me about him."

"He's the president of a company called Allied One Security. Looks like it's only about a year old. They provide security guards for a lot of Jones's properties. There's a little bio on the company's website. Let's see . . . he served in the army . . ."

That got Rachel's attention. "Really?"

"Yep. Eighty-Second Airborne. He was a cop too. Wait . . . damn."

"What is it?" she asked quickly.

"This says he used to work for the Lowry County Sheriff's Office."

Rachel looked at Braddock with alarm in her eyes. He mouthed, "What?" but she didn't answer. She scanned the scene in front of her, suddenly feeling exposed.

"You still there?" Parker asked. "Rachel . . . ?"

"I gotta go."

She put the phone away and whispered to Braddock, "Take me to your car."

He obeyed, wearing a confused look as they made their way through the crowd and up the driveway to the unmarked Crown Victoria parked on the side of the road. Rachel laid the blanket over the seat to keep the blood—most of which had already dried—from staining it. When they were in with the doors closed, she said, "Tell me about Derek Bishop."

"Derek?" He looked surprised to hear the name. "He was the chief deputy before me. He quit after that thing with the kid from the high school I was telling you about."

Rachel remembered the story. She looked around again at the uniforms milling about and said, "Can you take me back to Mrs. Shipley's? I want to get cleaned up."

"Yeah. Of course." He started the car, shifted into drive, and rolled forward slowly, squeezing between the half-dozen patrol units lining the street in front of them. When they were clear and up to speed, he asked, "What's going on? What does any of this have to do with Derek Bishop?"

"I don't know yet," she said. "I need to think for a minute."

They were almost at Shipley's when Rachel changed her mind and said, "Take me to Gifford's."

"Why?" Braddock asked. "He's still at the jail."

"Not Kevin's. Dylan's."

"Uh . . . okay."

Ten minutes later, they reached the intersection that had served as the staging area for the operation to arrest Dylan Gifford.

Rachel said, "Pull over."

"But it's up there another—"

"I know. Just pull over."

He parked at the edge of the road and flicked on the hazard lights. Rachel was out of the car and walking uphill before he could shut off the engine.

"What's up?" he asked, chasing after her.

"I want to see where the BearCat was when the call came in that Dylan was running."

He pointed ahead. "It was right up there."

As they walked past the spot, Rachel said, "This has gotta be it. I remember the driver saying they were twenty yards from the driveway."

She stopped a few paces later, looked farther uphill, and said, "I can't see the house from here. Can you?"

"No," he said, rising up on the balls of his feet to look through the trees. "It's up there a pretty good way."

"Exactly. From what I remember the other night, you can't see it until you're about halfway up the driveway."

"Okay?"

"So how did he know to run?"

Braddock looked at her, dumbfounded.

"If he couldn't see you from his house," she said, "how did he know you were coming?"

"I don't know . . . a neighbor?"

They looked around. It was a rural road with only a handful of houses, acres of wooded hills between each one. There was another dirt driveway about fifty yards downhill, but the house was hidden from view.

"I don't think so," she said. "Bishop's still talking to someone in your office. I think they tipped him off, and he told Dylan to run."

Back in the car, Rachel explained her revenge-plot theory, trying to make it sound a little stronger than it was. She recounted everything she had learned about the joint-smoking incident and Jamie Moody, about the Newfield shooting and her conversation with Jones. When she repeated his final words, Braddock asked, "You're sure that's what he said? Bishop?"

"I'm positive. He kept saying it over and over again. Right up until he died."

"Jesus Christ." He looked dizzy. "Can we use it?"

"As an excited utterance?"

He nodded.

"Maybe," she said. "But it won't be enough on its own. We're going to need a lot more."

"I know Derek. He was a good detective. He'll have thought of everything."

"I guess that explains how someone like Dylan Gifford could cover his tracks so well," she said. "He had a good teacher."

Braddock looked out at the road, gritted his teeth, and said, "That sorry motherfucker. He killed them."

Rachel got the impression that he was thinking more about Fisher and Howard than about the other victims. She reached up to scratch her scalp, felt the hair on the back of her neck matted by a mass of dried blood. "Maybe we should go," she said. "I really need to get cleaned up."

★ ★ ★

The shower felt good. Even after the water turned tepid, Rachel lingered. When she finally got out, she was shivering. She dried herself quickly, dressed in a sweat shirt and jeans, and went downstairs. Braddock was waiting in the salon. Shipley was fussing in the kitchen, heating up leftovers.

"Feel better?" Braddock asked.

She smiled, still towel drying her hair.

Shipley brought out two bowls of stew and thick slices of home-made bread. "I'm so glad you didn't get hurt, Miss Rachel. I just don't know what to think about all this insanity."

They ate while Shipley talked about the Lord and the power of prayer to heal grieving hearts. When they were finished, she collected the dishes and the wet towel and took them to the kitchen. She came back out long enough to wish them a good night, then retired to her room.

Braddock got a call from one of his deputies. Rachel used the time to look up the Allied One Security web page on her phone. She studied it while he rubbed his eyes and said, "Mmhmm," nearly a dozen times. A few minutes later, he was off the phone, and Rachel said, "Let's take a walk."

He nodded and followed her outside. They strolled along the edge of the road, heading away from town. She hugged herself against the cold wind and said, "He's going to get away with it."

"Don't say that," he said without confidence. "There's got to be something, right? A money trail? He didn't do this for free."

"There is," she said, "but it won't help."

"What are you talking about?"

"That security company he owns. I'd bet my life that Jones was his partner in it. Not to mention the fact that he gave Bishop the contract to provide guards for all of his properties. It's become a million-dollar business in less than a year."

"And you think there's nothing for us to find there?"

"Why would there be? It's the perfect deal. Looks like a legit investment from Jones's standpoint. But as far as Bishop is concerned, he might as well have won the lottery. I bet he'll be able to pay himself a hundred thousand in salary this year."

Braddock shuffled along with his hands buried in his pockets, a pained expression contorting his face. "You're right. He's going to get away with it."

They followed the road down to a turnoff and stopped at the river's edge. Stared at the water and the town beyond. The lights looked like fireflies hovering just above the ground, frozen in the night.

"I stayed behind to solve this thing," she said, "because I knew everyone else had it wrong. I thought I was trying to do what was right by the victims. By Shane and Melissa. Even Dylan Gifford . . . and Lauren Bailey. But now I think maybe I was looking for a little redemption too. Trying to fix something that was broken in me."

"How's that working out for you?"

"I should've gone home when I had the chance."

They gazed at the lights across the river for another minute, then Braddock said, "Seven people, Rachel. That sonofabitch killed seven people."

"Yeah."

"Shane and Melissa . . . Christ, he used to work with them." Rage was building in his voice. "I'm going to kill him."

She turned to him, tried to study his face in the dim light of a streetlamp. "No, Danny," she said weakly. "We can figure this out. There's got to be something—"

"No. He beat us. Plain and simple. There's nothing else we can do. Nothing legal. And you know I'm right."

"Yeah." Her voice melted into the churning water. "I do."

"I'm going to take care of him myself. It's the only way to make him pay. Not right away, but . . . someday soon. I'll catch him when he's not ready. After all this has blown over, and he thinks he's safe."

Braddock's face had turned resolute. Rachel had no doubt that he would go through with it. Or that he would try. Bishop was a cold-blooded killer. He had already proven his willingness to take out anyone who got in his way. And he wouldn't hesitate to do it again. One misstep, and Braddock would become his next victim.

Rachel couldn't let that happen. She had been the one to discover Bishop and convince Braddock of his guilt. If he died, it would be her fault. And she wouldn't be able to live with that. She had to find a way to protect him.

"Jensen's going to want to talk to me," she said. "Soon. Do you want me to tell him what I know about Bishop?"

"I'll talk to him. Him and Ted both. I'll pull 'em aside and make sure they keep quiet about it. At least until we can figure out who Bishop's source is in our office."

56

Monday

Rachel woke up before the alarm went off and got ready in a hurry. The sun was just coming up as she stepped out of her room and padded barefoot down the stairs, hoping not to wake Shipley. She tiptoed through the door, closed it behind her as gently as she could, then slipped on her shoes. Feeling safe, she started for the driveway. She was nearly at her car when she spotted a black sedan parked on the street and froze.

Ross Penter, special agent in charge of the SBI's Capital District, stepped out. "Good morning, Rachel."

She approached him slowly, trying to keep her emotions in check. Anger, resentment, admiration, affection . . . all boiled up within her. Penter had been much more than just her superior. Even more than a mentor. He had been a surrogate father, replacing the one she hardly knew. He had been there for her since the moment she had joined. Had ushered her through the difficult times when she had let her work overtake her life, completely engrossed in her cases, living among the dead. He had always been the one to bring her back. And she had depended on him for that, right up to the moment when he had asked her to betray her duty. To lie to Lauren Bailey's family. And, worst of all, to herself.

"What are you doing here?" she asked.

"I was worried about you." There was real concern in his eyes. "For Christ's sake, you almost got shot yesterday."

"Yeah, well . . . it happens. But I'm fine."

He laughed, took a step closer to her. "I'm glad. I've missed you, you know. Are you doing okay otherwise?"

She had to look away. "Yeah. Everything's great. Sorry you wasted your time coming all the way out here."

"Actually, I was in the neighborhood, as it turns out. I was in Asheville yesterday, getting to know the Western District office a little better."

"Why is that? You thinking of transferring?" she asked, though she tried not to care about the answer.

"I'm getting promoted. Starting in two weeks, I'll be the new assistant director for field operations."

She looked up and offered him a smile. "Congratulations, Ross. That's great."

"Thanks." He held her gaze for a moment and said, "You know, there's still a spot for you, if you wanted to come back."

"I don't think so. It's not where I belong anymore."

"Come on, Rachel. Where else are you going to go? You were born to do this, but you need someone to keep you in check. To keep you from getting lost again. And who's better at that than I am?"

Rachel shook her head in disbelief. "Good-bye, Ross."

She turned to go to her car, but he grabbed her by her arm and spun her around to face him. "Maybe I'm wrong. Maybe you'd rather waste away in some trailer park stalking a little boy whose mother you shot?"

She wrenched her arm from his grip. "Fuck you. How dare you say—"

"What? The truth?" he yelled.

"*Truth*? You weren't so concerned with the truth when you asked me to lie under oath. To tell everyone that I believed Lauren Bailey killed her boyfriend."

"Lauren Bailey *did* kill her boyfriend."

"Bullshit, Ross. No matter how much you want to believe that, you know it's bullshit."

"And you're so sure of that, you would have ruined our careers? Not just yours, which you obviously don't care about anymore, but mine too?"

Rachel wanted to scream yes at the top of her lungs, but she held it in. In spite of all the pain and disappointment, she had never wanted to hurt Penter. But that's exactly what she would have done had she told the truth about the Bailey case. Penter had pushed Bailey as a suspect from the beginning. He had insisted that the investigation be focused on her. And when he was certain that they had gathered enough evidence, it was his order that sent Rachel out to arrest her.

"Look," he said, softening his tone. "You've done a good job on this case. And you've embarrassed the hell out of Sanford, if that makes you feel any better."

"It does," she muttered.

"But they're on the right track now, thanks to you." He walked to his car and opened the door. "So the question is, what are you going to do now that it's over? Getting another job will be easy for you, Rachel. Whenever you're ready. But that's not the problem. The problem is you lose yourself too easily. Sooner or later, you're going to disappear down a dark hole again. And if you're not careful, no one will be there to pull you out. Not even me."

His words held her in check as he drove away. She stood there, staring at the empty road in front of her, and wondered if she could ever find her way back to working for him. There was still a part of her that wanted to try. But she didn't need to answer that just yet. After all, Penter was wrong about one thing—this case wasn't over. There was still work to be done.

57

As far as jails went, the Lowry County Detention Center wasn't a bad place to spend a couple of nights. Kevin had stayed in worse spots voluntarily. But that didn't change how good it felt to be free. With help from a few of his friends, he had managed to hire a bondsman just after sunup. They'd even scraped together enough to get his mother released as well.

Presently, he waited for her outside. Sitting on a park bench by the front door, he took out his phone and started making calls. Though his friends had been eager to contribute to his get-out-of-jail fund, finding a ride home had been a different story. Expecting someone to drive all the way from Whittier to pick them up was apparently too much to ask.

He skimmed his contacts and found a few people that still owed him favors. They were all asleep at this hour, so he left messages, hoping it wouldn't be long before one of them called him back. He was finishing his fourth attempt when a Tahoe from the sheriff's office rolled to a stop at the curb. The woman behind the wheel shifted into park, left it running as she stepped out and walked over to him holding a clipboard and a set of keys. She was tall and muscular, looked like she could have been American Indian. Maybe Cherokee.

"Kevin Gifford?"

"Yeah?" he said, holding his hand up to shade his eyes from the sun. "That's me."

"We're releasing your brother's truck," she said, handing him the clipboard. She held onto the keys. "If you'll sign for it, I'll give these to you, and you can pick it up whenever you want."

He unhooked the pen from the clip and read through the form.

"You just have to sign at the bottom," she said impatiently.

He looked around the parking lot. "Well, where is it?"

"It's in the back lot at the sheriff's office."

"Y'all couldn't bring it to me?"

"Afraid that's not my job."

"You keep away from my boy," Linda Gifford shouted from the door.

Startled, Kevin looked over and said, "Damn, Momma, calm down."

"To hell with that," she said, stomping toward them. "You already got one of my sons killed. You stay away from us, you hear? Just get away."

She was building momentum. Looked like she might charge the Cherokee woman.

"All right, Momma," Kevin said, jumping between them. "That's enough, now. I mean it."

Linda looked into his eyes, and the anger in her expression faded. "You sound like your brother."

Kevin hugged her and said, "It's gonna be okay, Momma. She's just here to give us the keys to Dylan's truck is all."

He signed the form and handed the clipboard back to the woman. She gave him the keys, thanked him quickly, and hurried back to her Tahoe. He said, "Wait here," to Linda, then ran after her, catching up to her as she was about to close the door.

"Hey, look," he said, "I know it ain't your job to be drivin' us around town and everything—"

"You're right," she said. "It isn't."

"I know, but . . ." He glanced back. "She's been through a lot, you know. And we ain't got no way to get home. It'd be a big help if you could just give us a ride back to the station. I mean, you're goin' that way anyway, aren't you?"

She looked past him, sighed, and said, "Yeah, okay. Get in."

He loaded Linda in the back seat, glared at her when she said, "It's the least she could do," then ran around to the other side and climbed in next to her. It was a quiet ride to the sheriff's office. The Cherokee woman let them out right next to the Sierra, which was parked in the back corner of the parking lot. Kevin thanked her as he closed the door, and she pulled away to find a spot closer to the building.

"Hop in, Momma," he said, unlocking the doors. "I'll take you home."

She leaned against the fender and started to cry, lost the strength in her legs and slid down to the ground. Kevin ran to her side, trying to pull her up by her arms.

"Come on, Momma," he said, his voice cracking. "We can't be doin' this right now, okay?"

But she only wept more forcefully. Her arms were limp as wet noodles. Kevin knelt down beside her and hugged her shoulders.

"I want . . . my baby boy back," she said between heaving breaths.

"I know." He squeezed her and rocked her gently. "I want him back too."

He wiped his eyes and looked toward the building. A pair of deputies stood by the back door, watching with dead faces. The Cherokee woman parked and walked inside without a glance in their direction.

"Let's get you outta here, okay? Come on, now. Let's get in the truck so I can take you home."

When she was finally inside, Kevin went around, hopped up into the driver's seat, and cranked the engine. He took a second to look around while it warmed up. It was an older pickup, but his brother had loved it. There was trash in the back seat and mud on the floor mats. Everything in it looked and smelled old. Everything except the cheap cell phone sitting on top of the center console.

He picked it up and turned it in his hand to examine it. There wasn't a single scratch on its black surface. Plastic film still covered the screen. It was brand new, and he couldn't recall ever seeing Dylan with it. It started to vibrate. He jumped and said, "Jesus . . ."

He didn't recognize the number.

58

The neighborhood would be beautiful once all the work was done. Most of the lots had been sold, and more than two dozen houses were in various phases of construction. A couple of families had already moved in by the entrance, next door to a trio of model homes that were decked out with expensive options meant to entice prospective buyers.

Bishop admired them as he drove by, making his way toward the back where a new batch of houses was just starting to come out of the ground. He rounded a bend carved into a hillside and spotted a concrete truck parked ahead. He pulled into a grassy spot in a lot across the street and watched the operation.

The driver would pull on a lever, the giant drum would spin, and concrete would run down the chute extending from the back of the truck. The chute dumped into the receiving end of a pump, which pushed the concrete through a long black hose. At the end of that hose, a worker fired the gray slush into a trench that would serve as the foundation for the new home. The crew had finished digging it on Thursday, had spent Friday laying and tying together the thin steel bars sitting inside it.

At a spot near the corner, just a few inches beneath the bottom of that trench, Bishop had buried his own bit of concrete work. He had gotten there two hours before sunrise. Had been long gone by the time the crew had arrived to set up the pump. Now he was back to make sure the evidence got covered up for good. He wouldn't feel at ease until there was a foot of reinforced concrete above the rifle barrels and the burner phones.

The foreman noticed his Wrangler and came over to make small talk. Bishop had seen him around before, had said hello to him once or twice. He rolled down his window and said, "Looks like a good day for pouring concrete."

The man shrugged, lifted the camouflage ball cap off his head, and scratched his buzzed scalp. "I'll like it better when it warms up a bit more."

"Yeah, but before you know it, it'll be too hot to do anything outside."

"Ain't that the truth. What's got you out here today?"

"Oh, just trying to figure out how many cars I'll need to patrol these mean streets."

"So basically, you're out here wastin' time for a little while," he said with a chuckle.

Bishop smiled. The workers had moved to the corner. Concrete was flowing directly onto the spot where he had performed the burial. "Something like that," he said.

"I hear the man that owns this neighborhood got killed yesterday. My wife was tellin' me she saw on the news that someone went and shot him through his back window."

"Yeah. I'm afraid that's true."

"Damn," the man said. "That's some crazy shit."

"Sure is."

"Course, now the damn Democrats will be tryin' like hell to take all our guns away again."

"You know it."

The engine in the concrete truck revved loudly, and the drum sped up. The worker at the trench dropped the hose and walked back toward the others standing by the pump.

The foreman spit and said, "Well, that'll do it for that load." He unclipped a large phone from his belt and started searching for a number. "I'd better make sure the next truck is gettin' close. You take it easy, my friend." And he walked away.

Bishop watched for a few more minutes, then wheeled back onto the street and left the neighborhood.

★ ★ ★

Pratt had cancelled their picnic date after the shooting, saying she had to canvass the neighbors around the Jones residence. He tried calling her after lunch, but she was still too busy to talk. And that suited him just fine. He figured it would be another month, maybe two before he broke it off anyway.

He spent the afternoon in his office in Asheville, meeting with clients and interviewing applicants for security officer positions. He finished the day with a call to his accountant, who told him he was going to owe more in taxes than she had originally antici-pated. Tried to tell him that it was a good thing, though it didn't feel like it.

At 5:00, Bishop said bye to the office manager and headed out. On his way to I-40, he decided to stop by the Wicked Brew res-taurant near downtown. He had dinner and a few beers and flirted with the bartender for a while. When he realized it wasn't going anywhere, he paid the bill and left. Pulled the soft top down on the Wrangler and enjoyed the cool air as he cruised through the mountains.

By the time he turned onto the gravel drive, it was dark. He considered leaving the Wrangler open but decided against it. There was a chance of rain in the forecast, and he didn't want the seats to be wet in the morning. He parked and put the top up, then took the shovel out of the back and brought it into the garage. He hung it on the rack by the side door, locked up, and walked toward the cabin, yawning.

Then he saw it. Out of the corner of his eye, a figure standing in a shadow beyond the fire pit. He kept his stride for two more steps, lifted his shirt, and drew the compact 9mm from the concealed carry holster tucked in his jeans at his right hip. He turned and lev-eled his sights on the silhouette. Behind him, a familiar voice said, "I wouldn't do that if I were you, Derek."

"Danny?"

Braddock circled into view. He had his own sidearm trained on Bishop. "Hand it over," he said. "Easy."

Bishop lowered his weapon and passed it to Braddock. His eyes were still fixed on the shadow in front of him. The figure approached, emerging into the moonlight.

"Good evening, Mister Bishop."

He smiled and said, "It's nice to meet you, Miss Carver."

59

"So," Bishop said, "which one of you wants to tell me what the fuck is going on here?"

Rachel peered into his eyes, trying to get a read on his expression, but there wasn't enough light to see clearly.

"We just came out to have a little talk is all," Braddock said, holstering his weapon. He removed the magazine from Bishop's 9mm, then the round from the chamber, and laid them in a chair by the fire pit. "Your name has come up in a murder investigation."

"A *murder* investigation," he said, sounding surprised. "*My* name?"

"That's right, Mister Bishop," Rachel said. "How well did you know Lawton Jones?"

"Pretty well, I guess. We were business partners."

"Were. I guess that means you've heard he was killed yesterday."

"Of course I heard. Hell, it's been all over the news. Just like the two of you." He looked at Braddock. "Jesus, Danny. Does she really think I had something to do with Lawton getting shot?"

Braddock shrugged. "It's her show, Derek. I'm just along for the ride."

"Since you mention it," Rachel said, "mind telling us where you were yesterday afternoon?"

"Home," Bishop said. He folded his arms, a defiant gesture. "All afternoon and all night. And no, I don't have an alibi. I live here alone."

"And Friday night?"

"Same thing. I was here. Wait . . . you can't possibly think I'm involved in . . ." His head darted between Rachel and Braddock. "Shane? Melissa? Jesus Christ. There's no way in hell I could hurt either one of them. Come on, Danny. You know me."

"You forgot someone," Rachel said.

"What?"

"Dylan Gifford. He was in the car too. Did you know him?"

"I don't . . . No, I don't think so."

Rachel had just scored her first refutable lie. She and Braddock had reviewed his case files earlier in the day. He had arrested Gifford on at least two occasions as a detective. She was about to remind him of that when a new voice said, "I'm gonna have to call bullshit on that one, Mister Bishop."

Braddock's hand moved to his sidearm, but another voice said, "Don't even fuckin' think about it, man."

There was the racking sound of pump-action hardware, hurried footfalls over rustling foliage. Bishop spun in a circle, looking in every direction. He said, "What the fuck?" as the men came into view.

There were three of them, all dressed in black, all wearing ski masks. Two of them carried shotguns. The third brandished a shiny chrome automatic. He put the muzzle in Bishop's face and said, "Why don't you invite us all inside, asshole? It's gettin' a little chilly out here."

Bishop led the way into the cabin. The shotgunner nearest Braddock took his weapon and waved him in. Rachel followed. Once everyone was in the living area, the man with the chrome handgun made Bishop drop to his knees in the center of the room. Rachel and Braddock were made to stand against a wall.

The chrome handgun appeared to be the leader. He stood over Bishop and said, "You know why I made you bring us in here? 'Cause when we take to shootin' your sorry ass in a minute, we don't want the noise to carry too far."

Rachel saw Bishop's jaw muscles flexing nervously. His eyes were fixed on a spot on the floor, but his mind seemed to be in overdrive, trying to figure a way out of this situation alive.

"That's right, motherfucker. We're fixin' to light your ass up, and it's gonna make quite a racket."

One of the shotgunners laughed. The leader joined in, then he suddenly got quiet and leaned down to get within a few inches of Bishop's face. "I'm gonna enjoy watchin' you die." He backed up and looked over at Rachel and Braddock. "You two ever seen what a pair of shotguns and a hand cannon like this'll do to a mother-fucker?" Back to Bishop, "You're gonna turn into one helluva mess."

"Why?" Rachel asked.

"What?" The leader looked at her, incredulous. "Did you say something to me?"

"I said why. Why do you want to kill him?"

She took a step forward, and Braddock seized her arm, gave her a sideways look that pleaded with her to keep quiet. But the leader didn't appreciate that.

"Whoa, ease up on the lady, man. She and I are tryin' to have a conversation." He looked her up and down for a second and said, "Step on over here, sweetheart. Let me get a look at you."

Rachel moved to the center of the room next to Bishop. The leader walked around behind her and examined her figure. "Not bad, huh, boys?"

One of the shotgunners said, "Looks good to me."

"I'll say." The leader came back around to stand in front of her. "Now tell me again. What is it you were sayin', pretty lady?"

Rachel tried to swallow, cleared her throat, and asked, "Why are you going to kill him?"

The leader feigned surprise. "You mean you don't know? Well, shit, girl, I guess I should fill you in. Then again"—he seemed to reconsider—"why don't we just hear it straight from the horse's mouth?" He leaned down to Bishop. "Go ahead, cocksucker. Tell the lady why we're here."

Bishop mumbled something.

"What's that? Speak up, asshole."

"I said, I don't know why you're here. I don't know what the fuck is going on right—"

The leader cocked back and struck Bishop's mouth with his pistol. Rachel yelled, "No!" and Braddock took a step forward, but a shotgunner pushed him back against the wall. Bishop was lying on his side holding a bloody lip.

"Get up," the leader said.

When Bishop moved too slow, he kicked him. "I said, get up, motherfucker." And Bishop lifted himself back to his knees.

"Since our host ain't shit for tellin' stories, I guess I'll have to educate you all myself. This sorry piece of trash went and murdered a good friend of mine. A fella by the name of Dylan Gifford. Ain't that right, asshole?"

Bishop, blood trickling down his chin, didn't respond.

"And you sorry sonsabitches . . ." He pointed his pistol at Braddock. "Y'all don't plan on doin' shit about it."

"That's not true," Rachel said, stepping between them. "The whole reason we're here is because he's a suspect."

"Then why ain't you arrested his ass yet?"

"It takes time to build a case. You just have to give us time."

"Time? I ain't got time to be waitin' on you all to fuck around. I got bullets, though. And shotgun shells too. I got plenty of them."

"That's right," one of the shotgunners said. "Let's kill this sumbitch and get outta here. What the fuck are we waitin' for?"

"I'm startin' to agree with my colleague over there. Anything else you wanna say to try and change my mind?"

Rachel turned to Bishop and dropped down to her knees. "Tell them. Confess. Give Danny enough to arrest you with, and maybe they'll let you live."

Bishop looked at her like she was crazy.

"Better to fight it out in court," she whispered, "than die here."

The leader laughed. "Nice try, honey. But I ain't takin' a chance that this shitbag gets out on some technicality. Besides, we didn't get all dressed up for nothin'."

He pulled Rachel back to her feet and out of the line of fire. The shotgunners leveled on Bishop.

"No, wait!" Rachel yelled. "None of you have killed anyone yet. If you do this, you'll all be murderers. No better than him."

"I can live with that," he said, turning to take aim. "You ready, boys?"

Bishop closed his eyes.

"Let's do this."

Rachel jumped forward. Braddock yelled, "Rachel, no!" as she hit the leader's arm. A deafening shot exploded. It missed Bishop's head by less than a foot, and he dropped to his side, panting as if he might hyperventilate. Rachel was on her knees again, ears ringing a dull tone.

Braddock grabbed her arm and tried to pull her away. The shot-gunners converged on him. One of them pressed the muzzle of his weapon against Braddock's cheek and drove him back to the wall.

"You're one crazy bitch!" the leader yelled. "And I admire that shit. But if you try that again, I will straight up *kill* your ass."

"I can guarantee that he goes to prison," Rachel said.

"What?"

"I promise you. I can guarantee it. Just don't kill him. Not yet."

60

"It's time to come clean," Rachel said. "It's time to confess, or they *will* kill you. And I'm not getting between you and another bullet. This is it. Prison or death. Your choice."

Everyone had calmed down. Bishop was back on his knees with Rachel standing above him. One of the shotgunners was seated on the sofa. The other was leaning against a wall, watching Braddock. The leader was pacing, circling the room anxiously.

"I did it," Bishop said. "I killed him."

"That's not good enough," she said. "You need to tell us the whole story. Convince us that you know things you shouldn't know."

He closed his eyes and exhaled. He seemed to be thinking, trying to conjure a story. Perhaps one that would satisfy the gunmen but leave him with enough room to fight his way out of a conviction.

Rachel leaned close to him. "I want you to understand something. I believe wholeheartedly that you're responsible for killing seven people. As far as I'm concerned, it would be justice served if I let them shoot you. The only reason I saved you is because I want the truth more than I want you dead. Beyond that, I have zero incentive to help you get out of this alive. If you don't give me enough to put you away for life, I'm going to tell them. Now get on with it."

He looked into her eyes for a long moment. The fear in them turned to defeat. She saw his head drop and his shoulders slump, and she knew he had accepted his fate.

"It all started with Lawton's daughter," he said.

"Jamie Moody."

"Yeah. She killed herself last year. Lawton was crushed. Apparently, they had been fighting the night she died. He had accused her of using him for his money. And she said he hadn't supported her enough when she was a kid. She said that no one knew what she had gone through when she was a teenager and how it had messed her up."

"Did she tell him she had been raped?"

He nodded. "She told him it happened the day she was kicked out of school. Two boys had done it while another two were acting as lookouts. She even told the school resource officer, but no one believed her. Lawton didn't believe her either when she told him. He thought she was exaggerating. Then she turned up dead, and that changed his mind. He figured she wouldn't have killed herself over something that was just in her imagination. It had to be real."

"How did you get involved?"

"I was still chief deputy at the time. Lawton paid me to look into it. Asked me to investigate, to see if there was any chance of bringing charges against the four boys."

"What did you find?"

"Not much. There was the officer's report, but that was about it. He took her statement, but nothing came of it. When I talked to him, he said that Jamie had a bad reputation back then, so no one took her seriously. The school administrators got her in a room and told her she could be charged with a crime for falsely accusing those boys. They said they were doing her a favor by expelling her for the drugs, so they wouldn't have to tell her mom she'd been busted having sex with two boys. I guess that scared her enough to keep quiet about it. For a few years, anyway."

"Did you talk to Coach Grisley about what he saw?"

"Vernon Grisley died six years ago. Nobody knows what he saw."

"So what did you tell Jones?"

"I told him it was a lost cause."

He shifted his weight to one knee. The leader stepped over and tapped the back of his head with his pistol and said, "Sit still and keep talkin'. You don't want me to think you're fixin' to try somethin' stupid."

Bishop rubbed his thigh. "I told him that without Jamie to testify against the boys, there was no hope of getting a conviction for rape. Not to mention the fact that they were only fifteen when it happened. Even if by some miracle we could prosecute them, they would never get the punishment they deserved."

"How did he react to that?"

"Not good. He was inconsolable. Couldn't let it go. He kept asking me if there was anything else that could be done. Over and over again. Then one day, he came to me and asked what would happen to him if he killed the boys himself. If I thought there was a way for him to get away with it."

"Is that when you offered to take care of it for him?"

He glanced at Braddock. "The bullying case last year . . . when the one kid beat the other one so bad he ended up in the hospital? I was frustrated after that. The bully got away with it, just like the boys who raped Jamie Moody got away with it. So I resigned and told Lawton I'd take care of his problem for him."

"How noble of you."

"Yeah, all right, I got paid. He got me started with my company, but that made him money too. Or it would have."

"This is takin' too long," the leader said. "I wanna hear about Dylan."

Rachel said, "You heard him. Tell us about Dylan."

"I liked him. He was tough, resourceful. He knew how to get in and out of places without getting caught. The only time he ever got in trouble for breaking and entering was when he decided to get one of his idiot friends involved." Bishop glanced over his shoulder at the leader. "And I knew he would kill too."

"How?"

"The last time I busted him, he had beat this poor bastard unconscious outside of a bar. The guy was completely helpless. But Dylan pulled out a lock-blade knife from his pocket and put it to the guy's throat, then looked around like he was making sure no one was watching. There's only one reason you do something like that. I stopped him from killing that guy. No doubt about it. He even admitted it to me later."

"Okay. So how did you convince him to work for you?"

"Money. Lawton set aside forty thousand to pay him."

"Bullshit," the leader said. "He was scared. Scared you was gonna kill his mom or his brother."

"I wouldn't have—"

He kicked Bishop in the back. "Don't lie to me, motherfucker."

"All right," Rachel said. "That's enough."

He stepped back and eyed her, then reached under the ski mask to scratch his jaw. "This damn things gettin' itchy. Do you have what you need, or do we get to shoot him?"

Rachel understood everything now. Jones's motive had been revenge for his daughter's rape, the trauma of which had contributed to her suicide. Bishop had used that to his advantage, fashioning a deal that would make him a lot of money while appearing to be legitimate. And he had forced Gifford to kill for him, threatening the safety of Gifford's family but offering to reward him if he did what he was told.

Bishop was the center of it all. His greed had set Jones's revenge fantasy in motion. His desire for self-preservation had swept Gifford into his plans. And when it had all started to go sideways, he simply tried to cut his losses and walk away, no matter who died in the process.

"We have what we need," Braddock said. He gave Rachel a look that begged her to agree. "We can put him away forever now."

"Not yet," she said.

Braddock looked shocked, but Rachel wasn't finished. It wasn't enough to know the story. She wanted physical evidence.

"Where's the rifle?" she asked.

"In the garage," Bishop said. "Most of it, anyway."

"What do you mean?"

"I got rid of the barrel. Beat it with a sledgehammer and encased it in concrete. Then I buried it at a construction site. They covered it with a concrete foundation this morning."

"That sounds pretty thorough. We're still going to need it, though." She reached into her pocket, which caught one of the shotgunners' attention. She withdrew her Steno pad and pen slowly, holding it out so they could see it. Then she turned back to Bishop. "What's the address?"

He gave it to her, and she wrote it down.

"Is that it?" the leader asked.

She shook her head. "No. I need something more."

"Rachel . . ." Braddock said.

She ignored him. Stared into Bishop's eyes and said, "There's something else. There has to be."

She thought about everything she knew about the case. Every note she had taken. Every idea that had crossed her mind since the beginning. Every assumption she had made when she was trying to get a picture of the killer. And then it struck her.

"You knew the victims too well. Dylan didn't know them. You taught him everything he needed to know. You must have been watching them, studying them, for months. Where's your computer?"

Bishop smiled. "It was the last thing I was going to destroy. Just as soon as I was sure I wouldn't need it anymore."

The chrome pistol tapped the back of his head. "Where is it?"

"My bedroom closet. On the shelf above the clothes."

"Watch 'em," the leader said and went to find it. A minute later, he returned with the laptop, carried it over to the dining table, and powered it up. When the login screen came up, he asked, "What's the password?"

Bishop hesitated.

"Don't make me come over there."

"*B–D* seven two eight two."

Rachel wrote it in her pad as the leader typed it. A second later, he was in. "What am I lookin' for?"

"Mind if I take a look?" she asked.

"Go right ahead."

It didn't take her long to find it. Photos, videos, audio files . . . an immense amount of data, all divided into four folders—one for each target. Some of the media had even come from *inside* their homes, as if Bishop had bugged them.

"Holy shit," she said.

"What is it? Did you hit the jackpot?"

She looked at Braddock and nodded.

"Well, all right," the leader said. "I guess we can get outta here, boys." He walked over to Bishop and waved the gun in his face. "Looks like you lucked out, buddy. If you call livin' in a cage for the rest of your life lucky. Then again, I hear they've brought back the death penalty. Maybe your ass is doomed after—"

It was a quick motion of the hands, and he hadn't been ready for it, not that he could've stopped it anyway. Bishop had twisted the gun free of his grip and was holding it, pointing it straight at his face.

"Shit!" The shotgunners shook off their surprise and aimed their weapons. "Drop it!" one of them yelled.

Braddock had his hands in the air. "Whoa. Everybody just stay calm, okay? No one needs to die here tonight."

"Derek," Rachel said. "Put the gun down."

Bishop backed away toward the corner of the room, shifting his aim between the shotgunners, who glanced at each other nervously, unsure of what to do. The leader sank to his butt and scurried backward until he ran into the sofa.

Rachel stepped forward. "Derek, look at me. It's over. You're not doing any good right now. There's no way out of this situation as long as you're holding that gun."

"I beg to differ," Bishop said. "Danny, I'm sorry about Shane and Melissa."

He put the muzzle of the pistol beneath his chin, closed his eyes, and drew in a sharp breath.

"Wait!" Rachel shouted.

The room was completely silent for an instant, as if everyone was holding their breath, waiting for the pop that would end Derek Bishop's life. But it never came.

Bishop exhaled and dropped the pistol. It bounced off his foot and slid away from him. Rachel lunged forward and grabbed it, then trained it on Bishop, keeping her distance in case he thought of trying to disarm her. But there didn't seem to be any fight left in him. He leaned against the wall and slid to the floor.

"Man, what a pussy," said one of the shotgunners.

Rachel looked over her shoulder. "Get out of here. All of you. Go."

The leader scrambled to his feet, took a second to look Rachel in the eye, then gave her a nod and ran for the door. The other two followed right behind him. As soon as they were out of the cabin, Braddock got on his phone and called the Buncombe County Sheriff's Office.

61

No one said anything on the trip back. Kevin spent most of the ride staring out the passenger window, lost in thought. When they were almost at the drop-off point, he shook it off and asked his cousin, "You doin' all right?"

"I'm good," Clayton said, trying to sound poised.

He veered onto the shoulder and shut off the engine and the lights.

"That was some crazy shit back there," Kevin said. "But I guess we did all right by Dylan."

"Yeah. We done what needed to be done."

There was a soft snore behind them. Kevin turned around to look at his other cousin, curled up in the back seat. "I don't know how in the hell that boy can be asleep right now."

"Who knows," Clayton said.

Kevin got out and walked around to the driver's side. Clayton lowered the window as he knelt down next to him.

"You'll be good gettin' rid of them shotguns?"

"Leave it to me, cuz," Clayton said.

"Well, here then. Get rid of this for me too." Kevin dug into his pocket and produced the burner, handed it over.

"Will do." Clayton dropped it into the cup holder. "That was a good trick, leavin' it in your brother's truck the way she did. You think you'll ever see her again?"

"Listen, man," he said, ignoring the question, "you two gotta keep this quiet, all right? Forever. There ain't no one you can ever trust with it. You understand?"

"Yep. You ain't gotta worry about that, cuz. Trust me."

Kevin looked at the black hillside ahead, silhouetted by the waning moon. His property was on the other side about a mile away. He would have to find his way back in the dark and sneak in undetected. The SBI surveillance team was still watching his trailer, but Kevin had a solution for that. He had told the woman about it on the phone earlier that morning. After their third conversation, when she had finally convinced him that she could help him get revenge for his brother's murder.

A couple years back, Kevin had cut a hole in the floor of his closet. It was meant to serve as a trapdoor where he could store money, drugs, and guns. But it also worked as a secret escape route. The night that the woman and the chief deputy had paid him a visit, he had used it to get outside without being seen, which was how he had sneaked up on them so easily. And earlier today, he had used it again to make his way outside, into the woods and down to the road where Clayton had picked him up.

"When this is all over," Clayton said, "you should get outta this place. Just like Dylan told you. Get your mom and head west. Make a fresh start somewhere new."

"Yeah, maybe. She always talked about wantin' to see the Grand Canyon."

They stayed quiet for a minute. Kevin looked up and down the road and scanned the hill ahead like he was getting ready to take off. But then he looked back at Clayton and asked, "You think Dylan woulda been proud of what I done?"

"I know he would. Now go on and get before I have to chase you outta here with a damn shotgun."

He chuckled. "All right."

"And be careful."

Kevin wandered off down the road and slipped into the shadows of a row of oak trees. He imagined himself walking with his brother, talking for a while until there was nothing much left to say. Then Dylan started to fall back, encouraging Kevin to keep on. He couldn't pinpoint exactly where he'd lost him. He had turned around every so often to look for him. Had seen him standing on the road, waving. But at some point, it wasn't him anymore. His eyes could only find a sapling, wavering in the spring breeze. Moonlight danced on its leaves.

62

Tuesday

It seemed like the whole town had shown up for the memorial service. Too many to fit inside the old Lowry County Courthouse. The stately, white, federal-style building had been converted into a museum of local history, and the fire marshal said it could only accommodate two hundred at a time. So the organizers moved everyone to the gardens out back, which worked out nicer anyway, save for the lack of seating. Those that could stand for the duration were asked to. Folding chairs were set out for the ones who couldn't.

Rachel stood in the back with Shipley, who sang her rendition of "The Star Spangled Banner" right along with the young girl on the PA, and Shipley's was better. Then there were speeches. Pritchard went first, followed by the chairman of the county commission. Then they sang a hymn. Everyone but Rachel seemed to know the words to it. That was followed by a lengthy law-and-order-type speech from a congressman and a short address from the lieutenant governor.

Together, they talked for more than an hour. Rachel spent most of it staring at the photographs of Fisher and Howard, official portraits standing on a pair of easels next to the lectern. Their faces were fixed with broad smiles. They looked far too young to be wearing uniforms.

Rachel cried every time she thought about that.

After the service, Chief Miller found an opportunity to break away from the crowd and wandered over to Rachel. "Didn't take you long to cause a stir, did it?"

"No, I guess not," Rachel said.

"Well, I'd say you earned your pay. There's a check waiting for you at the office, if you feel like swinging by on your way out of town. Or we could mail it, whatever's easier."

"Who said I was leaving?"

"Aw, hell."

"Back off, Rich. I saw her first."

They looked over to see Pritchard and Curtis walking toward them.

Miller nudged Rachel with his elbow and said, "I think he might want to fight me for you."

"You wouldn't stand a chance, Rich." Pritchard took his sunglasses off and put a hand on Rachel's shoulder. "I just wanted you to know I think you're one hell of an investigator, Rachel Carver."

"I appreciate that, Sheriff."

"Having said that, I thought I'd let you know my cousin has been chastising my ass all morning about the way you and Danny went over there last night without giving him a courtesy call."

"Yeah, I'm sorry about that. I guess we weren't thinking."

"Uh-huh. Good thing you didn't need backup to make it outta there in one piece. But I suppose you don't let anything scare you anymore, do you?"

"I wish."

"Well, all kidding aside, that was a hell of a thing you did last night. Keeping your head and getting Derek to incriminate himself . . . all while facing off with a damn firing squad. And I'm sure the SBI appreciates it too, though you probably won't hear that from them. I understand Jensen is at the Buncombe County Jail as we speak. Having a little talk with our former chief deputy."

"Still can't believe it turned out to be Derek Bishop," Curtis said.

"Hell, I can't believe any of it," Miller said. "Lawton Jones? Who the hell could've imagined that? Whole thing's just so damn bizarre."

290 I J. R. Backlund

"Yep," Pritchard said. "Sure is. I'm just glad it's over. Course there's still a lot of work to do to put it all together for the DA. Then we've got to figure out what, if anything, we can do about Caleb Rucker's role in the Moody girl's rape. And then there's the matter of hunting down those three fellas who wanted to execute Derek." He was looking directly at Rachel. "I don't suppose you'd consider staying around a while longer to help out?"

"I appreciate the offer, Sheriff," she said, "but I think I've done all the good I can in these parts. Time for me to be heading home."

"I figured as much. Probably couldn't afford you anyway."

She laughed. "Just wait till you see what you already owe me."

"Huh? What d'you mean?"

Curtis flashed her a crooked smile as she walked past him.

"Wait . . ." Pritchard said. "Hang on, now . . . how much are we talking about?"

★ ★ ★

Rachel packed up, thanked Shipley for her hospitality, and accepted a pair of homemade blueberry muffins in a paper bag for the trip home. Carly and Braddock were waiting outside by the Camry. He hefted her suitcase into the trunk while Carly gave her a long hug and whispered, "Thank you. For everything."

When she finally let go, she turned to Braddock and said, "See you back at the office, boss."

They watched her get in the Tahoe and pull away. Then Braddock said, "She's in a little bit of trouble."

"Why?" Rachel asked.

"She released Gifford's truck yesterday. I guess she thought that since he was dead, we didn't need it anymore."

"Rookie mistake."

"Yeah. Anyway, Jensen wants us to get it back. Shouldn't be a problem, but still a pain in the ass. Oh, by the way, I think I know how Bishop got tipped off about the raid. As soon as Tina heard the news this morning, she broke down. Started crying hysterically. Turns out, they've been seeing each other for a few months.

He asked her to keep it a secret, since there were some hard feelings between him and Ted after he quit."

"Was she feeding him information?"

He shook his head. "I doubt it. Probably just gave it up by accident."

"Well, I feel bad for her if that's the case."

"Yeah." They stood quietly for a moment, then he said, "Oh, shit, I almost forgot."

He ran to the Crown Victoria, stuck his arm inside, and returned with a four pack of sixteen-ounce cans of Monster Energy.

"Aw, Danny, you didn't have to do that."

He set the drinks in her passenger seat. "There. All set and ready to roll. Unless you wanted to change your mind. We've got an opening for a detective, if you're interested. I'd be willing to put in a good word."

She smiled and hugged him tightly, kissed him on the cheek, and said, "I'm glad we got to work together again."

"Yeah, me too." There was a little sadness in his voice. "Hopefully it won't be the last time."

"I'm sure it won't," she said.

That brought a smile to his face. "You take care of yourself, Miss Carver."

★ ★ ★

A few miles away, Kevin stopped in at his brother's house. Bert had been by the previous afternoon to fix the door the cops had kicked in. It would hold for a little while, but Kevin figured they would need to put in a new one before trying to sell the place.

He cooked eggs and sausages for a late breakfast and sat Linda down to talk about the future.

"I talked to Clayton yesterday," he said. "He told me he thinks he can hook me up with a pretty good lawyer."

"Why would he do that?" she asked.

"'Cause he wants to help, I guess."

"You really think he wants to help you after the way he and your brother got on?"

He shrugged and rolled a sausage link around with the tip of his fork. "I dunno. He's still family."

"Mmhmm."

"Anyway, he says we'll probably get community service or somethin', since we ain't ever done nothin' else wrong. And I was thinkin', when it's done, maybe we oughta think about gettin' outta this shithole."

"Watch your mouth, boy. I didn't raise you to talk like that."

"Sorry."

He went back to eating, figuring he could bring it up again later. But after a minute, she asked, "Where was you thinkin' about goin'?"

"Arizona maybe."

"Hmph."

She stood up and went to the living room, sat on the sofa, and turned on the TV. He gathered the dishes and brought them to the sink, cleaned up a bit, then joined her to watch a reality court show. They laughed at other people's misery for a while, and Kevin tried not to think too much about anything.

During a commercial break, Linda lit a cigarette and said, "I always wanted to see the Grand Canyon."

★ ★ ★

On the drive home, Rachel called Parker and made good on her end of their deal. First, she filled him in on all the developments in the Lowry County case. Then the conversation turned to Lauren Bailey. She told him her doubts about the official version, how she had come to believe that Bailey was innocent. She answered his questions and gave him as much detail as she could while trying her best not to blame the special agent in charge—the soon-to-be assistant director of field operations, Ross Penter.

"So even though you had doubts, you still decided to arrest her?" Parker asked.

"It wasn't my decision alone," she said, "but, yes, I did."

"And because of that decision, you ended up in a standoff in Bailey's house that ultimately led to her death."

"Yes."

"Do you think another agent . . . had they been in your shoes at the time . . . do you think they would have fired on Bailey?"

"Yes, I do," she said without hesitation.

"Okay. Do you think that another agent . . . had they been in your shoes . . . would have made the decision to arrest Lauren Bailey in the first place?"

She thought for a moment and said, "I . . . I don't know."

The question stuck with Rachel after they hung up. Her honest answer would have been no, but she hadn't been able to say it. It shined a light on what had been her biggest weakness as an agent—her devotion to Penter. It had allowed him to take advantage of her, to push her aside for political expediency. During the past week, she hadn't felt that weakness. She had been free to tackle the case on her own terms or not at all. And that was exactly what she needed.

Her mind was made up—she would not return to the SBI. She cracked a can of Monster Energy and thought about what career might offer her the freedom she desired. It didn't take her long to settle on becoming a legal investigator. She could work for defense attorneys and set her own hours, take the cases she wanted and ignore the rest. It might even be better pay. Penter would call her a traitor, of course. He would accuse her of using her expertise to help criminals go free instead of putting them behind bars. That thought should've bothered her, but it didn't. In fact, the more she considered it, the more it appealed to her.

Rachel Carver, legal investigator.

She liked the way that sounded.

Acknowledgments

To the following, my sincere gratitude:

The entire team at Crooked Lane Books. Especially Matt Martz, for seeing the potential in this novel and for pushing me to make it better. Peter Senftleben, my editor, for keeping me focused on what makes a good story. Sarah Poppe and Jenny Chen, for their efforts and patience as I learn what it takes to produce a book.

Every great journey needs a guide, and without Rachel Ekstrom Courage of the Irene Goodman Literary Agency, my agent, I would be lost.

Eric Weaver, for his counsel. Sean Wiggins, for his expertise in all things prosecutorial. And Officer Katie Anderson, for teaching me about law enforcement in North Carolina.

My wife, Thu Ngo, for her unwavering support.

20x